KRIS BUTLER

TATTOOED HEARTS DUET

PART ONE

Riddled Deceit

Tattooed Hearts Duet

Part One

Kris Butler

First Edition: August 2021

Published by Kris Butler

Cover design: © 2021 by Bookish Duet Author Services

Proofreading: © 2021 by Black Lotus Editing

Formatting Design: © 2021 by Bookish Duet Author Services

Created with Vellum

"I'll meet you under the stars."

Contents

Playlist

Music plays a part of this story in unique ways. I wish I could embed certain songs at certain parts so the music could add to the scene as music has a way of enhancing emotions. There are four songs sung in the book listed below and they can be found on the playlist included below.

Riddled Deceit Playlist on Spotify

Here are the chapters and songs

Chapter 9

Jewel, "Foolish Games"

Chapter 16

Lady Antebellum, "Need You Now"

Lewis Capaldi's, "Someone You Loved"

The Chicks', "Not Ready To Make Nice"

Foreword

This is a why-choose novel, meaning the main female character doesn't have to choose between love interests. This is a contemporary romantic suspense with some dark themes including grief, mental health, and stalking. This is a medium burn with MM. This is an adult romance and is intended for readers 18+ due to language and content. Cuss words are used throughout, and sexual scenes are explicit. This book ends on a cliffhanger. Part 2 will be available shortly.

To my reader group—you guys are amazing. Thank you for helping me build this book. It transformed into an amazing story, more than anything I'd ever anticipated, so I hope you like it.

Chapter One

LENNOX

SQUEEZING MY EYES SHUT, I held the needle in my hand as I attempted to breach the cartilage. With my surgical gloves on, I felt a bit like a surgeon ready to dismember this earlobe! Not that I would say that to the client, they tend to get a little iffy when you want to lop off body parts. Truth be told though, I hated watching the needle part.

No matter how often I did this, I always got nauseous. And well, when it was your job, it wasn't something you advertised. I'd devised a way to stop from passing out on people. It was simple, really. I squeezed my eyes closed just before I plunged the needle through. Brilliant, right?

"Um, are you supposed to have your eyes closed?" the nasally voice of the overly perfumed soccer mom asked, breaking through my concentration.

Ugh, I hated when they noticed. Couldn't they just let me have my process? I didn't go to their jobs and tell them how to calculate numbers or some baloney-maloney mumbo jumbo! Geez, people and their expectations these days.

Mumbling to myself in response, "*Keep your eyes open.*" I realized too late it might've been louder than I intended. Not to mention, possibly a bit mimicky. Okay, there was no might. It totally did and it wasn't the smartest thing I'd done today. I tended to forget that regardless of my eyes being closed, it didn't mean they couldn't still see me.

Apparently, my object permanence hadn't advanced past childhood because I still believed if I couldn't see the monsters, they couldn't see me. Tragic really.

"Did you just *mock* me?"

It was on the tip of my tongue, but I held back the urge to do it again. See? I could be a grown-up when it called for it.

Squinting to appease the harpy, because yes, despite her calling me out, I still had my eyes closed. I lifted one eye to check if the needle was hidden from my purview. It was a bit of an ironic thing, to be a body piercer and yet hate the sight of needles. It really hindered my ability to stab people with sharp objects. Which double irony, I also enjoyed! This job should've been right up my alley. It was just the whole 'eyes closing near needles thing' people kept complaining about.

Seriously, people were the worst.

"Nope, that's something I *definitely* did not do, darlin'. Now, hold still and I'll get you fixed up real nice. I've almost got it."

Sticking out my tongue, another part of my process, and keeping one eye closed, I angled myself to push the needle in the correct placement on her ear. The stupid cartilage was always so tricky. Like, why did it have to be so hard?

"Okay, on the count of three," I began, but before I could say one though, she interrupted me.

"Wait! I'm having second thoughts."

Ignoring her, I counted off in my head. *One, two, three*. Pushing it forward, I squinted again as the needle pressed through. The customer tensed, but I ignored her and slid the hoop into the hollow needle, and then pulled it completely out. Snapping the clasp closed, I tossed the needle into the sharp's container, happy to be rid of it and did a little 'ta-da' with my hands.

Stepping back, I felt proud of myself and smiled at my handy work, but as usual, no one appreciated the effort it took for me to do this job, nor my jazz hands. They were severely underrated. The customer looked at me in shock, a hand clutched to her chest. Furrowing my brow, I tried to figure out what was going on.

"What? Do I have something on me?" Patting myself down, I didn't feel anything in my search. Instead of answering, she hopped up and stormed out of the store, knocking into people as she went.

"You're welcome," I called after her. "Don't forget to clean it twice a day!"

The other employees turned at my shout, before rolling their eyes, and returning to whatever they were doing. They were used to me by now, and quite frankly, her only storming out was a better ending than most of my piercing jobs.

Cleaning up my area, I put everything back just the way Tatzilla liked it. The boss was very particular about certain things, and unless I wanted to reorganize the entire supply room *again*, I made sure to at least do as requested, even if I grumbled about it while doing it. I could follow directions when I wanted to. It was the *wanted to* part that was the key.

"James!"

"So close."

Muttering, I dropped my head and shuffled my feet in my platform shoes to the back office. I caught Bubba snickering behind his hand as I walked by, making an "ooooh, you got in trouble" face at me. Being the ever-classy Southern Belle I was, I stuck out my studded tongue at him. At least it was decorative.

"How can I help you today, Evans?" I cooed in my best charming voice while I blinked my eyes at him. I even held my hands behind my back, the perfect picture of innocence as I teetered on my feet.

Tatzilla sat behind his desk, his tattooed arms crossed as he glowered at me. His dark espresso eyes lasered into me, and I didn't recall a time when the man wasn't making some sort of disappointed, angry face in my general direction. He was only a few years older, but half the time, I felt like an errant child who'd disappointed him simply by breathing. He very much had that 'being called down to the principal's office' vibe about him.

"Cut the shit, James. Why did your client run out of here like her ass was on fire?"

Tatzilla glared, daring me to lie as he lifted his perfectly pierced brow. Which, thank you very much, I did! Now, *that* piercing was a fun one!

Zeroing in on his eyes, I ignored the way my pulse spiked at the intensity I found there. Every time I was in a room alone with the tattooed beast of a man, I simultaneously wanted to punch him and make out with him. It was a bizarre feeling.

"Oh, you mean the completely satisfied customer I just had?" I countered with my best sickly-sweet voice.

"Is that what you call *satisfied*?" I ignored the sexual innuendo and kept up my act.

"Yeppers! She was as happy as a lark, too! In fact, she couldn't wait to get home to show her family. Now, if that's all, I reckon I better get back to the front. The boss is a stickler for those sorts of things."

Faking a cringe, I tossed my hands up in a 'what can you do' gesture like I wasn't talking about him. Very carefully, I began to make my way out of the office as I walked backward, never taking him out of my eyesight, knowing full well who the alpha was here. I was so close to salvation when he spoke up, halting my steps.

"James, sit your taco-loving ass down. *Now*."

In my defense, he only had himself to blame for what happened next. He had brought up my butt and love for tacos in the same threat, after all. Tatzilla had insulted my outfit—the black taco dress I wore was one of my favorites—and commented on the amount of junk I had in my trunk! And yet, it was the '*now*' in his phrase that really got under my skin.

Tilting my chin up, I glared daggers at his devilishly handsome face.

"What did you say about my butt?"

My voice was raspy, my breathing ragged as I tried to calm myself down, my face heating. Evans leaned over his desk, his arms flexing when he clenched his fists, his jaw tight as he scowled hard back at me. It was a staring contest for the ages, one of the highest caliber, our stubbornness battling it out between us.

His look had my pulse racing for an entirely different reason this time.

"I *told* you to sit your ass down. So do it. *Now*."

There it was again, that '*now*' tacked onto the end, a *dare* if I ever heard one. Crossing my arms, I planted myself right where I was, glowering back just as hard at the overbearing jerk.

"Or *what*?"

Yeah, it wasn't the brightest response, but I also knew how this would end despite telling myself to stop every time.

I never did.

I pushed the darn button every single time that started the domino effect.

What was Tatzilla's button? Obstinacy and sass, and I had heaps of both.

Like clockwork, he pushed back from his desk, his 6'4" frame filling the space as his dark black hair fell into his eyes. He brushed it back, his tattooed fingers moving it behind his ears. Tatzilla continued to stalk toward me, nothing stopping his trek until his body was towering over me as he eyed his next meal.

His nostrils flared, the movement sending flutters straight to my hoo-hah. There was no doubt I was his prey in this situation, even if I was too stubborn to admit it out loud. Tatzilla moved closer, erasing all the space between us. Instinctively, I backed up despite knowing I'd already been caught.

My body didn't care, it screamed at me to do it anyway.

When my back hit the door, I knew I was trapped. I mean, I'd known that ahead of time. This wasn't a new thing with us. *Oh no*. This was a familiar dance between the alpha male and his dinner.

Me—I was his dinner.

My chest rose as my breath quickened, the buttons on the top of my cardigan threatened to give way. His eyes zeroed in on the fabric as it stretched, and I watched as he licked his lips, wetting them with his tongue as he clicked the stud over his teeth.

This was our thing, our whole shtick. Tatzilla and I hated each other with a fiery passion, which resulted in constantly pushing one another's buttons until we erupted, preferably in orgasms.

Slamming his hands around me on the door frame, I sucked in a breath at the sound. Tatzilla's dark eyes bore into me, causing me to hold my breath.

"Do you want to try that again, *Peach*?"

Ah, crap! He'd gone and used his sexy nickname for me. The one he only used when he *purred* it. Lifting my chin, my stubbornness flaw was going strong, and I held my ground despite my legs shaking from the lust coursing through me, and I repeated, "Or *what*?"

It was all he needed as his lips crashed down onto mine, demanding entrance. I heard the lock snick seconds before he lifted me by my hips, my legs naturally wrapping around him.

I hated how naturally we fit together.

I hated how good his kisses made me feel.

I hated how I both craved and despised every second of our encounters.

"You need to be punished, Peach, for your sass, and I know just the way to remind you who's in charge."

He growled it into my neck, his hot breath licking up my body, promising me *all the things.* This close, his woody leather scent invaded every part of me, stopping any attempt I could make to halt this.

There would be no stopping now.

The clink of his belt froze me in place, as I started to backpedal. Okay, maybe we wouldn't go down this road today, after all. We'd never done anything like this before, and I wasn't sure I wanted to. Tatzilla felt my body tense at his action and pulled back. Observing me closely, he peered into my eyes, another challenge rising.

"You're not scared, are you, *Peaches*?"

How he knew precisely which question would flip my fear into reckless stupidity, I never understood. But somehow, Tatzilla could read me better than I could myself and always understood *exactly* what I needed. And when he added the extra adoration onto Peach, I was a goner.

It was sexy man witchcraft if I ever heard it. Tilting my chin, I stared back, dead on.

"What's there to be scared of? *You*?" I chuckled, the sound a bit manic as it rushed out. "I can take whatever you dish out, Evans. Haven't you learned that by now?"

"Oh, Peach, your mouth is cashing checks I don't think you can afford. Time to play and see."

He wrapped his belt around my wrists, binding them over my head. Looping the belt back together, he placed it on the coat hook on the back of the door. Since it was currently summer, it was empty, and my hands slid down easily before pulling taut. His gaze as he took me in was devilish and reminded me exactly who I was dealing with.

"That's more like it. *Now*, you can't run away or try to take control. I have you exactly where I want you."

If he didn't look and sound so sexy when he said it, I might've kneed him in the groin. Tatzilla licked up my neck and swirled the stud around the curvature. I wanted to hate it. I even tried to push him away. But even with the excuse of my arms bound this time, I was never successful at stopping him. It felt too good to care.

Tatzilla's hands roamed my body, treating me like I was a masterpiece. Despite hating one another 98% of the time, it was the other 2% where he made me feel *worshipped*. He made me feel like the sexiest woman alive when we were together, and, being on the curvy side, it was something I craved. Maybe it was why I always caved to him, but in reality, I knew it was because it felt too good to give up.

You could say whatever you wanted about making love, but I'd come to believe lust-filled hate sex was a top contender for the ultimate horizontal tango.

"Time to remind you who's boss at this store, Peach."

I should be nervous or worried, but my body was so taut with sexual tension and turned on, all I could think about was the pleasure he could give me. If he didn't touch me soon, I was afraid I'd combust from sexual frustration. In a surprising move, he dropped to his knees, and for a moment, the belt pulled, digging into my wrists. I winced at the sting as the belt held all my weight. The small bite of pain had been unexpected, gravity taking control. Hanging on the door, I couldn't even touch the ground, my toes barely scraping the surface.

Thankfully, the alphahole didn't leave me suspended for long and settled my legs over his shoulders. The move helped to redistribute my weight, providing me with relief from the belt. When Tatzilla nosed himself under my dress and into my crotch, I jumped. He rubbed his face across my panties, and I could feel my wetness seeping through the fabric. Tatzilla's hot breath fanned over my skin, and I was on edge as I waited to see what he'd do next.

His tongue dipped around the edge of my panties, his stud hitting my clit briefly before he lowered them down. Lifting one leg up, he pulled the fabric off before lifting the other to do the same. I'd become so distracted by his actions, I hadn't paid attention to where his focus was as he settled my knees on his shoulders.

Within seconds, his tongue plunged into me, his stud scraping along the sides of my walls before coming up to flick my clit. It was the most fantastic feeling in the world, and a long moan escaped me as I gave in to the pleasure.

Tatzilla growled seductively as he pulled back, a

smug expression on his face. "Mmm, seems you like that, Peach. Now, it's time I had my cream."

I couldn't even make out his words as he kept tongue loving me, sending waves of intense satisfaction through me with each stroke. When Tatzilla started scissoring his fingers as well, I was seconds away from orgasming on his face. Just as I began to feel my body tighten, he pulled away and dropped my legs. The pain of the leather bit into my skin again, but it was the loss of the orgasm that had me crying out to him.

"Mother of Pearl! What do you think you're doing, or more like *not* doing?" I screeched.

Taking in his smug smile, I knew then it'd been intentional. What I hadn't noticed, though, was when he'd stood, he'd lowered his pants just enough to allow his manhood to pop free. So, as he distracted me with his smirk and fuddled my mind with the loss of orgasm, Tatzilla stroked himself.

"I'm showing you who's boss, remember, *Peaches*?"

He'd moved closer, his words a caress over my mouth, breathing them into me. When he grabbed my legs, I instinctively wrapped them back around him. Tatzilla was a sex master, skilled in distraction techniques and misdirection. While my brain focused on shouting at him, he'd cleverly moved into position to dominate me.

Right as he reminded me I was *his* peach, Tatzilla slammed his cock into me in one fluid movement. I'd opened my mouth to tell him off, but instead, a loud moan escaped, my body's welcoming call to him. His lips lowered back to mine a second later, swallowing the last of the sound. With my hands bound above me, and his hands clenching my butt, I stayed perfectly immobilized while he screwed me against the door. The force of his movements banged us against the door, the frame rattling with each thrust.

There was no point in being quiet. Everyone in the shop knew we hate-humped on the regular, and I was pretty sure they took bets on how long we'd go between them. This period of time had been long, and after four weeks, I didn't want to admit I'd missed it.

Slamming into me over and over, my body started to rebound its earlier orgasm. This was the kicker, really. Because as I stared into his eyes during these brief moments of intimacy, I could almost make out—

"*Lennox*! Can you turn on the stove for me? I want to make some mac n' cheese."

Jumping up at the noise, I blinked at the interruption as I came back into the land of the living, waking from my sex dream. Dagnabit! And right before the good stuff too. For some reason, I felt I was doubly robbed of an orgasm now. Fake or not.

Wiping my mouth with the back of my hand, I peeled the book cover off my face that had somehow adhered there via the stream of drool I'd excreted over the past few hours. I'd fallen asleep at my desk while reading my newest smutty book. My mom had needed me to watch Noah for a few hours, but since he was twelve, he didn't need to be entertained. I'd given in to the call of my new book. I'd also started sketching a new tattoo design, and as I lifted my other hand, it was stuck to the piece of paper I'd been working on.

Well, fiddlesticks! I liked that drawing.

Unfortunately, my latest creation was now smudged from the drool river that had run through it.

Rubbing my face to wake up, I was surprised when I glanced down at my hands and spotted ink all over them. Crapola, I bet I'd smeared it all over me now. Lovely.

A poke in my arm reminded me there had been a reason I'd awoken, and I came face to face with the object of the poking. My brother, Noah, stood staring at me, patiently waiting for me to answer while I woke up. When he caught sight of my face, he let out a loud hoot.

"Oh man, your face."

"What?" I played dumb. "Is there something on my face?"

Moving, I acted like I was going to wipe it on him causing him to take off running. Grinning, I popped up to chase him. Noah was one of my favorite people in the world, and despite our fourteen-year age difference, we got along splendidly. He was one of the few people I didn't loathe being around on a regular basis. As I skidded to a halt in the kitchen, I ran smack dab into a body that wasn't meant to be there.

"What the hell, James?"

Ignoring the voice, I grabbed onto the shirt of the body I was pressed against to keep from falling. I managed to right myself, my socks slipping on the freshly waxed floor just as Noah chased the cat into the kitchen from the other direction, and inevitably right into the middle of my huddle.

That was all it took, and down we went in a tangle of arms and legs.

In a surprise move, the body shifted before we hit the floor, and I landed with a resounding 'oomph' on top of the one person I never wanted to be this close to. The air was knocked out of us both as we laid staring at one another in mutual hatred and shock.

"Lennox James! What in tarnation are you doing, young lady? Get off the nice Mr. Evans right this instance!"

My mother stood over me, stomping her foot as she stared down at me in shock for presumably embarrassing her. As if the matter couldn't worsen, my father, the police chief, entered along with my roommate and best friend, Simon. I just loved having an audience to my humiliation.

Si busted out laughing when he saw my predicament and how I couldn't manage to figure out how to get out of it. Noah chuckled along with him, and my father shook his head, used to my shenanigans by now.

"Is there a reason you haven't gotten off me yet, *James*?" the tattooed Adonis below me whispered.

Cheeks flaming, I scrambled and rolled off him, lying on the floor. I was unable to get up any further, the weight of embarrassment keeping me down.

Just kill me now. This day was going to be fan-freakin-tabulous.

Welcome to my life, where I just didn't get crapped on. I got double-dipped crapped on. Pulling myself up to standing, I turned and looked at the crowd in the kitchen. When no one said anything, I tossed my hands up and pointed at the sexy man who was now smirking at me.

"Y'all going to tell me what the heck *he's* doing in our kitchen?"

Huffing, I planted my hands on my hips as I waited for an explanation. Unfortunately, it only caused them to burst out laughing for my effort. Glaring daggers of hatred at them, I waited for someone to explain. Finally, my mother pulled herself together enough to answer me.

"Sorry, dear. Mr. Evans helped me out when my car got a flat, and he offered to give me a lift home while they towed it in since my spare was also flat."

Nodding, I accepted my mother's response. Dropping my hands, I started to relax when my father spoke up next.

"Now, can you tell us all why your face looks like you had a fight with a zebra?"

"Jiminy Cricket!" I yelped, turning, and racing from the kitchen into the bathroom. Before I shut the door, I stopped and listened to their banter, wondering why he'd stuck around.

Slade's dark rumble was doing things to me I didn't want to admit. I could picture him with his smirk, basking in the enjoyment of my humiliation as he leaned against the counter.

Yelling, "I hate y'all," I finally closed the door and looked in the mirror. I couldn't help the chuckle that escaped as I took in my face. Grabbing a rag, I began to rub it off, clearing myself of any ink smudges. If Slade hadn't been here, I would've laughed right along with them, not even blinking an eye at the embarrassment.

But his presence changed things and brought out the worst in me.

The part I was in denial about, though, was how good his body had felt beneath me.

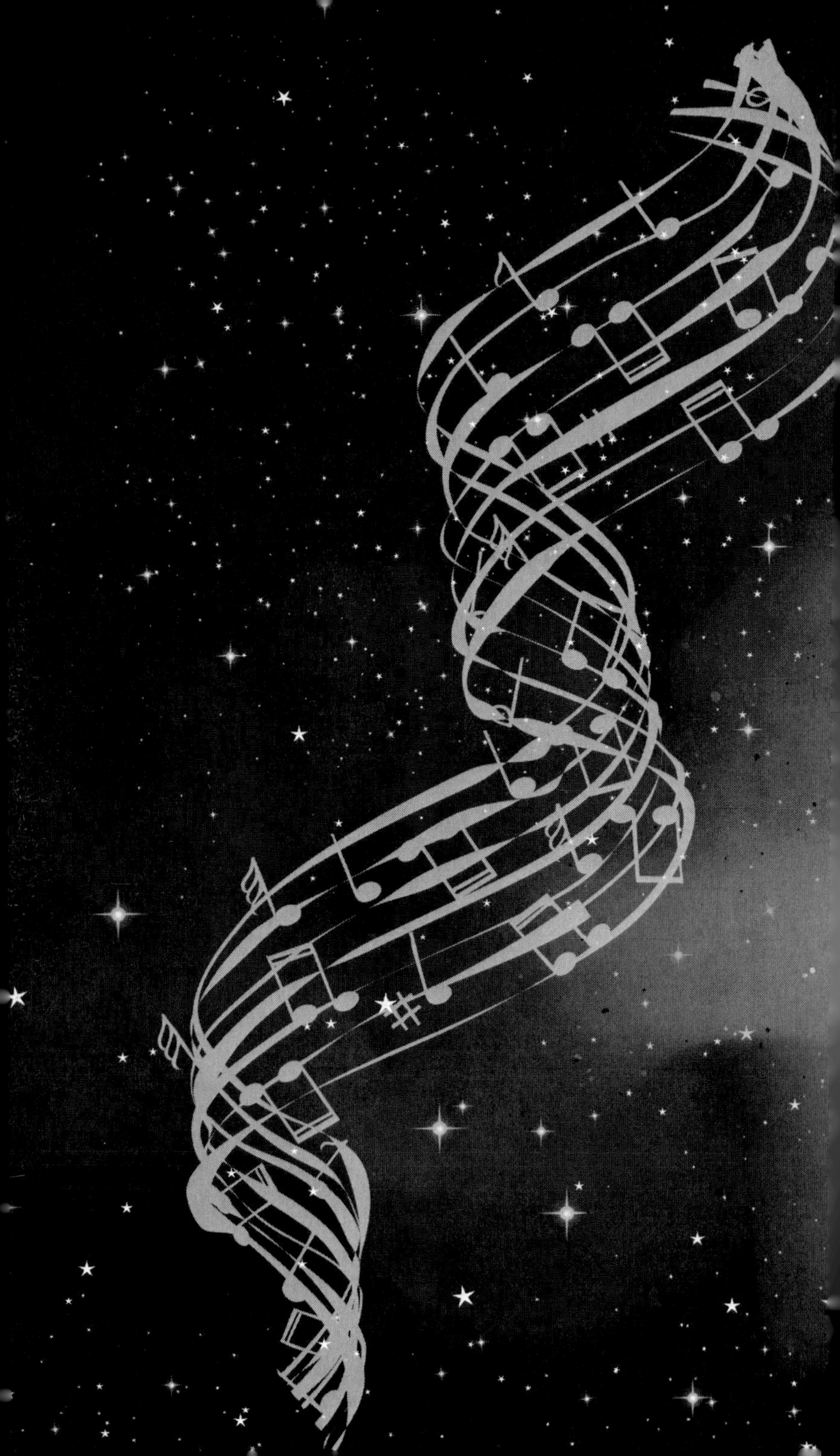

Chapter Two

LENNOX

THE HUMID AIR blew through the shop as another customer entered the place. It was August in Kentucky, meaning it was as hot as Satan's balls and as humid as Hell itself. I didn't look up from my sketch pad, not caring who it was until they absolutely needed me.

My boss would yell at me later, but it was a semi-regular occurrence, and I'd gotten used to his shouting by now. Besides, some days, it was the most he spoke to me, and I think I'd become conditioned to expecting it. I tried to ignore how hot it was watching him get angry and kept *that* hidden desire to myself. My subconscious apparently wasn't down with the idea, though, if my dream yesterday was anything to go by.

Slade and I weren't exactly sworn enemies, but you couldn't call us besties either. The best term was boss-nemy and we merely tolerated each other. I didn't know what his beef was, but from moment one, he'd had a stick up his rear toward me. I'd honestly been surprised when he called to offer me the job since he'd spent the entirety of the interview glaring at me, and then grilled me on proper piercing techniques and my commitment to work for the last five minutes of it.

It was probably why I'd been an incompetent

employee in my dream. Nothing like a lucid memory to make your insecurities glaringly obvious.

So, I've had a few jobs. Big whoop. Life hadn't been the easiest for me, and after several failed directions, I'd finally found one I'd stuck with, even if it had taken me a while to get here. I was about to turn twenty-six and it wasn't a crime to not know your future, despite how he made me feel about it.

I hadn't wanted to accept the position, knowing I'd have to work for him, but jobs were scarce in our town, especially for piercers. When you added in the salary, a job I enjoyed, and flexible scheduling, I couldn't turn it down.

A bonus was my best friend worked next door at the hair salon, making it an overall win when I truly thought about it. I just had to suffer through Mr. Bad Attitude on the daily. Of course, he was too freaking hot for his own good, so I spent half my day creating ways to creatively torture him and the other half drooling.

It was a fun game to pass the time.

My attraction to him wasn't a proud one, and I wouldn't admit it out loud if you paid me. Our heated battles were well known in the shop, and I didn't want to look like one of those girls who gave it up for the bad boy.

So, Slade Evans was my bossnemy—end of discussion.

We'd been slotted into our opposing corners on day one, and both of us were too stubborn to come out of them in real life. 'Dream Me' might want to bang him, but 'Real Me' knew where to draw the line. Preferably far, far away from one another.

A clearing of a throat had me lifting my eyes to find a middle-aged man staring down at me. Welcome to Bowling Green, Kentucky, a small town with a big city feel, or at least that was what the sign proclaimed. Our biggest achievements were the University and the Corvette Museum. Everything else was small-town America, and you tended to know everyone who lived here your whole life.

Being a hop, skip, and a jump from Louisville, Kentucky and Nashville, Tennessee, we'd become a pit stop for travelers, and this man was clearly one of them. I'd go with a truck driver based on the stench alone if I had to guess.

"Welcome to Emblazed Tats. How may I help you, sir, on this fine day?" I chirped, overexaggerating my southern accent. Just as I'd expected, the man softened, my greeting dripping in warmth and charm. No one could hate a Southern Belle; it was a proven fact.

"Well, aren't you just a pretty thing?" The foul-smelling man grinned, leaning his beer belly and sweaty, hairy arm against the counter to leer at me.

"Just as my momma made me. Can I get your name and what you're in for? Are we wanting body art or metal accessories today?"

"The name's Dwayne, sugar, but you can have more than that, if you want it."

Dwayne's attempt at flirting fell flat, his stale breath hitting me square in the face. The smell of beer and corn nuts overwhelmed me as he continued. "I'm here for a tat, and I hope it's with *you*."

"Ah, shucks, Dwayne," I pouted. "I'm not a tattoo artist. Something about trusting me with guns," I cringed into a fake laugh. "You shoot one guy in the foot during 7th grade wilderness camp, and no one ever lets it go!" As I hoped, he pulled back some, clearly not wanting any of my crazy near him. "But it does look like you're with Bubba, and I know he'll take *real good* care of you. One sec, hun."

I spun around on the stool, hopping off as I did, the move perfected at this point. As I walked away, I prayed the skirt of my dinosaur dress wasn't stuck up my buttcrack for Dirty Dwayne to peeve on.

Slade had thought it would be hilarious to make me sit on the stool as a jab at my height. The joke was on him though, I liked it. I had fun spinning around on it. On slow days, Bubba and I would see how many twirls we could go round before toppling off. It was a hoot as long as I didn’t get sick.

My platform espadrilles gave me extra height today, and I danced to the song in my head as I strutted over to the burly bear of a man. Bubba was the type of guy you expected to find at a tattoo parlor. Shaved head, long ginger beard, with more tattoos than you could count, and his customary leather vest made him appear unapproachable to most. But to me, he was a sweetheart.

"Oh, Bubbbaaaa," I sang, doing a spin as I got closer.

"Yes, sweetheart?" He grinned. "What can I do for you today?"

"You're so good for my ego, Bubba. You've got a live one upfront." Raising my eyebrows, I let him know he was in for a real treat with this one.

Chuckling, he nodded, giving me a big toothy grin. "I'll be up in five."

"Toodles!"

I finger waved at him, skipping off to head back upfront. When I spun, I smacked into the all-familiar chest of Tatzilla. Groaning, I backed up, holding my head. I did not want to end up on the floor with him under me two days in a row.

"Son of a bee sting! Do your pecs have to be so hard, Evans? It's like you purposefully try to injure me."

Rolling my eyes, I shook him off to return to my post, except his invasion had soured my mood, making my steps flatter, no longer feeling my dance.

"Yes, *James*. I purposefully workout just to knock you out with my muscles." His deadpan was on point, and I didn't want to admit how it made me smile. Stupid hot boy magic at play again.

"Sounds like something you'd do, turd," I muttered, trying to dispel the lust wanting to course through me.

"For the love of tacos, James, use a real fucking cuss word, will ya?"

I stopped in my tracks, shocked at how eerily close his words were to my dream. Had it happened in a past life? Did I suddenly have glimpses into the future via my dreams? Shaking it out of my head, I turned on my heels, my smile so sweet.

"I'll have you know, *Evans*, that I am a lady! Nothing dirty will be coming out of this mouth."

I realized too late what I said, the words having already flown out of my mouth. I wanted to catch them in the air and shove them back down, never to be heard. Quickly, I spun around, my face flaming, and speed walked as fast I could on my stubby legs. My dress tracked my movement with each step, swishing around me as I went by in a flurry.

I wasn't certain, but I could've sworn I heard, *"I have something dirty that can cum in your mouth,"* uttered in a low growl, but I would deny hearing it if anyone asked.

Flustered beyond belief, I'd forgotten about Dirty Dwayne as I hastily sat back on my stool, spinning around to the front. Tapping my pen, it wasn't until he cleared his throat again, I remembered he was there.

"Oh! I'm so sorry, sir. Bubba will be right with you."

"Now I see why my flirting didn't work on ya, sugar. You're a claimed woman already."

"I-no, it's not like that. He's just my boss, and he hates me," I rambled, for some reason feeling the need to divulge this information to a complete stranger.

"I might not know a lot," he admitted kindly, making me like him a little bit more, "but I *know* when a man's claimed a woman." He lifted his eyes over my shoulder, and I turned to look at his gesture. Slade still stood leaning against the wall, watching us with a critical eye. Turning back, I shook my head again, denying what he claimed.

"It's not like that," I repeated.

"If you say so, sugar." He smiled, appeasing me. It seemed Dwayne wasn't so bad after all. Bubba walked up then, and I saw Dwayne straighten, taking in the bearded giant.

"I'm Bubba. What tattoo we doing today?"

Bubba pulled Dwayne away, looking at his phone as they discussed possible images. Once they were gone, the front fell back into the quiet haven it usually was for me when I didn't have bodies to stab. Popping my earbud back in my ear, I started my current work playlist, the musical tones soothing me as they drifted through. I found the zone again and went back to drawing.

A while later, I felt eyes on me pulling my attention. Glancing over my shoulder, I was confused when nobody was there. In the reflective mirror, though, I caught sight of the back of a black t-shirt as it went around the corner. *Slade*.

Swallowing, I turned back to the front and dislodged the lingering feelings of lust sparking as I remembered his hard chest. Slade was a walking piece of dynamite. Anything between us would be explosive, but whether we lived to tell the tale or not was debatable.

I'd stick to dream Slade. He at least used his mouth for good.

HUMMING ALONG to a song in my head, I browsed a dating app on my phone. In a fit of desperation, I'd signed up a few days ago but then promptly logged out and ignored it. The thought of dating gave me hives, but the dream today after reading one too many smutty books had to be a subconscious cry for help. The problem was, I had a horrible track record with men. It was so bad, they could write a whole sitcom on Lennox's dating woes.

Age 16: I had my first kiss and lost my virginity the same night to my best friend. The morning after, Simon told me that he was gay.

Yeah, ouch.

Age 17: I dated a nice guy from school for several months. We met through the school play. It was great for a month, but then he moved out of state over winter break, and I never heard from him again.

It had been the ultimate ghosting.

Age 18: I had a summer fling with a guy I met through my summer job. I thought it had potential. That was until I discovered he was engaged.

That had been an epic slushy in the face moment.

Age 19: I casually dated a guy I met in Nashville one weekend. We dated for a month, and when I was about to ask him if he wanted to become serious, he broke both of his legs and had to move back home to recover.

My dream of being his Florence Nightingale washed down the drain.

Age 20: I met the perfect guy at a Throwback Karaoke Party. We sang and danced the night away, ending it with a perfect kiss goodbye. Unfortunately, it really was goodbye because I managed to lose the napkin with his number on it the next day. One of the rules was no phones, wanting everything to be authentic.

Well, authenticity sucked. How did people do this in the 90's? I hadn't even known his real name, just Zach from Saved by the Bell.

Age 21: Well, this one was just embarrassing. On a blind date, it ended when I puked all over the table at a Cracker Barrel after a night of drinking. Did I mention it was my 21st birthday? Rookie mistake.

It was really hard to be cute when you had puke breath.

Age 22: Well, I liked to block that year out of my memory completely. It was better that way.

Age 23: At first, I didn't date anyone, and then I tried a one-night stand. When that went horribly wrong, I started texting with a guy online. We talked for months and had great chemistry. Yet, when we met, all he did was talk about my size and curves. He was proud of being what he called a "chubby chaser" and felt I owed him for being interested in me.

Dude, the only one concerned about my waistline was you. I was not a charity case bang. I might have hips, but I wasn't stupid or low on self-esteem. Boy, bye.

Age 24: Well, the guy I'd been seeing proposed after the third date. A few restraining orders later, and I decided I needed a break.

Romance books and my vibrator became my go-to Friday night plans after that.

So yeah, dating never went well for me. Now, I was almost twenty-six and hadn't dated in over a year. Books had been my escape and never disappointed me. They were always there for me when I needed them.

I'd gotten so into reading, I'd started a romance blog. Weirdly enough, people read it. Apparently, I was good at it! Take that, fourth grade teacher who said no one wanted to listen to me! I had a considerable following and presence online. No one in my real life, outside Simon, even knew it was me. It was a fun way to pass my time by sharing all the books I loved in quirky ways and remove myself from being Lennox.

Noxbooks didn’t have baggage unless it was books.

Here lately, though, I'd wanted a little more. I couldn't be cursed forever with dating, or at least that was my hope.

The problem was, it was difficult to meet people I hadn’t known since I was in diapers. I couldn’t even date any of the guys at Emblazed Tats. I mean, I loved them all, but they were mostly older men and not exactly my type. Well, outside of Slade because let’s face it, *he was everyone’s type.* Until he opened his mouth at least.

Bubba had even asked me to marry him multiple times on a lark to make me laugh. He was almost as old as my dad though, and was my bearded guardian angel. Outside the creepy customers hitting on me, I wasn't fighting the guys off with a stick. My social pool was, sadly, very small and consisted of my gay best friend, twelve-year-old brother, and a forty-year-old biker.

Swiping through the messages, I deleted all the ones that screamed ‘dick pic’ guys. I did not need that on my phone. Just my luck, Noah would pick it up, and then I'd be charged with exposing a minor to lewd images. My dad wouldn't care if it was me or that I hadn't been the one to ask for it. He’d arrest me to prove a point.

So, yeah, nope. I didn't need that. I was not one for jail. I would not survive. I had accepted this about myself. It kept me out of trouble most days. You'd think my father being the police chief would stop me from breaking the law, but he was a big teddy bear most of the time. Noah was the only exception. We were all protective of that kid.

Clicking on a guy's profile, I hummed a country song as I read his profile. Someone walked up behind me, placing their hands on my hips before whispering in my ear, "Whatcha doing, short stuff?"

Jumping, I reared back, almost nailing Simon in the head, but thankfully, he had quick reflexes. His hands tightened on my hips, and I sucked in a breath. *It was truly tragic to be in love with your gay best friend.*

Part of my heart had broken the day he told me he was gay. I think in a way, I've been gun shy since then, the pivotal moment my curse was born. It was probably some form of a self-fulfilling prophecy, but when it was your life and your disasters, it felt safer to be gun shy.

"Sugar toast! Si, I could've killed you."

I spun around to face him, pasting a glare on my face to cover the lust. The move also helped to dislodge his hands from my waist, bringing my heart rate to a normal level. Crossing my legs, I smoothed the cute dinosaurs on my dress to calm myself.

Simon Fisher was too good looking for his own good. Standing at 6 ft tall, he was fit without being too muscular. We both hated to sweat, so his muscles had naturally developed from hard work and life. His dyed silver-grey hair cascaded over his eyes, the top long as it swooped over, the sides shaved close.

His eyes were almost the same shade, and I swear with his hair that color now, it made them glow in the right light. When he'd gone to barber school, he started dyeing his natural brunette hair and never looked back.

This, though, was my favorite look. It made him appear rugged in a sexy city-country way. Add in his light stubble, and I had to physically stop myself from biting my lip in want. I wouldn't even get started on how good he smelled. The man was my kryptonite, and he wasn't even an option.

I got distracted checking him out, and it cost me.

Simon grabbed the phone out of my hand, and like cold water being thrown on me, I immediately sobered and scrambled to get it back from him. Reaching out, I forgot about my shoes and the stool, and tripped, falling into his arms. He caught me, laughing at my clumsiness before righting me.

"You throwing yourself at me today, Lenn?" he chuckled, holding my phone out of reach. It was at this point, I gave up and hoped the embarrassment would end soon. I didn't trust myself to move anymore. Leaning back, I huffed as I crossed my arms.

"What do we have here?" he grinned, but when he saw the dating app, a weird look crossed his face.

"You're *dating* again?"

Shrugging, I kept quiet. Simon had held my hand and eaten ice cream with me through each break-up and heartbreak. "I'm just looking, okay. Just to test out the waters."

"Are you even ready for that? You know, after everything that's happened. Are you ready to challenge the curse again?" Simon teased, but it had a biting edge I didn't usually hear from him.

Grabbing my phone, I clicked it off and shoved it in my bag below the counter. Spinning on the stool in one quick movement, I leaned against the counter, effectively ignoring him. I didn't need to be reminded of my failures in love, especially not from him.

Simon wasn't one to be deterred, though, and he walked around to the front like he should've done in the first place. Because our storefronts were in the same strip mall, the back doors let out to the same alley. He took advantage of this fact, even if to just avoid the girl at the front desk of the salon. Crystal was one of those girls who thought that she was all that and a bag of chips. It didn't compute to her how Simon could turn her advances down, despite him telling her repeatedly he was gay. I think the poor girl thought he just hadn't had the right va-jay-jay.

Sorry, honey, not that mine was made of gold or anything, but if he was ever to pick one, I'd hope it would be me.

I feared she was one step away from drugging his drink and raping him to prove her point. The crazy was *that* tangible in her eyes.

"Hey, Lenn. I'm sorry, okay? I'm just surprised. That's all. I didn't mean to be a jerk. We usually do these things together. And after everything that happened with your pen pal, I just thought you were done with trusting the internet. Okay?"

I could hear the hurt in his voice, and I instantly felt horrible. I had hidden it from him on purpose. The pen pal being the biggest reason, another pain I didn't want to relive. Sighing, I looked up at him. He was giving me his kicked puppy dog look, and I caved. How could you resist *that* look?

"I know. I know. I just thought, I don't know," I paused, shrugging my shoulders, "maybe if no one knew my date ended in a disaster, then maybe it wouldn't hurt as bad."

His face fell, a look of guilt crossing it for a brief second before this trademark smile returned. "I get it, Lenn. I do. You can tell me, though. I promise not to make fun. You know, for at least a whole hour." Simon laughed, not even able to keep a straight face, and I threw my pen at him.

"Ha, Ha. Why am I friends with you again?"

"Because you love me."

"Yeah, I do. I love you, Si."

I tried to hide my true feelings, but I could've sworn a look of lust flitted in his eyes at my words. Simon had been all over the place today, sending me weird signals. I didn't know how to deal with it.

"I have an idea," he started. "Let's grab Chinese for dinner and have a Real Housewives of Beverly Hills marathon. Just the two of us."

And this was why having a gay best friend was the best. Smiling, I nodded, scared to let my emotions leak through my voice.

"Your ends could use a touch up too. You want to pop over to my chair before we head home?"

Picking up the turquoise ends of my hair, I looked at them critically before realizing he was right. Simon was a magician and the curator of my look. He did my hair for free in exchange for having carte blanche to do whatever he wanted with it. When he'd suggested doing a turquoise ombre look, I'd thought he'd finally lost it, but it had become my favorite. My hair was naturally dark and wavy, but he managed to make me look cuter than I felt most days.

Good hair was the best confidence booster.

Nodding, I checked the time and realized I had about two hours left. There hadn't been too many piercings today, making it slow. I filled the time doing odd jobs around the shop, keeping the schedule, and answering the phones when I wasn't stabbing people. When I had all that done, then I read, drew, or played on my phone. As much of a fartknocker Slade was, at times, with other things, he didn't micromanage. Whether it was to avoid me or not, I didn't care to explore.

"Yeah, sounds perfect. Hopefully, Crystal will be gone by then too."

We both grimaced at her name. While she *loved* Simon, she hated me for being his best friend, and in the moments she was lucid in her crazy obsession and believed he was gay, blamed me for it. It was ludicrous, but not a thought I hadn't had myself. Being reminded of it by her put me in a sour mood. She was a brand of crazy I didn't have the patience for today.

"Okay, babe. I'll see you then."

Simon smiled, kissing my cheek before walking

toward the back exit. I spun around again and leaned against the counter as I watched him walk away. I hated how it felt like he took a piece of me with him each time he left, and I feared at some point, he wouldn't return it to me.

Once he was out the door, I twirled around again and stared at my bag like it might bite me. Biting my lip, I pulled out my phone and clicked the app open. I stared at the picture of the guy with brown hair, brown eyes, and a kind smile. He appeared reasonably sane and at least had a job, even if it was washing windows.

Deciding not to overthink it, I typed in a message and hit send.

Noxbooks: I'd love to. How about tomorrow night at Rookies we grab drinks?
TimSqueegeeClean: Right on. Sounds like a solid idea. 7 pm?
Noxbooks: Sure. I'll see you there.
TimSqueegeeClean: It's going to be lit, babe!

Sighing, I didn't feel as elated as I'd expected at the prospect of dating. Forcing myself to think positive, I sent happy vibes out into the world that it would go well.

If online dating was a bust, I was becoming a nun.

Chapter Three

LENNOX

FIXING MY HAIR, I twisted one more piece and placed a bobby pin. The color popped after Si had touched it up, and I was in love with the vibrance. I might not be able to style it as well as Simon, but over the years, I'd taught myself some tricks. YouTube and reality shows counted as formal classes in my book.

Tonight, I'd chosen to go with a twisty braid bun that pulled most of it off my neck. It was humid today and having my hair down guaranteed sweat would be rolling down my boobs in under two minutes flat.

I was hoping to save the sweaty part until later, you know, assuming things went well.

Turning my face in the makeup mirror, I scrutinized every angle in the magnifying panel. My cat eye was on point, another YouTube taught skill, and my lipstick was matte perfection. Some women thought about makeup as their war paint, the armor they put on before going into battle. For me, it was a creative way I could express myself. Nothing more, nothing less.

I'd given up long ago on impressing other people or even feeling like I had to fight them.

Growing up with a father who was the police chief hadn't won me many friends when their parties were busted up. And my mother, well, she had moments that made life difficult as a teenager. I'd learned to evaluate the importance of things early. High school girls' approval didn't even make the worry list. Which had probably been good, because otherwise, I imagine high school would've been hella difficult for me.

I didn't fall into the preppy girl category. Come to think about it, I hadn't fallen into any category. I wasn't a smarty geek, athletic, emo, or country-western either. Experimenting with my look and style had kind of always been my thing. I'd been dubbed the "quirky weird girl" in ninth grade when I started wearing dresses.

It was the summer after puberty had hit, and my body changed from a flat-looking boy shape into a curvy girl. Suddenly, I had boobs and hips, and no clue what to do with them. Jeans and t-shirts would no longer cut it, fitting all wrong on my short frame. I'd eventually found my style, landing on dresses that were modern-retro to quirky-cute looks.

That summer had been pivotal for me in owning my self-worth.

My brother had been born at the beginning of the year, and it had changed things in my home. The biggest was discovering my mom suffered from Bipolar 1 Disorder. My parents had hidden it from me, not wanting me to worry, but when an episode occurred, they could no longer deny it. My life became very different after that, and I'd realized I'd experienced things my other peers hadn't, no longer feeling connected to them.

When you let go of teen girls' expectations, it freed you to find your own.

After that summer, the only friend worth keeping was Simon, and when we started high school that fall, I was a new person. Them calling me quirky worked for me. I embraced it and stopped caring what my peers thought. They'd already all proven I couldn't count on them when I needed them. So, why would I put value in their opinions? I didn't.

"Simon, I need help! I can't fit into any of my clothes, and Shelley Adams invited me to her pool party at the country club! Can you believe it?" I shrieked, turning to look at him.

Simon rolled his eyes, not caring about Shelley. She'd told the whole school he was a lousy kisser last year after a boy-girl party where they spent 'seven minutes in Heaven'. He hadn't forgiven her yet since no other girls would go out with him now. He spent the whole eighth-grade dance against the wall, drinking punch. He wouldn't even dance with me, saying it was out of pity.

It hadn't been because of pity though.

Because despite what Shelley said, I thought Simon would be a great kisser. Maybe it just needed to be with the right person.

I wanted to be the right person.

I shouldn't be having these feelings for my best friend, but Mom told me it was natural as you got older to think about it. He was the boy next door, and we'd been playing in the dirt together since birth. I'd rolled my eyes at her at the time, but she'd said at some point, all my hormones would course through my body and make me see boys differently. She'd been right, but he was the one I saw the most.

Even now, as he sat on my bed reading a comic, his shirt raised a little, I found myself drooling. He was in shorts and an old t-shirt I've seen him wear hundreds of times. It was only now I noticed the way they fit him, and I imagined his chest underneath it all. When he looked up and caught me staring, he gave me a funny look.

"You get sunburned earlier, Lemon Drop? Your face is all red."

He scrunched his nose as he looked at me, moving to get off the bed. Quickly, I turned back to my closet, trying to hide the reason I was so flushed. It didn't help when he called me Lemon Drop. He came to stand behind me and I sucked in a breath. Simon had grown a few inches this summer and now stood a head taller than me.

He placed his hands on my shoulders, resting his head on top of mine. Simon joked I was the perfect height now to be his headrest. I tried to keep my body in lockdown as he stood there. His thumbs casually rubbed my shoulders, and I wondered if he even knew he was doing it. We weren't shy in our affection for one another. It was just part of our relationship. We would even sleep in the same bed and cuddle on the couch when watching movies.

I'd never questioned it. It was natural for us.

But now, I read into every touch and look. I hated how much of a typical teenage girl I'd become in those moments. Simon reached over and flicked through my clothes, and when he didn't find what he wanted, he dropped them, his arm hanging over my body, dangerously close to my boob. I sucked in a breath as I waited.

"Well, it's decided then. I think we need to convince your mom to drop us off at the mall. We're fourteen now. We're capable of going without her. And you're right. You need new clothes. I don't think your boobs will fit in any of those shirts unless you want them to be crop tops," he teased.

Elbowing him in the gut, I turned and crossed my arms over said boobs he'd just casually mentioned. The fact he'd noticed made me self-conscious. Sticking out my tongue, I diverted his attention.

"Hey! You can't talk about my boobs like that." Yeah, way to divert, moron.

"Why? We talk about everything, Lennox."

He looked at me oddly, an eyebrow raised in question. I couldn't find words to answer him when he was making valid points. Stuttering, I screamed out my frustration.

"Boys!"

Throwing up my hands, I stomped out of the room to find my mom. Simon had a good idea about the mall, at least. I found her in the kitchen, taking all the pans out of the cabinets. It was odd, but she'd been more restless lately with baby Noah. They were scattered everywhere, and I even spotted what looked like half a bowl of something she'd started to make, but stopped.

"Um, Mom?"

"Yes, dear?"

"Do you think you could drop Simon and me off at the mall? I need new clothes. Nothing fits, and I was hoping we could go by ourselves since we're older now."

She looked up from her frantic organizing and regarded me. Nodding enthusiastically, she smiled wide before stand-

ing. Wiping her hands on the apron she wore, she grabbed her keys and started to immediately move for the door, apron still on.

"Yes, yes, that will be good. Let's go!" She spoke so fast, I had a difficult time catching it all.

"Hold up, Mom! Aren't you forgetting something?"

When she turned, she looked confused, a furrow in her brow. The monitor went off right then, and I saw her wince at the sound. She hadn't been sleeping much and I felt guilty now for asking her to take us somewhere.

"I'll get Noah. You grab his bag, and I'll meet you in the car. Sound good?"

"Yes, yes! Perfect, honey. I knew I could count on you. You're the best big sister."

She kissed my cheek and jogged out of the kitchen. Shaking my head, I went into Noah's room and pulled the turd out of the crib. He was six months old now and starting to get to the fun stage. He giggled at me and started pulling my hair as I carried him into my room.

Simon looked at me when I entered and smiled at the baby in my arms. Handing him off, he took him gladly and started blowing raspberries on his tummy.

"My mom said she'd drop us off. So, I just need to grab my stuff, and we can go. You tell your parents?"

"I'll text them. They won't care if I'm with you."

Smiling, I buckled my sandal on and grabbed my cross-body purse. It was the newest Vera Bradley pattern of blue flowers and swirls. It had been a gift from my parents for my birthday and starting high school. It was my favorite thing I owned, and I couldn't wait to show it off at school.

Taking Noah back, I placed him on my hip and nudged

Simon out my door. When we walked by the kitchen, he stopped, and I bumped into him.

"What happened in there?"

"Mom was rearranging or something. It's fine. Come on, let's go, move it!" I chuckled, grabbing his arm to pull him.

"Are you sure she's okay?"

"She's fine. Mom just gets antsy sometimes. She'll be okay in a day or two."

"Okay...."

"Gah! Simon. Quit trying to find problems, and let's just go to the mall already. This turd bucket is heavy, you know."

He stopped resisting, looking shocked at finding me with Noah, apparently having forgotten. Shaking his head, he walked out the front door. I managed to lock it while holding a squirming baby. Mom was already in the car with it running. She had a massive grin on her face and made a "let's go" motion with her hand.

Picking up the pace, I opened the back and latched Noah in. I was barely buckled in myself before she pulled out of the driveway and backed out into the street. Speeding off in the direction of the mall, I wondered if maybe Simon had been right to worry. Biting my lip, I pulled out my phone and sent a text to Dad. He'd know what to do. Feeling settled, I laid my head back on the seat and sang along with Mom as the music blasted through the speakers.

We were all dancing and singing by the time we got there, and I ignored my earlier doubt. Kissing her cheek as I got out of the car, I promised to see her in a few hours. She hurried us along and sped off in a different direction. Simon and I shrugged before I grabbed his arm and headed in to find new clothes.

Pulling myself out of the memory, I smoothed out the black A-line dress with little cherries on it. It was my own creation that I'd mocked off a vintage dress but added in slits on the skirt part and a see-through overlay on top to give a peek-a-boo look. You could see the red bra I wore. It was racy and classy, my perfect aesthetic. Wrapping the ribbons of my favorite red espadrilles around my calves, I tied them in a bow. I was officially ready to rock this date.

Simon was working late tonight, so I didn't have to worry about sneaking past his room. I hadn't told him about my date yet. It was one of the first times I'd kept something from him, but I wasn't sure how supportive he would be after his reaction to the app.

I was tired of being on the sidelines, and the only way to get in the game was to take a chance. Hopefully, it would go well, and I could prove him, and myself, wrong about my dating curse.

TWO STRAWBERRY LEMONADES and a fried pickle appetizer later, I regretted my decision to try online dating. Si was right. I should've known better about online relationships after my pen pal.

In our freshman year of high school, Simon and I thought it would be fun to do the coast-to-coast pen pal exchange. It was something we saw advertised through our favorite TV show back then, Letters from Space. It was about a high school set in space, and they wrote letters to another high school on Earth. Of course, there were a lot of other plots, but it was interesting to watch these two schools and how similar they were. Spoilers —the high school in space was in the future!

The show had set up a Letters from Space Pen Pal program. Anyone, from anywhere, of any age could sign up and be paired with someone. We were told not to give any identifiable information and not to even use our real names. Our letters were sent to the headquarters and then mailed from there, so it was completely anonymous.

Of course, I'd thought this was a brilliant idea and was eager to meet someone who didn't know about my family history. Not that I let it bother me, but hearing the constant whispers from classmates and the sympathetic looks from teachers got old after a while. Simon thought it was stupid but went along with it for me.

The first pen pal I got stopped responding after five letters, and the ones I'd gotten had been minimal at best. Not the experience I thought it would be.

Simon, on the other hand, had a decent pen pal, but had told me he didn't want to keep doing it. I'd found his reluctance strange since he appeared to get excited when he received a letter, but I didn't force him to share.

I'd brilliantly taken it upon myself to reach out to his person, the perfect plan in my head.

Dear Mystery Person Aka Blaze,

You don't know me. I'm not the person you've been corresponding with. That's actually my best friend. Unfortunately, he's kind of a dork and doesn't think this thing is cool. I guess from his eyes, I'm the dork. My original pen pal bailed on me after five letters. I know, I know… how could they not think this was fun?

Well, I'm hoping you think this is fun. ~~Simon~~ won't let me read your letters, so your confidentiality is safe. But I know you wrote him back, and that's something I'm looking for.

So, I have a proposition… we become pen pals.

The following are the reasons I think this would work.

1. I'm awesome

2. I like to write

3. I'm loyal and dedicated to doing this, making it a priority to mail you a letter each week

4. Did I mention I'm awesome?

5. I can regale you with funny stories from life with a 2-year-old (before you ask, yes, this is Kentucky, no, he's not mine).

If none of that interests you, then you're not the soulmate pen pal I believe you to be, but if it does, then I think our relationship is off to a good start.

Write back within the week if you're interested, and I'll know you've accepted. If not, I hope you have a great life, Blaze.

Sincerely,

Nox

I THOUGHT I was clever using part of my name and making it gender neutral. To my surprise, because I thought they would roll their eyes and trash my letter, they wrote back, and a long-distance friendship was born.

Simon gave me grief, often stating I'd stolen his friend, but he never had the patience to actually write letters and didn't seem to enjoy it as much as I had. I told him I would stop if it really bothered him, but he shook his head, not saying anything.

Throughout high school, I wrote back and forth without fault every week. When the time came to graduate and move on, I proposed we upgrade our penpalship to online. Once we started emailing, it was an almost daily thing. We talked about everything. Sometimes, he was soft and sweet, and other times, more of a brusque know-it-all that gave good advice and made me laugh, but no matter what, he was always there.

We dropped the act of not knowing one another's sex midway through the first year. It was pretty obvious based on the handwriting, and the things we discussed. It didn't matter to me, though, because we'd become friends. He was a few years older than me, but it didn't seem to matter.

There was a part of me that wondered what he looked like and what his real name was, but I brushed it aside. It was nice not being hindered by those things. At some point, I did start to develop feelings for him. It was hard not to. On paper, or in writing, he was the perfect man and never disappointed me. Of course, I would fall in love with him.

Especially after the disaster with Simon, it felt inevitable.

But I kept quiet, not wanting to lose a good friend. I was surprised when he told me he would be in Nashville for the summer and wondered if I'd be up for meeting in person. Everything in me buzzed to life, and I anxiously awaited our meeting, but it never happened. A pain I didn't like to remember.

Before I could think about everything that followed, a person sat down next to me, breaking the mental trap I'd fallen into. I'd been unconsciously swirling a fried pickle in the dill dip. It was aimless motion allowing me to recollect memories of my past.

This was the problem with being alone. I thought too much.

Taking a pull on my straw, I sucked up the last bit of strawberry syrup as it made that slurping gurgle sound.

"That looks good. Could I buy you another?"

Twisting, I was momentarily awestruck by the most beautiful man sitting next to me. Soft blue eyes, closely cropped dirty blonde hair, and a smile that dazzled me with his perfect teeth were attached to a 6 ft, muscular frame. I blinked, assured I was dreaming or perhaps in a sugar coma.

"You okay, Cherry?"

"Cherry?" I managed to mutter, still dazzled by his pearly whites and baby blues. He was so put together and squeaky clean that he looked out of place in this dingy bar.

"I don't know your name yet, and your dress has cherries on it, so I improvised."

Looking down, I was amazed to find that there were indeed cherries on my dress. My brain had melted, and I could no longer process my environment.

"Huh, you're right."

Looking back up, I was hypnotized again by his smile and eyes. He was just so pretty!

"So, can I get you that drink? Or is your boyfriend returning soon?"

I knew it was a ploy, but I'd never had anyone use it on me before, so I giggled. I giggled like Shirley Temple and even covered my mouth. I was beginning to think they'd put alcohol in my drink or laced those pickles with something because I was acting crazy.

"Nope, no boyfriend. I had a date, but it looks like he stood me up. Unless you're Tim? Though you don't look like the picture, and if you are Tim, and you look like *you*, why would you lie about your appearance? Crap on a stick, I just blurted all that out, didn't I?"

Turning back toward the bar, I tried to motion down Ricky, the bartender, but he was too busy flirting with Darla Sue. Shiitake mushrooms, I needed to get out of here! Deciding I knew the total, I pulled out some cash to leave on the bar when a hand stopped me.

"Has anyone ever told you how cute your accent is? Please, don't leave on my account."

His touch halted me, and I paused, thinking about how I felt with his hand there. There weren't a million butterflies fluttering inside me, but I didn't hate his touch either. Perhaps, this could be a good thing. A test out the waters, so to say experiment. The thought grounded me, and I found myself relaxing. Shoving my wallet back into my purse, I turned and blasted him with my best southern smile.

"No, they haven't, actually. I'm Lennox, in case you want to call me something other than Cherry."

He smiled warmly at me, satisfaction ringing in his eyes that I'd stayed. Something about it felt weird, but I didn't even care because he was so good-looking, my mind kept getting befuddled by it.

"I kind of like Cherry, but it's nice to meet you, Lennox. I'm Thane. *Now*, can I buy you that drink?"

"Yes, I'd love that. It's just lemonade, strawberry lemonade. I don't drink alcohol. It doesn't bother me if you do, though," I started to ramble again. "It's just not something I enjoy."

Nodding, he waved down Ricky, who apparently thought Thane was a better reason to move away from flirting with Darla Sue than me. I gave Ricky the stink eye as he listened to Thane, ensuring he felt my rage at the slight.

"What can I get y'all?"

"I believe the lady is drinking strawberry lemonade, and I'll take one as well. Seems they're rather *tasty*."

Thane grinned, turning to me, and I swear he licked his lips deliberately. Heat flushed up my neck at the gesture, and I had to hold my hand down not to wave it in front of my face to cool off. My death stare must've worked on Ricky because he filled our order the quickest I'd ever seen him. Those drinks were shaken and in front of us in record time.

"So, Lennox, tell me more about your adorable self?"

"Wow, okay, pulling out the big guns there, Thane. I don't really do well on the spot, so FYI, you'll probably get a mixed bag of crazy."

He leaned forward, his hand brushed mine, and I instinctively pulled back, surprised by my movement, but then he spoke again, and I lost all thoughts.

"I can't wait to unravel this bag you're talking about."

I swear the way he said *unravel* had me clenching my legs together. Thane was a smooth talker.

Our chairs naturally turned toward one another, his legs bracketing mine as the rest of the bar faded. We talked about nothing important, but somehow, it seemed like the best conversation I'd had in awhile. I'd never flirted so effortlessly before, and while I barely knew him, it seemed right to find myself pressed up against his Jeep a few hours later as he left me with a kiss.

His body pressed into mine, the hard planes of him rubbing against my nipples. Thane's hands were in my hair, the carefully crafted braid no longer intact. Moaning into his mouth, I was tempted to jump in the front seat and take things further. The voice inside my head that tended to be more practical reminded me how much I liked the date and not to rush it. Slowing things down, I pulled back, our breath now mingling between us.

"I'm really glad I stopped in here tonight."

"Me too," I grinned.

"Can I see you again?"

"I'd love that."

"Here give me your phone."

Handing it to him, he quickly sent himself a text before handing it back. Kissing me briefly, he walked me to my car a few spots over. My old Honda Civic sat alone and I unlocked her as I got in. Going through my startup routine, I was relieved when Betty roared to life. I found Thane watching me, his gaze intense before he jumped into his Jeep. He was a little intense, and, at times, I felt unsure, but my libido responded to him, so it had to mean something.

Driving back to the apartment, I felt confident I'd finally broken the curse—the remnants of his strawberry kiss and his number in my phone as evidence. Things were finally looking like they were coming up Lennox.

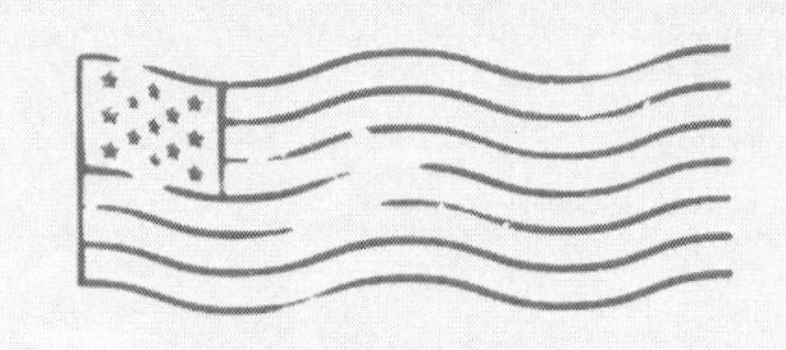

PEN PAL LETTERS

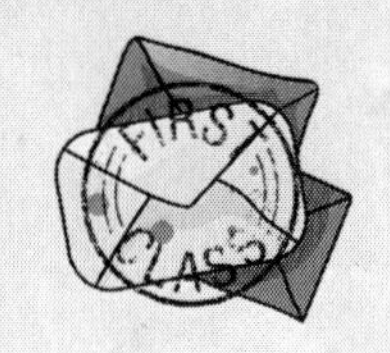

I SUPPOSE I CAN TAKE YOU UP ON YOUR OFFER TO BE PEN PALS. THOUGH, YOUR FRIEND WASN'T A BAD ONE. I'LL MISS HIS FUNNY LETTERS.

YOU DO MAKE SOME INTERESTING POINTS, AND FUNNY TODDLER STORIES ARE A SELLING POINT. I DIDN'T THINK HE WAS YOURS THOUGH, SO SLOW YOUR ROLL. I MIGHT BE FROM THE WEST COAST, BUT I'M NOT A TOTALLY CLUELESS PERSON.

I'M NOT SURE WHERE TO START. WHAT DO YOU WANT TO KNOW? YOU'VE CONVINCED ME TO WRITE, BUT WHAT DO WE WRITE ABOUT? WELL, MY DAY HAS BEEN LAME. MY BROTHER AND I GOT INTO A FIGHT AND I'M NOT SURE HOW I FEEL ABOUT IT. THINGS HAVE BEEN DIFFICULT LATELY. I'M HOPING YOU CAN DISTRACT ME.

I DON'T KNOW WHAT ELSE TO SAY NOW, SO I'LL KEEP THIS FIRST ONE SHORT. PERHAPS WE CAN ASK EACH OTHER A SILLY QUESTION, A PERSONAL QUESTION, AND A RANDOM QUESTION TO MAKE IT EASIER?

I'LL GO FIRST.

1) IF YOU HAD TO CHOOSE BETWEEN NEVER BRUSHING YOUR TEETH OR NEVER SHOWERING, WHICH WOULD YOU CHOOSE? AS GROSS AS IT MAY SOUND, I CAN'T STAND NOT BRUSHING MY TEETH. HOPEFULLY, MY NATURAL ODOR IS GOOD.

2) TELL ME SOMETHING THAT FRIGHTENS YOU. CLOWNS. THEY'RE EVIL.

3) FALL OR SPRING. FALL ALL THE WAY.

SINCERELY

Blaze

Chapter Four
LENNOX

SIMON HAD BEEN in his room when I returned last night, with the door closed. I hadn't had to face him yet about my date, and the dread pooled in my belly. Pouring some cereal into a bowl, I kept my eyes focused on his door, waiting for him to wake up. I knew I was being ridiculous and a tad bit obsessive, but when it came to Simon, it had always been that way.

I didn't know how to be anything but full throttle with the boy, even if just friends.

It felt like he'd been upset with me yesterday, or worse, *disappointed*. Having Simon displeased with me was the absolute worst feeling. This obsession wasn't healthy, this need for his approval. I could recognize that. But it had been our dynamic for so long, I wasn't sure I could stop. Or that I wanted to. I didn't care what others thought, but Simon wasn't just anyone.

He was my rock, my person, and if I didn't have him in my life, I wasn't sure what my life would be like. He'd been there for every important moment so far. To do something without him felt wrong.

Of course, I wished for more, but I'd accepted nine years ago that it never would be. My brain and heart just hadn't communicated that fact very well, though.

I started to pour the milk when Si's door opened, and I found myself distracted. Simon's bare chest, the way the dark hair of his happy trail led down to the waistband of his boxers, and the sleepy adorable look he rocked had me drooling. When I felt wetness hit my toe, at first, I thought I had a spontaneous orgasm with *squirting*. But then common sense flitted in, and I realized the milk had overflowed from my bowl.

"Ah, fiddlesticks!"

Quickly, I grabbed some paper towels and started mopping up the spilled milk. On my hands and knees, my butt in the air, I chastised myself for being so klutzy. Simon walked over, surprising me when he came up behind me.

“Need help, Lenn?”

Popping up to my knees, I spun and got an eyeful of his junk, which, I was surprised to find, was *very happy* to see me this morning.

"Um, Si, I think your rocket is confused. Either that or I look like a guy from behind."

Twisting, I tried to take in my backside to see if it looked masculine. I had on my sleep shorts and Captain America tee. Maybe that had been the cause? Shrugging, I found Simon staring at me oddly. He hadn't said another word, just had this weird look on his face.

Standing, I waved my hand in front of his face, "Simon, are you having a stroke? What's going on?"

The movement seemed to wake him up, and he blinked at me a few times before looking down at the floor covered in milk still.

"Were you trying to float your Cheerios, Lenn?" he teased.

Shaking my head, I rolled my eyes before finishing up and disposing of the soggy mess. Looking back to Simon, I found him focused on my rear again. I twisted around, worried I missed something.

"What is it, Si? Do I have something on my bum? Why do you keep staring at it?"

"What? I don't keep staring at it!" he exclaimed, jumping up and shoving his paper towels into the trash. "Not everything is about you, Lenn."

He stormed off to the bathroom, shutting the door hard, leaving me alone in the kitchen. I was officially flummoxed, my Cheerios a soggy mess. Giving up on them, I dumped them into the sink and retreated to my room, my brow furrowed.

Simon was acting weird. The fear that he was keeping something from me filled me. Grabbing a skirt with lemons on it, a white tank top, and a green cardigan, I headed into my bathroom to get ready for the day. Maybe reminding Simon of the nickname he used to have for me would bring him back to me.

Other ideas of how I could fix things floated through my head as I readied. I could try making something for dinner tonight and getting Simon to talk to me then. My brain was in full problem-solving mode as I fixed my hair.

I'd dubbed these my 'mirror conversations', a time to lay out the things troubling me. It sounded better than admitting I talked to myself. Sometimes, it worked, and other times, it left me even more befuddled.

Today, I felt even more lost than I had when I started. It was hard to know the solution when you didn't even know the problem.

Heading out, I chose to keep my shoe choice simple and slipped on my grey canvas flats. My klutziness this morning didn't bode well for heels today.

Simon's door was open and dark, meaning he'd already left. He hadn't even said goodbye. Disappointment flared in my chest, and I vowed to do something today. I didn't like feeling this disconnected from him. Nothing made sense when we weren't on the same wavelength.

The drive to work was quiet this morning, and I enjoyed the music as it blared through my speakers. Betty puttered along as normal, and I made the same plea I made every morning. *"Just get me to work one more day, Betty."* It was silly, but it felt like she listened to me and tried to deliver on the promise.

Making it to the parking lot, I breathed a sigh of relief for not breaking down on the side of the road. Grabbing my stuff, I made my way up to Emblazed Tats' front door and unlocked the several locks installed. Slade insisted on having four of them. I think he forgot this wasn't Los Angeles, but instead was Bowling Green, KY. It was his store, though, so I only poked minimally at him over it.

Opening everything up, I blared the music as I got the shop ready for the day. Sometimes, I hated being the unofficial receptionist in combination with body piercer, but at times, when I could dance around without an audience as I prepared the stations for the day, I enjoyed it. I'd been working here for three years now, and everyone was my family. I loved taking care of them and helping make their day better.

Even Slade, despite his dickish nature the majority of the time.

I chuckled at myself for using the word. It was hard to get past my manners at times and say *naughty* words out loud, but every now and then, I would catch them slipping in my head. It threw me for a minute, the word foreign to my inner dialogue, until I inevitably would laugh at it.

I didn't remember when I'd decided not to cuss, just that at some point, I did. I didn't hold it against anyone else. It just wasn't how I chose to communicate. My southern roots had been sowed in me strongly. I think the fact it annoyed Tatzilla was also a bonus.

Finishing up my sweeping, I turned to find someone had snuck in while I was busy singing. Slade was in his usual pose, arms crossed as he leaned against the wall, watching me. Sticking my tongue out at him, I carried on doing what I was, not caring if he liked my singing or not today.

Some days, it bothered me more than others, him not liking me. I strove to be a nice person and kind to everyone even if I griped about it. I never went out of my way to be mean, even if sarcasm was my go-to response.

Slade, however, was a whole other category. I think I was coming to terms with him only ever being my bossnemy. My lady parts cried out in despair, but my heart knew I'd never be able to take the pain he was sure to bestow on me.

"What's eating you today?" he asked when I dumped the broom pan.

"Nothing."

"Hmm."

"Hmm, yourself all you want. It doesn't mean I'm going to tell you anything."

Seriously? Why did I engage?

Continuing to get the day ready, I pulled out my stool I used for the cabinets and stepped up. They all laughed at me for needing one, but without it, I had to jump on the counter, and that was a bad decision with how many dresses and skirts I owned.

I was pulling down some of the ink colors the stations were low on when he came up behind me.

"James, I'll be heading out early today and need you to cover."

Jumping, I whirled around to tell him exactly how I felt about being told instead of asked about covering for him. My canvas shoes didn't have the best traction on them, though, and when I spun, my equilibrium was off, and I started to topple over the side.

Slade grabbed my hips, steadying me. My shirt had slid up some with the movement, coming untucked in the process. I felt his thumb brush against the bare flesh sending goosebumps to the surface. Sucking in a breath, I held his gaze, forgetting what I was about to yell at him for.

"You don't have to throw yourself at me, James. Desperate isn't a good look."

His obnoxious remark had my mind re-circuiting, and I remembered what I'd spun for. Pulling myself back, I crossed my arms and glared. With the stool, I was at eye level with Tatzilla. His hard stare bore into me, and we found ourselves in a staring contest again. His jaw ticked and it seemed like he was upset for having to touch me.

"First of all, just no. Take your cheesy pickup line elsewhere. There isn't anything desperate about me. Second, what makes you think I'll just cover for you?"

"Well, I'm the *boss*."

"So? There are still rules. You can't just boss me around."

"Actually, I think that's exactly what it means. It's in the title... *boss*."

His voice took on a quality I wasn't used to hearing from him. It almost sounded... seductive. I wasn't sure how I felt about it. We clearly had our roles, and if he went and changed them, where did that leave me?

It was much easier and safer to keep him in his box. Dream Slade could do all the dirty things to me I wanted because it had no consequences.

Boss Slade was wrapped in bad decisions and a million consequences of why I should never even entertain the thought. If you looked up 'bad boy heartbreak', Slade Evans' picture would be there. I couldn't do that again. *I wouldn't.*

"Cat got your tongue, James?" I swear he licked his

lips at the word tongue, but I forced my gaze to remain on his eyes.

"Why do you need me to cover for you?" I finally asked.

"Personal."

"*Personal*?"

"That's what I said, isn't it?"

"I've never seen you take a personal day in almost three years. What's so important?"

"Are we besties now, James? Did I miss the memo where we traded friendship bracelets?" His nostrils flared and it looked like he bit back his words. "Do as I ask and stop with the questions, will ya."

He spun on his feet and stomped off toward his office, slamming the door as he entered. I jumped at the sound. The music had stopped, making the space dead quiet. Centering myself, I finished up my tasks before locking up and heading over to the coffee shop a few storefronts down the strip. It was a local hole in the wall and better than any Starbucks, in my opinion.

The door jangled with my entrance, and the familiar smell surrounded me as I entered Coffee Grounds.

"Lennox! How are you, lovey?" the exuberant owner greeted me.

"I'm doing well, Mrs. Patty. How are your grandkids?"

"Oh, you know, rotten as ever and the apple of my eye," she beamed. "Your usual?"

"You know it. Gotta keep those artists caffeinated."

She started on the drink order as I perused her baked goods selection for the day. It was a weird thing I did. I drooled over the baked goods, but I never bought one. The smell alone was amazing enough. I was afraid it would go straight to my rear if I had one bite, and it didn't need any help there. Sweets were my weakness, and if I indulged once, it was a slippery slope. Best to just stay away. So, while inhaling the delicious scents, I imagined eating them. When she set down my drinks, I looked up in shock, constantly amazed at how fast she got them all done.

"You talk to Slade again about apprenticing?"

Shaking my head, I avoided her gaze, not wanting to disappoint her. Every time I thought about it, I chickened out for some reason. I didn't think I could handle him laughing at me or rejecting the idea like he had two years ago.

"Hmph," she huffed. "Lovey, you're never gonna fly if you don't spread your wings."

"That your greeting card advice for today?" I cheesed.

"Hey, knock my theory all you want, sugga. Those greeting cards *are* cheesy but powerful. Take it and put it into action. And here, I can see your drool for this brownie. It's on the house today, so you're not allowed to say no."

"Mrs. Patty! You know it will only go to my hips," I whispered.

"I know, and you'll thank me later." She winked, the old hoot trying to play matchmaker.

With whom I never could figure out, but she was always trying to fatten me up, and I was already a curvy girl. I embraced my body and all that went along with it, but it didn't mean I wanted to add more. I enjoyed food and loathed exercise, so there had to be a balance.

But as everyone knew, my weakness was manners, and no part of me could deny her generosity. So, I begrudgingly took the brownie as I gathered the drink trays. And people wondered why I was so sarcastic at times? This was the reason right here.

Looking down at the tray, I realized she'd given me Simon's too. I felt weird dropping it off today after how this morning had gone. I didn't know why, or what had done it, but things were off between us.

Deciding to stop acting like a scared little girl, I choose to face it like a grown-up. Using my hip to open the salon door, I ignored Crystal as I made my way to his station. Simon's back was to me since he was talking with someone I couldn't see. When I heard my name spoken, I slowed my steps.

"It's literally killing me. I don't know if I can live with her anymore. Not like this, man."

Pain shot through me at his words, and the tears were falling before I could even stop them. Pulling out his coffee, I walked around him and squeezed between the two of them. Quietly, I placed it down on the counter as a hush fell over us. Continuing to ignore them, I pivoted and kept walking out the back.

Taking advantage of the back entrance, I scurried to the door making a quick exit if only to hide my tears. I heard Simon calling my name, but I didn't stop. I just kept walking. I stepped into the alley and quickly made my way over to the tattoo shops' door. It was hard to open with my hands full, but I managed to get it just as I heard the other door. Pulling it closed, I threw the latch to lock it and leaned back against it.

Tears streamed down my face in silent tracks as I stood holding the coffee trays. I was kind of amazed I hadn't spilled them in my distress. Slowly, I slid down the door, no longer having the energy to hold myself up, my legs giving out under me. A moment later, Slade walked out of his office and stopped when he saw me there. I didn't even care at this point because my heart had already broken into a million pieces.

"James, your other half is asking for you upfront. He said the door was locked. But, I'm guessing you did it on purpose. Trouble in paradise with you two?"

I stared at him, no ability to move, his words echoed over and over in my head. I didn't miss the tilt of his smile in the corners, the pleasure he was gaining from my pain. Tatzilla knelt in front of me, and I thought for a moment he was going to be nice for once.

"Pull yourself together, James. You have a job to do. I thought you were better than this."

His vitriol hadn't been what I expected, and I reared back like he'd slapped me. Why I'd been surprised was anyone's guess. Nothing with Slade ever made sense. My vulnerable state might've made me more sensitive, but it also gave me the courage to speak my mind and ask the question I'd always wondered. He'd started to walk away, presumably back to the front when I asked it.

"Why do you hate me?"

It came out sounding teeny, my voice so small. I

wanted to berate myself, but the fact I was able to put words together was a win. He stopped, his back rigid before he responded.

"I don't hate you, James. I *nothing* you. You're an employee. That is the extent of our relationship. You have five minutes to get yourself presentable for work."

Not once did he turn around, and in that moment, I felt as inhuman as a person could feel. Distractedly, I stood up, but everything was out of focus and spinning. I left the coffee on the floor and made my way up front, using the wall to guide me as everything swam in and out of focus.

When I made it to my stool, I plopped down on it, but the world continued to spin, and I soon found myself falling further. I gave in to the sensation, so tired of fighting for a future that was doomed. I closed my eyes, hoping it would all fade away as my body became weightless.

My heart was broken, and I'd just lost my best friend. It was the perfect day to just say *fuck* it.

Blaze

I'LL ADMIT, I WAS SURPRISED TO HEAR BACK FROM YOU. I MIGHT'VE DIMINISHED MY LAST PEN PAL'S ABILITY TO

PARTICIPATE. IT USUALLY CONSISTED OF FART JOKES AND A DIRTY COMIC. GRANTED, THE COMIC WASN'T HALF BAD, BUT IT GOT OLD REAL FAST. I HAVE A 2-YEAR-OLD BROTHER IF YOU RECALL AND GET ENOUGH POOP RELATED CONTENT IN MY LIFE.

I'M SORRY THINGS HAVE BEEN DIFFICULT. I FIND MYSELF STARING AT THE STARS WHEN MY LIFE IS OUT OF CONTROL. SOMETHING ABOUT IT MAKES ME FEEL BETTER. DURING ALL THE CHAOS, THE STARS REMAIN, AND REMIND ME HOW BIG THE WORLD IS.

THERE WAS AN INCIDENT THIS SUMMER WITH MY MOM, AND THINGS HAVE BEEN DIFFICULT SINCE. I LOVE MY MOM AND WILL ALWAYS SUPPORT HER. IT DOESN'T MEAN MY PEERS ARE AS FORGIVING. IT'S MADE ME REALIZE WHO ARE TRUE FRIENDS AND WHO ARE JUST IN IT FOR THEMSELVES.

I think your question sounds perfect. I'll answer and then ask my own.

1. You make a convincing argument, but I think I'd have to go with showering. Unless you literally mean you can't take a shower, and then I'd just take baths and pick brushing my teeth.

2. Full disclosure, storms scare me. It's not the cool answer, but we have a lot of tornados here and there have been about four bad ones in my life already. The last one was really scary. I didn't know if we would make it.

3. Fall

Okay my questions:

1. Silly? Would you rather only eat pizza or never eat pizza again? I'd go with never eating it again. Not a fan.

2. Personal? Have you ever been in love? I dont know how to be any other way.

3. Random? Favorite hobby? Toss up between reading and drawing. Oh wait, I love to sing too, and make clothes. Yeah, I can't pick one thing.

Sincerely

Nox

Chapter Five

SIMON

THERE WERE moments in life when you knew you royally fucked up. This was one of them. In fact, it was possibly the biggest one of my life. I didn't even have to wonder how I ended up here, watching my best friend fall to the floor as her face went white.

Running to her, I wasn't fast enough, and she hit the filing cabinet, slicing open her head. "Fuck! No! Slade, call 911." Cradling Lenn's bleeding head in my hands, I attempted to stop the bleeding, applying pressure, the moment too eerily similar for my liking.

Moments were funny like that.

The one where my life seemed to have gone off course had been seared into my memory as the best and worst moment of my life. It was the catalyst that shifted everything nine years ago when my fear, insecurity, and hormones collided in the fuck up of the century.

Simon and Lennox, age 16 (Nine years ago)

"Mm, this tastes similar to what I'd expect you to taste like, Lemon Drop," I slurred.

We'd stolen a few Mike's Hard Lemonades from my

parents' garage fridge. It was the one where they thought they hid the "bad things" from me. But I knew. It just made it easier to pilfer a few every now and then without their notice.

Some of the older boys in the neighborhood would hit me up for them from time to time, giving me an ounce of street cred. I didn't want to admit how good it felt to be seen that way by Lennox. She was so above it all, the peer pressure and popularity contests. I didn't want to admit I still cared about it.

Currently, Lennox danced in the grass, her arms spread wide as she made dives like she was a bird or something.

"Oh yeah?" she giggled. “Do you *often* imagine what I taste like, Si?”

Her breath was heavy from the exertion of dancing for as long as she had, not even stopping to answer me. Lennox was rarely ever still, a constant motion of color I could never take my eyes off of. I never understood how she didn't catch me staring at her a hundred times a day. I didn’t want to admit it was probably more. Some time during freshman year, I had an epiphany.

I was in love with my best friend.

The thing was, I didn't want to be in love with my best friend. She was my *best friend,* and I needed her to stay in that role.

But no matter what I said or did, Lennox James was the star of all my fantasies, dreams, and desires. No other girl at our school compared to her. *No one.*

I’d also come to the conclusion I wasn’t like other kids in our grade when I had my first boy crush on my pen pal, Blaze. When Lennox took over writing him, I'd been jealous at first but also relieved in a way. In one of our last letters between us, we'd both kind of admitted having confusing feelings. I'd written some things back, and then like a chicken, never mailed it.

But then last year, he sent me another message and despite having told Lenn I didn't want to write to him, I found myself doing it, but in *secret*.

I carried a lot of secrets now, they weighed heavy on me. I feared one day, they'd all crack open, spilling out like a piñata. Only it wouldn't be a celebration of candy treats, but my insides in a curdled mess of lies.

I'd been *jealous* of Lennox getting to know Blaze because I wanted to keep them both for myself. Blaze wasn't like the boys here and I knew he'd see how cool and down to earth she was. But I saw how happy she was to receive them, having someone interested in what she had to say. And in a weird way, it kept me in his life. Lenn read me each letter, and I got to catch glimpses of him from her perspective. It was interesting to see how different they were with each other than me.

Lennox smiled at me, and I found the alcohol buzz giving me confidence to say things I normally wouldn't.

"Yeah, I do, actually. I should taste your lips to confirm, Lemon Drop."

She stopped spinning, her hair fanned out until it settled back to her shoulders and for a second, I worried I went too far when she only stared at me. A quiet and still Lennox was unheard of.

"Did you just say you wanted to kiss me, Simon Fisher?"

Her sweet little twang came out, and I smiled at the blush that spread across her cheeks. Getting up off the picnic table, I managed to swagger over to her without falling on my face. Towering over her, I bent down, my frame casting her into shadow.

"And what if I did, Lennox James?"

"I-I-I-, I don't know!" she whispered. Her eyes never stopped looking into mine, moving so fast back and forth like I held the answer to something there.

"I think we should try it, you know and see. Who else would be a better judge of you as a kisser than your best friend?"

All joking had left me, and I knew I wanted this to happen. I watched as she thought about it, the waiting period was agonizing as she tapped her finger against her lips. The very same ones I longed to kiss. When she finally stopped, she dropped it and squared her shoulders, her decision made.

"You're right. We should. In fact, I have a counteroffer."

"I'm listening." My heart sped up, excitement pumping through me at what my sassy best friend had decided.

"I think we should go all the way. Get it out of the way from all the pressure. Because you're right, who better to have your first time with than your best friend? That way, it doesn't have to be awkward or anticlimactic, or like a dumb prom thing. It would be something between us, the person who knows you the best."

My breath caught. Was she? Did that? My pulse

skyrocketed as my brain got stuck on what she was implying.

"Did I just break your brain, Si?"

Nodding, she laughed at my action, and her melodious sound covered my skin, sending shivers down me and straight to my dick. It was very much on board with this plan. Lennox had the voice of a true songbird, and any time she graced me with it, I wanted to swoon in her vicinity.

"When?" I managed to utter.

She shrugged, and I worried she was changing her mind. "How about right now? We're sleeping out here already. Our parents aren't expecting us home until tomorrow morning. It's the best place and time where we won't get interrupted."

"It's scary how logical you sound about all this."

"Why can't it be? Maybe if we take out all the nonsense, we won't feel all weird about it. Plus, we've seen each other naked before and you know everything about me. I don't have to hide who I am with you. You're my person, Si. You know that."

It was the truest statement, and yet, I didn't know if she meant it the same way I wanted it to mean. Was I her person out of shared history? Or was I her person because the thought of living without me was too unbearable? I wanted to be the latter.

"But, but," I started, worried now that I had this ball set in motion.

"No buts, well," she paused thinking, "no, no butts, except naked ones." Giggles exploded out of her again, and I knew there was no way I'd be saying no. Clasping her biceps, I steadied her as I stared down into her familiar hazel eyes.

I wanted to believe something more was hidden there in the depths than her normal love and care for me. I wanted to believe it so bad, I didn't know if I imagined it into being. Slowly, I dipped my face down to meet hers, and our lips touched, igniting a fire in me from just the press of them against mine.

I started to carefully move them against hers, and before I knew it, we were kissing. It was the best kiss I'd ever had, and now, I feared it was just a practice kiss to her and not the earth shattering one it had been for me. Pulling back, I tried to gauge her emotions before I lost my heart completely.

"Shelley was wrong." Her voice was breathless as she peered up at me with hunger. My breath caught at the sight, but I struggled to understand what she meant. Giving her an odd look, I was a little annoyed she was thinking about Shelley while kissing me.

"You're not a lousy kisser."

Her words pushed a memory loose of the summer before freshman year when I'd gone into the closet with Shelley for seven minutes in Heaven, and she'd told everyone at school that year I was a "lousy kiss". I found myself smiling at the implication she thought about what kind of kisser I would be, my confidence returning.

"Oh yeah, what kind of kisser would you say I am, Lemon?"

"The greatest." She smiled. “So, do I?”

“Do you what?”

"Taste like lemon?"

I smiled, realizing her question. "Better."

Diving back in for another kiss, it soon turned into a frenzied mess of hands exploring bodies. I couldn't get it out of my head that I was finally touching Lennox, feeling her beneath my palms, and it wasn't just a dream. Shoving her shirt off, I paused for a moment to take in her boobs.

They weren't the first pair I'd seen, but they'd just become my favorite. I continued to stare, frozen in my view of them when she slowly unhooked her bra, dropping it to the ground. I grabbed my shirt and pulled it off, kicking off my shoes in the process. Never once did I take my eyes off her, needing to remember this for the rest of my life. Her boobs were beautiful, and I couldn't wait to touch them.

I unzipped my pants, careful not to fall over in my rushed state, and I watched Lennox lower her skirt, leaving us both in only our underwear.

Taking her hand, I pulled her into our tent and closed the zipper. The moon shone through the moon roof, and an electric lantern was lit in the corner, giving us a small amount of light. Lying down on our sleeping bags, we stared at one another, taking in each other's bodies, noticing the changes since we last saw one another naked. Despite what she said, it had been years, and our bodies had changed tremendously.

Lennox was all soft curves and skin, and I wanted to trace every peak and valley. My cock jutted out in excitement at getting to take in our dream girl.

"Can I touch it?" she asked quietly. Nodding, I

sucked in a breath when I felt her hands dip below my boxers and wrap around me.

"It's different than I expected. It's smooth and yet hard. Does it feel good?"

"Very," I groaned, trying to keep myself together, my eyes closing involuntary.

"Um, do we have, you know?" I started, realizing the one thing that might stop this before it even occurred. I hadn't thought this would ever happen, so I didn't have any condoms on me. Peeking open my eyes, I saw Lennox nod as she moved to her bag.

"My mom puts them in all my bags now, so afraid I'll end up pregnant despite me telling her I'm not having sex."

"Well, it's not the craziest thing she's done."

"Yeah." She nodded, but I hated how sad her voice sounded, and I regretted my choice of words instantly. Pulling her to me, I wrapped my arms around her, needing to feel our skin touching.

"Are you sure this is what you want?" I felt her nod into my chest as I rubbed up and down her back.

"Yes, I'm sure."

She lifted her head, and I lowered my mouth back to hers, and the heat and passion returned. Before I knew it, we were out of our underwear, and I was pulling a condom over my length. Bracing myself, I slowly sank into the most incredible feeling in the world as I tried to be easy, knowing that it had to hurt for her.

I felt her tense, and I slowed until I saw her nod to continue. I picked up speed, and before I knew it, it was over. I worried she hadn't enjoyed it, but the smile on her face comforted me that maybe she had. I wrapped her in my arms, and we fell asleep holding one another. It was the most intimate experience of my life, and it had happened out of the blue.

I woke up feeling happier than I ever had before, and I'd made a conscious decision to tell her how I felt, to tell Lennox that I was in love with her. Maybe we could have round two after.

She wasn't next to me though and I found the zipper flap partially blowing in the breeze. Peeking my head out, I could make her out over by the table where this had all started.

It looked like she was on the phone, so I dressed and made my way over to her. I figured she was talking to her mom, checking in as she was known to do. Lennox never stopped worrying about Robin or Noah, not after that day at the mall. I felt partially responsible for her obsession, but I also didn't know how to change it. So, I supported her and tried to be there when she needed me.

My feet were silent on the grass, the dew seeping into the soft canvas and I guess it was why she didn't hear me. It's the only reason I could explain to myself after overhearing her words because nowhere in my mind did they belong. Nor would Lennox say them to hurt me. That wasn't who she was.

"Yeah, I know. Can you believe it? After all this time, it finally happened. I'm so happy. I can't wait to tell Simon."

Wait, why did she need to tell me about it? I was there.

"Oh yeah, he’s a good friend, but he's not the one I'm in love with, you know that. I need to tell him. Now that things have developed, it doesn't feel right."

Devastation sat in my gut, and I knew it had all been as she said—something special between us, but nothing more. It was an opportunity to get it out of the way, a practice.

And I'd almost ruined my relationship with my best friend by admitting my feelings. I couldn't do that. I needed Lennox in my life, and if I only got to be friends with her, then I would be the best friend she would ever have.

It still stung to hear her say those words. I was a teenage boy, and being rejected, even if unintentionally hurt, so for some reason, when Lennox saw me a few minutes later and said she needed to talk to me about something, I blurted out a phrase I had no idea would set my life into a chiasmic tailspin.

"Lennox, I like boys."

It was the one phrase, the one moment that set everything else into motion and led me to this point.

VOICES SHOUTED around me as time sped up, people handing me things to press to her head before the paramedics took over. The world spun fast, but me, I was in slow motion as the implication of what this meant hit me.

I was going to lose her.

Lifting my head, I caught Slade’s eyes, and I stared

back. Regret, fear, and self-loathing swirled around him, but I wasn't sure who it was directed at. It didn't matter right now. Only Lennox mattered.

Following the paramedics, I left him to deal with his own emotions for once.

Dear Stranger,

HI, I SUPPOSE. I DON'T REALLY KNOW WHAT TO SAY TO YOU. IT SOUNDED LIKE A COOL IDEA WHEN MY BEST FRIEND SUGGESTED IT. WE LOVE THE SHOW AND IT SOUNDED FUN. BUT NOW, STARING AT THIS PAPER AND HAVING TO COME UP WITH SOMETHING TO WRITE, I WONDER HOW GENIUS IT ACTUALLY WAS.

IT'S JUST THAT MY BEST FRIEND, SHE'S KIND OF THE COOLEST AND MAKES EVERYTHING FUN. WHEN SHE ASKED, I SAID YES, LIKE I ALWAYS DO. I DIDN'T REALLY THINK ABOUT HOW I WOULD BE DOING IT WITHOUT HER THOUGH.

I GUESS I CAN TELL YOU ABOUT MYSELF. THAT'S HARD TOO WITHOUT GIVING ANY PERSONAL DETAILS. WELL, HMM. I LIKE COMICS. I READ THEM A LOT AND HAVE A MASSIVE COLLECTION. I SPEND MOST OF MY TIME WITH THE GIRL NEXT DOOR. IT'S SAD WHEN I THINK ABOUT IT AND HOW MOST OF WHO I AM IS WRAPPED UP IN HER.

HOPEFULLY, YOU HAVE A BETTER TIME WRITING AND THIS TAKES OFF.

SIMON'S COMIC BOOK IDEAS

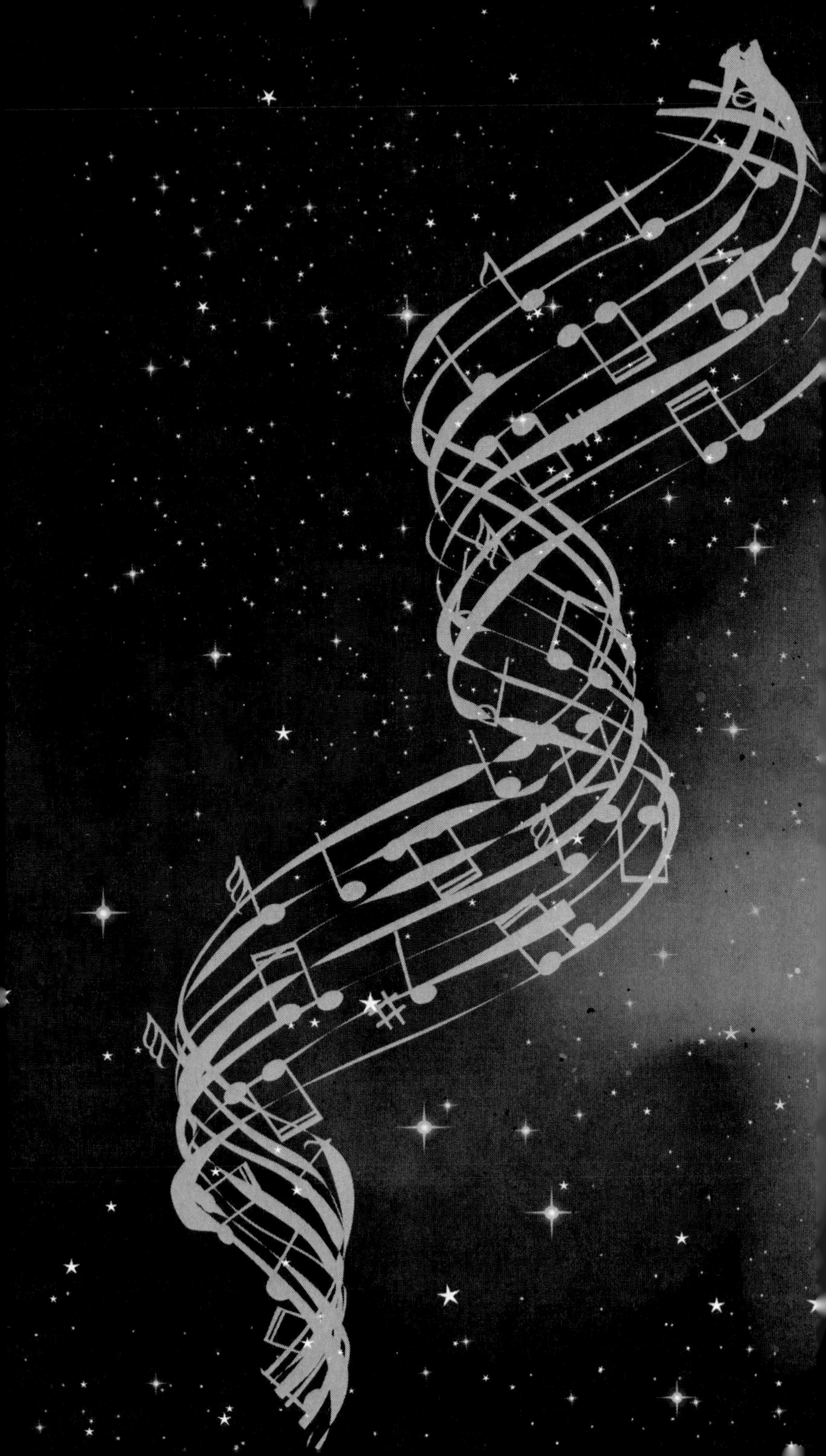

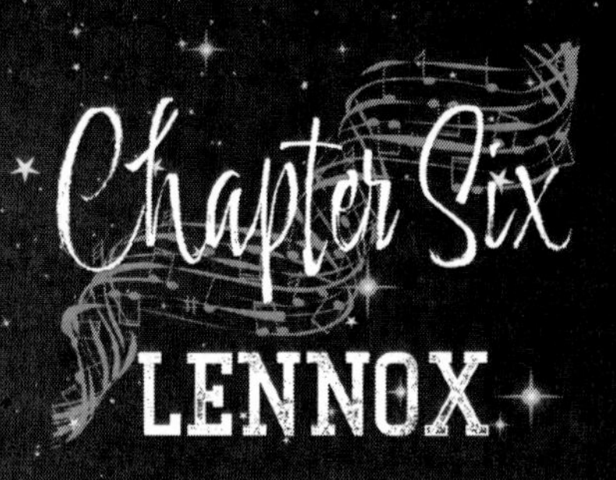

Chapter Six
LENNOX

MY HEAD WAS POUNDING when I woke, and I couldn't remember where I was or how I got here. I hadn't drunk last night, I hadn't really drunk anything alcoholic since my 21st birthday, so I couldn't be hungover. Reaching up, I touched the part of my head that ached and immediately regretted it.

"Ow," I winced, the soreness stinging when I put pressure on the spot. My cry of pain alerted whoever was in the room with me, and I felt them draw closer.

"Honey, Lennox, are you awake?"

"Yeah," I mumbled, the pain making me nauseous with everything spinning. "What happened?"

"What do you remember?" my mother asked, squeezing my hand.

Trying to remember, I drew a blank. Nothing except getting ready for a date lingered in my head.

"What day is it?"

"You don't know?"

"I mean, I think it's Thursday, but I can't remember anything since Wednesday night, so I don't really know."

"That's good, honey. It is Thursday." I heard the relief in her voice as she squeezed my hand again. The door opened, but I kept my eyes closed, the light too bright to bear.

"Ah, I see our patient is awake. How are you feeling, Lennox?"

It was Dr. Barnes. I smiled as I recognized his voice. He was a kind man and had been good to our family over the years. Sadly, we'd gotten to know him on a regular basis. I'd say first name basis, but that was unheard of in the south to ever utter his first name. It just didn't happen.

"Hello, Dr. Barnes. I've felt better. My head feels like I took an ice pick to it, though."

"Well, dear, you kind of did. Let me set you up and check you over."

He raised the bed I was in, and the light shifted out of my line of sight, making it easier for me to pry my eyes open. Blinking, I found my mom on the left side of the bed sitting in a chair. Her face was white, and she wore a grimace. I instantly felt terrible for putting her in this position. *Mom hated hospitals*. She hadn't had a good track record here, so I didn't blame her. Most people treated her with kid gloves at best and incompetent at the worst.

Grabbing her hand, I squeezed it, giving her the comfort now. My mom had her issues, but she was still my mom, and I would do whatever I needed to protect her, even if from herself.

Dr. Barnes checked my pulse and blood pressure before listening to my lungs. He made me follow his finger as he shined a light into my eyes. He kept scribbling things down, not saying anything, and it had started to make me worried.

"Well, all things considered, Lennox, I think you're going to be alright. Can you tell me the last thing you remember?"

"I uh," for some reason having to share I was meeting up with my online date in hopes to score had me blushing from my head to my toes in front of the doctor. "Just last night. I remember getting ready to go out, but everything else is a blur."

"Hmm, it could be temporary from the head wound, but I want to keep an eye on it. I'll need you to come back in a week for a check-up, but if any symptoms worsen, then sooner. Do you understand? You'll need to be monitored for the next day or so, but you don't appear to have a concussion. I'll write you a note for work. I think it would be good for you to take at least three days off."

Nodding, I instantly regretted it when pain sliced through me. Yeah, I could get behind no work. The thought of the tattoo guns buzzing had me wincing already.

"She can come and stay with us," my mom interjected before I had time to think about it. I'd moved out two years ago when Simon had a roommate opening. It had been a hard decision to leave my family, but I'd been ready. I'd already put so much of my life on hold at times, and I couldn't live at home forever, forcing me to finally make the leap. Smiling at my mom, I was grateful she was here with me today and being the adult.

There were times when it hadn't always been the case.

"What do you think about this, Si? Does it look dorky on me?" I twisted and turned in the cute dress I'd found. It was mint green and hit me at my knees. It was probably meant to be shorter on taller girls, but I was happy with that length. I kept swishing the skirt back and forth, watching it spin.

Simon looked up from the rack of clothes he was searching through, "Uh, yeah, Lenn, that looks nice. Not dorky at all. Now, hurry up and try on that swimsuit. I want to go talk to Clarissa over at the pretzel place."

I tried to ignore the flare of jealousy as I hurriedly tried on the swimsuit. It was a tankini, which I liked since it covered most of my stomach without making me look like I was wearing a grandma suit. Redressing, I headed to the cashier to pay for the dress and swimwear. I was starting to get excited now for the party because I had clothing that looked nice on me.

Simon was talking to some guy at the front of the store, so I headed up there after paying for my things. When he saw me approaching, he broke off and met me at the store entrance.

"Is that the guy from your little league team? Justin something?"

"Yeah, it was."

"What did he want?"

"Nothing."

"Okay. Weird much," I started. I was about to give him

a hard time for keeping secrets when we came upon a commotion.

"Ma'am, we're gonna need you to leave," a very stressed store clerk stated at the front of the store.

"But I need these things! It will be ruined if I don't have them. Please, just let me grab a few more."

"Ma'am, we already asked you once."

"Is that your— "

"Mom!" I answered as I took off running. Something wasn't right. She was acting all over the place and didn't resemble the mother I knew. When she saw me, she started to tug my arm to get me to talk to the man.

"Baby, tell this man," she urged. "Tell him I need these things. They will look great in our house. We can have tea parties and go on adventures together. Won't it be the best?" She was smiling ear to ear, and I wanted to join in on her excitement, but something felt wrong. Looking around, I realized what it was.

"Mom, Mom," I said over and over to get her attention. Simon had joined me in the store and was looking at me curiously as well.

"What, baby? Do you want it in a different color?"

"Kid, is this your mother?" the store clerk directed to me, officially giving up on getting through to my mom.

I tuned them all out, needing my mother to answer my question.

"Mom, where's Noah?" Fear and ice-coated my skin when she didn't immediately answer.

"Who?" she asked, looking at me strangely.

"Noah, my baby brother, your son." She tilted her head, confusion on her face. In a voice I'd never heard before, she

responded nonchalantly, dismissing my fear. "Oh him, I left him in the car. He's not very fun. Always crying that one. Not like you. You're fun. So, what do you think? Purple or pink? Hmm?"

Turning to Simon, I saw the same fear reflected on his face. "Stay with her. Call my dad. Call 911."

And then I took off, running the fastest I'd ever run in my entire life, my sandals smacking the ground, my bags banging against my leg with each step. I ducked and weaved around customers, pushing my way through the mall. Darting through the glass doors, I searched around me, looking for the car.

Taking off in a direction, I started turning my head side to side on the side of the mall she dropped us off earlier. Finally, about five rows down from the door, I spotted the familiar blue Camry.

My breath was uneven from the exertion and fear as I ran, sweat dripped down my neck, the humidity suffocating in the early summer heat. When I got to the car, I yanked open the door handle only to fall on my butt from the force. Crapola, it was locked!

Standing, I dropped my bags and started to look around for a way around the lock, checking all the doors to see if one had been left up. I could see Noah in his seat, but he was quiet. He blinked when he saw me and reached out his little hand to me. Tears streamed down my face, and I started to bang on the window, unsure how to get to him. Where was a clothes hanger when you needed one? A rock? Anything!

I was panicking but I didn't know how to solve this. I needed my dad.

Wiping my tears, I searched the ground again, going a

little further out this time. I heard footsteps approaching and hoped it was the police. When I looked up though, it was to be met with soft blue eyes. Shaking myself, this was not the time to be consumed by thoughts of hot boys.

"Can I help?"

"I'm trying to get in the car. My brother's in there, but the keys are with my mom, and I don't know how to jimmy it."

The boy nodded, taking in the seriousness of the situation, and ran past me to pick something up. Returning, he had a medium size rock in his hand and looked to me for permission.

"Please," I begged, nodding, the tears never stopping.

He braced himself, turning away from the passenger window as he smashed the rock down on it. It took a few smacks, but eventually, it did splinter. It was the shatter-proof windows, though, so even though it was broken, it was still all intact. Without hesitation, he whipped his shirt off over his head and wrapped it around his hand and smashed his fist into it. Once it went through, he pushed the unlock button, releasing all the locks.

Jumping into motion, I lifted the door handle to the backseat and quickly unlatched my brother from the car seat. The car was sweltering, and I tried to keep a brave face for him, not wanting to scare him more. Pulling him out, I took off his shirt and pants as I sat on the ground holding him.

The mystery boy handed me a bottle of water he'd magicked out of somewhere. I was thankful and started to feed Noah tiny drops of it. I used some to cool him off as well, wetting his hair and dampening his skin. Just as he started to revive, I could hear the ambulance in the distance. I turned to tell the boy thanks for helping me save my brother, but he was no longer next to me. Standing, I watched him disappear as the ambulance wails grew louder.

"Thank you," I croaked, clutching Noah to me.

He turned, winking but kept walking, blood trailing down his hand onto the pavement. It was the thing I focused on later when I'd been questioned, that he'd been real, his drops of blood proof.

That was the day I learned my mother was Bipolar. She'd stopped taking her medication for the pregnancy and had wanted to breastfeed Noah. It meant monitoring her symptoms on her own and it had been approved by her doctor. They'd been watching it at her visits, but what they hadn't anticipated was the post-partum depression. It complicated things, masking a lot of her symptoms until she was in a full-blown manic episode.

There had been a lot of backlash for my father and mother after that. Mom lost her job at the real estate firm she worked for. DCS got involved and threatened to remove Noah. My father being the police chief, was the only thing I think that stopped them. He ensured he'd get her help and assistance for Noah's care. I think my dad felt guilty for not noticing as well. Mom went back on her meds and stayed in a facility for a few months, leaving me to help raise Noah that summer while my dad tried to dispel the rumors and public opinion.

But it didn't matter. People thought what they wanted in the end.

Simon was there for me when all my supposed friends

started to pick on me and call my mom the "crazy car killing mom".

It was the summer I quit caring about my peers' opinions, the summer my body changed, forcing me to find my own style, and the summer I vowed to always be there for my family.

I quit making plans to leave Kentucky that day and changed my career path to something I could pursue at the college in town. I often wondered what happened to the blue-eyed boy who helped me, but I never saw him after that.

My job changed over the years as I bounced around to different things, attempting to find my passion. I wasn't an accountant, despite what my diploma said. I'd always been there for Noah and my mom. That meant something to me, even if no one else understood why.

Blinking back into focus, I heard Dr. Barnes tell my mom he would send someone to discharge me shortly. Mom helped me get out of bed and change into some clothes she'd brought me. When we walked back into the room, Simon was standing there, a hesitant look on his face. I walked over and hugged him, just happy to see him. His arms slowly came up and wrapped around me as well.

"Si, I'm so glad you're here."

"You are?"

"Yeah, why wouldn't I be?" I asked, pulling back, and taking in his face.

"Well, because of what happened."

"What do you mean?"

"Before your injury? You don't remember?"

Remembering not to shake my head this time, I answered with my words. "No, I don't remember anything after going out last night. Do you know how I got hurt?"

Slowly, he filled me in, lifting his eyes to my mom behind me. "You overheard something I said and ran off. I couldn't get into the backdoor, so I ran around to the front. When I got inside, you looked like a ghost. Slade was trailing you, a weird look on his face too. He gave me a death glare, and in those few seconds where we both had our eyes off you was when you fell off the stool. I watched as you hit your head on the corner of the filing cabinet unable to get to you."

"Oh wow, that sounds painful, and scary. I'm sorry you had to go through that. I feel bad that I got blood all over the floor. I bet Slade's upset about that. Did a lot of people see? Was my underwear showing when I fell?" The most random things filtered through my head as I thought about the information he'd told me.

"So, you're not mad at me?"

"Why would I be mad? I'm sure whatever it was, I'll get over it. Besides, I bet Slade was to blame. He's always saying mean things to me."

He nodded slowly, uncertainty plaguing his features as he held me close.

"I'm going to stay with my mom for a few days per doctor's orders, that way, you don't have to worry about monitoring me while you're at work."

"Oh," he nodded, "yeah, I guess that makes sense. I'll come by and hang out, though."

"Okay, sure. Sounds great."

The nurse entered then, and I signed everything, grateful to be leaving. The three of us headed out the door, and I gave Simon a hug before heading off with my mom. Something niggled at the back of my brain that I needed to remember, but it hurt when I tried to pull at it, so I left it alone.

Dr. Barnes had said I could possibly regain the memories after a few days, or they might be lost forever. Considering it had only been a few hours of the day, I wasn't too worried. How many life-altering things could've happened by 9:00 am anyway?

Simon had brought my stuff from the shop, so I pulled out my phone and checked my messages. Looking at the screen, disappointment filled me when I didn't see any messages. I didn't know who I expected to text me since it was early, and Simon had been with me. But it felt like I was missing something, something I'd been excited about. Again, before I could grab ahold of it, it vanished. I started to put my phone away when a message popped up.

Bossnemy: I'm sorry, James. I'm glad you're okay. You scared me. I didn't like it. Take all the time you need to recover.

I read the message over and over as anxiety whirled in my gut. Just what was he apologizing for? What had *happened* in those few hours I was blocking? Maybe I did need to remember.

Especially when the butterflies took flight at the

kindness in his words. I didn't know how to handle this version of Slade. If he started to be friendly, it would be tough to ignore how much I wanted him to devour me. Thoughts of two guys swirled in my head, making it a jumbled mess, and I realized I was in a world of trouble. I couldn't like either of them.

We stopped for milkshakes at the Dairy Barn, my mom's go-to treat for anything bad, before heading home. I focused on the things I could control as I sipped the cold treat.

I couldn't do anything but wait to see if my memories would return.

I couldn't do anything about my attraction for two guys.

But I could focus on healing and enjoying my books and dreams. I could hope everything else would work itself out later.

Fish

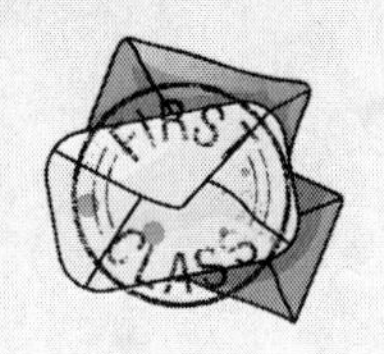

I'm curious how you got your name. Are you a good swimmer? Like a fish? Or perhaps you look like one? Hopefully it's not because you smell like one.

I think it's cool you have a friend who pushes you to do things. I sorta have that in my brother. We're twins, but opposites. He's the preppy, do gooder with the perfect grades. I'm the dark horse, always getting into trouble, and almost flunking out of school. But despite that, being a twin means I always have a built-in best friend. We do everything together, and he knows me better than anyone.

Or well, he used to. I kind of have a secret, but I don't know how to share it.

I think that's why I joined this program. The extra credit is also a bonus because I need it to pass. But I do think the concept is cool. It's kind of refreshing to talk to someone you'll never meet and share things with them. You might not be in the future, but it feels similar to send scribbled secrets.

I like comics too. What's your favorite? I've been getting into graphic novels lately. Art is a passion of mine and they seem to capture me and speak to my artistic nature. I'm kind of a loner otherwise. We move around a lot, and this is the third school I've been to this year. My twin always makes friends easily, but not me. I just stick to myself and wait for us to pack up again.

Swim, swim Fish.

Blaze

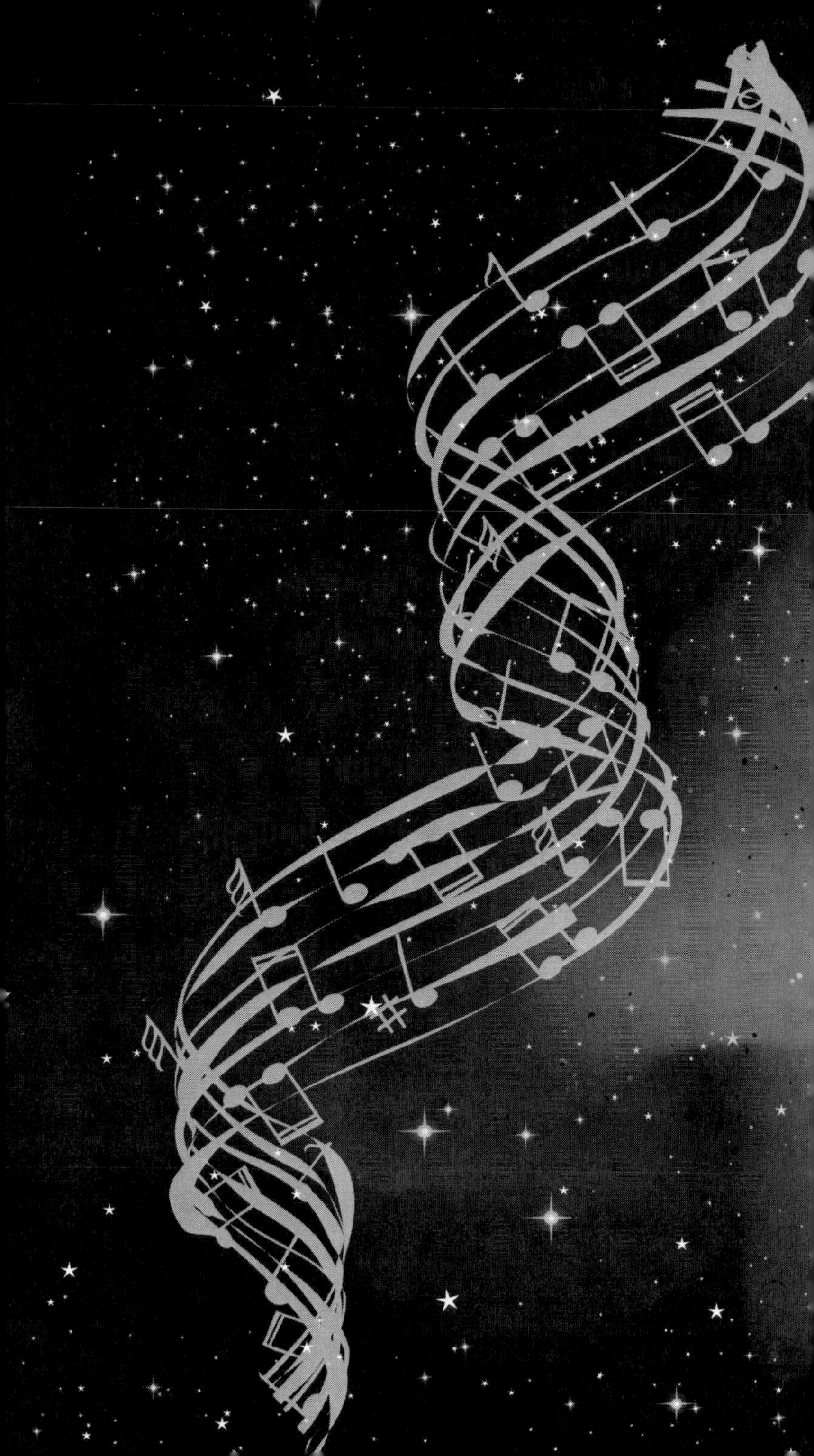

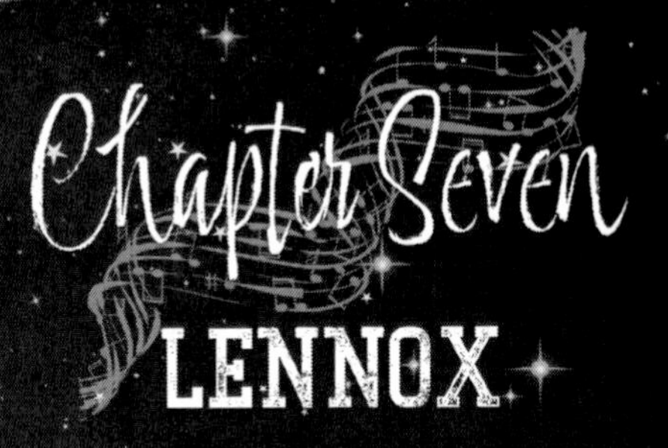

Chapter Seven

LENNOX

FLIPPING THE PAGE, I found myself immersed in a book world. Being on bedrest at least gave me the perfect excuse to read. I had to read slower than usual, or I'd forget whole sections, but it was still better than staring at the wall. Currently, I was reading a book about a treasure hunt, and I already had ideas for my blog post.

"Knock, knock."

Looking up, I found Simon in my doorway. Smiling, I motioned him in as I flipped the page. Si knew the drill now after years of friendship. I returned to my page, my rule to be allowed to finish the chapter while he found a spot on the bed. After countless years of fighting, we'd come to an agreement. He gave me the time to finish the section I was on, and I promised not to keep reading past it. Of course, the hard part was stopping.

Slowly, I tried to turn the page so he wouldn't know I was starting a new chapter. But of course, he knew. Simon always knew.

"Not so fast, *Lenn*. If you start another chapter, then I'll have to enact the code."

Gasping, I clutched the book to my chest, a look of shocked outrage on my face. "You wouldn't dare!"

"Oh, I so *would* dare."

He smirked, and the only way to ignore the way my heart pitter pattered from the look was to distract. Or, at least, that was the excuse I was going with.

"I don't believe you."

Sitting back in my papasan chair, I flipped to the next page with all the sass I had. I flipped it so good, there had to be legions of people cheering me on with a "Yassss, Queen".

I watched through my eyelashes, not even focused on my page anymore as Si's jaw ticked, and his nostrils flared before he vaulted off the bed, surprising me. He braced his hands on my chair, trapping me, his rainfall scent enveloping me in the space.

"What was that, Lenn? Are you feeling *feisty* today?"

I ignored the way my breath came in and out, I ignored the way my heart raced, and I especially ignored the slickness growing between my legs at his move.

"Whatever do you mean?" Batting my eyelashes, I played the innocent card I used with the customers.

"Oh, I think you know exactly what I mean. It's just unfortunate I'm going to have to remind you of the *code*."

Swallowing, my eyes never left his gray ones. They swirled thick with emotion, and I wanted to dive into them. I wasn't sure who'd moved, perhaps both of us had, but as I prepared to respond back to him, I found us nose to nose. His breath was hot on my face at the proximity.

"I double-dog dare you."

My lips ghosted over his as I taunted him, and I wondered if I'd hit my head harder than I'd realized. I'd flown past playing with fire and had lit the matches and thrown gasoline on them. Simon's nostrils flared even more and when his eyes started to flutter closed, mine followed, anticipating a kiss on the horizon.

"Ew, gross!"

Noah's shout had me opening my eyes, as a bucket of cold water figuratively drowned me. Simon had stayed perched over me, and using Noah's distraction went in for the kill. Licking up my nose, he jumped back, a proud look on his face.

"And that's how you teach your sister a lesson, little man!"

"Uh, no thanks. I don't want to lick any part of her."

He scrunched up his nose, making a gagging sound and Simon doubled over in laughter. I was still frozen in my chair, not having it in me to argue. Had I imagined that? If Noah hadn't walked in right then, would we have kissed? Was my eyesight waning as well or had I imagined the bulge in his pants when he got up? Blinking, I focused on the two laughing hyenas and decided to ignore it for now. My head hurt too much anyway.

"Did you need something, Noah?"

My question had them sobering, and Noah turned back, remembering he'd come in for a purpose.

"Oh yeah, dinner. Simon, you're staying, right?"

"Uh, yeah. Sure, bud."

He looked at me, an odd look crossing his face, but I had no idea what it was in regards to. I hated feeling like I'd missed something. Especially when it felt like a significant thing. Placing my book down, I followed them into the dining room. Everything smelled great, but as I sat at the table, my appetite was lacking.

Conversation took place around me, but I zoned out, the sounds becoming background noise as I tried to piece things together. A bang a while later had me jumping, and when I looked up, everyone at the table was looking at me, the dishes held aloft in their hands.

"I asked how are you feeling, Lenn? Any memories return?" Simon stared at me, concern edging his face.

"Um, I'm feeling better. A little dizziness here and there, but nothing to be concerned with."

"How did you hurt your head anyway?" my dad asked.

"Oh, um, not sure. But apparently, I fell off my stool and hit it on a filing cabinet."

"Was blood everywhere?" Noah asked, a grin on his face.

"Yeah, there kind of was," Simon supplied, making a face at him. Those two had become thick as thieves over the years.

"Nice."

Rolling my eyes, I went back into my zone until I heard my mother ask a question. Playing with my fork in the mashed potatoes, I eavesdropped as I peered up from under my eyelashes attempting to appear innocent.

"So, Simon, are you seeing anyone new these days?"

Simon looked baffled for a minute, stunned he was being asked. "Um, nope. I'm not."

"Oh, that's too bad, sweetie. I know the one's out there for you," my mom reassured.

"Yeah," he swallowed, looking at me. I raised an eyebrow, unsure what he was getting at. If I hadn't known he was gay, I'd swear he was looking at *me* with longing, and lust.

Noah took over the conversation after the awkward pause and proceeded to update us on the moves he could now do on his skateboard. It was a nice break from the leading questions, at least.

When everyone was finished, I felt relieved and quickly cleared my plate from the table. I started gathering the other dishes, needing to do something active. My mom joined me, and I could tell a question was on her mind. Waiting her out, I kept washing as I scraped off the food.

"Honey, have you ever," she started, but I stopped her before she continued.

"Mom, drop it. Simon doesn't have feelings for me. He told me to my face after we had sex together, both our first times, mind you," I reiterated. Giving her the eye, I used my soap covered fingers to make air quotes. "That he, and I quote, 'likes boys'. So, please, tell me where that's open for interpretation. He had sex with me and was like, 'nope, vags aren't for me, dick all day'."

"Lennox Elaine! Language."

My face heated as I realized how many body parts

I'd just said to my mother. I focused back on the dishes and hoped she would drop it.

She did not.

"All I'm saying, dear, is that maybe, he's changed his mind now?"

"After nine years?" I deadpanned, rolling my eyes. Concussions made me testy, apparently. "Mom, just drop it, *please*. It's hurtful to keep bringing it up. He doesn't like me like that despite my feelings. I'm sorry your and Mrs. Fischer's plans of a joint wedding aren't going to happen. We're friends, end of discussion. Can't that be good enough?"

I hadn't realized I was on the verge of tears until she pulled me into her arms. My soapy hands got her all wet as I hugged her, but she didn't seem to mind. Tears fell as my mother held me, and I blamed it on the head wound. I'd grieved years ago, so why was I getting so emotional about it again?

I was chalking it up to today having been a weird day.

"Oh, honey. I never meant to make you sad. I just see how you both look at each other and the love that's there. I just want you to be happy, though, so I'll drop the Simon thing."

"Thanks, Mom. I think I'm just going to lay down. Are you okay with finishing?"

"Yes, honey. Go rest. I'll check on you in a few.

Wiping my nose, I walked back to my room, not in the mood for any company. Logging onto my computer. I checked my blog site to see how my views were today on my last blog post.

Books, Tats, & Bad Boys Reading Sphere

Views: 2300
Likes: 4053
New Subscribers: 34
Total Subscribers: 3000

Just as I finished scanning the page, a new message popped up on a post I'd done last week.

Unrequited love or Fated Mates? Which is your poison?
Blue_eye_rescue: Hi! I love your insight. Thanks for the great book recs! Fated Mates are my favorite.

Ah, well that was nice. Deciding to reply, I typed in a message.

noxbooks_tats_&_badboys: Thank you, I just love to read! Happy to meet a fellow reader!

The ping came through quickly, surprising me and I found a message waiting in my DM's. Well, they didn't waste any time sliding up them. I swear every time I thought I met a genuine reader, it would be some creep who'd send me a dick pic. Tapping on the message, I squinted to avoid having my retinas burned by a stranger's dong. Surprisingly, it was an actual message. In fact, it was kind of a letter. Opening my eyes fully, I began to read it.

Hey Nox Books,

Hopefully it's okay for me to shorten your name, if that is your name. I just didn't want to type out the full thing, but if that's what you prefer then I will. Thank you for responding back, this is my first time on a blog site, and I wasn't sure what the procedure was.

I do appreciate your book recs and the insight you have into the characters. I especially like the art you add with it. It brings the story to life in a whole new way by seeing how you saw it.

Well, I hope you have a good night. It was nice to meet you.

B.E.R.

My finger hovered over the reply button, and I debated whether or not it was prudent to respond. Simon's laughter drifting down the hall for some reason had me pushing it. I remembered my determination the other night, tired of feeling alone, or waiting on someone to find me worthy enough to pursue. Perhaps it was the ordeal of this day, or maybe it was just my own mortality staring me in the face, the trip to the hospital reminding me how short life could be. I was done waiting on the sidelines.

Hey B.E.R.!

Hope it's okay to call you that. Nox suits me fine as well. Welcome to the site! I'm not too crazy or fancy, but I'm pleased you like my concept. It's really the perfect way for me to combine a lot of my loves. Let me know which book you read and what you think. Look forward to discussing more with you.

Nox

Signing off, I slumped back into my chair, picking my book back up from where I'd stopped earlier. I could always depend on a book to send me into a magical world.

Knock Nox,

I have a joke for you. I'm going to pretend you answer back for this to work.

Knock knock. (Now you say, who's there?)

Cow says. (Now you say, cow says who?)

No, silly. Cow says moo.

Are you laughing? I hope you're laughing. I'm horrible with jokes, but I saw that one and it made me think of you. You mentioned Kentucky once and I feel like you must have cows in your backyard or something. I don't really see them on the West Coast, so it interested me. Read into that if you will, but yes, I do think of you at times.

Thank you for your last letter. I'm sorry to hear your peers are cruel. Sometimes, family things make life difficult, but they're family, and that's important. At least I feel that way. Some days I do question my sanity.

I tried your trick with the stars, and I was surprised. Not that I doubted you, but yeah, I was surprised it worked. So, thank you for that.

Your answers? Very clever, Nox. I didn't think about the bath part. I'd like to edit my answer as well.

I've never been in a tornado. Weather phenomena do interest me, but I doubt I'd enjoy it if I was in the middle of a cyclone. I need to get you a thunder shirt. It works for my dog. I'm glad we agree the best season is fall. We can continue to be pen pals now.

IN RESPONSE TO YOUR QUESTIONS.

1. PIZZA ALL THE TIME. I DON'T KNOW HOW YOU COULD HAVE A DIFFERENT ANSWER. SERIOUSLY, I'M DEBATING BEING YOUR FRIEND NOW. I'LL HAVE TO CONVINCE YOU.

2. NO, I DON'T THINK I'VE BEEN IN LOVE, NOT REALLY. I FEEL LIKE THERE'S A STORY TO YOUR ANSWER. I WANT TO PUSH YOU TO SPILL, BUT I WON'T DO THAT. BUT YOU CAN, YOU KNOW... SPILL. IT'S KIND OF THE BEAUTY OF PEN PALS. SHARING SECRETS WITH SOMEONE YOU'LL NEVER MEET.

3. HOBBY? I ALSO LIKE ART. I DRAW ALMOST EVERY FREE SECOND I GET AND IT DOESN'T MATTER WHERE. NOW MY PARENTS AND TEACHERS HAVE DIFFERENT OPINIONS ABOUT THAT, BUT IT DOESN'T STOP ME. I ALSO LIKE MUSIC. I FIDDLE WITH THE GUITAR, BUT I WOULD NEVER PLAY IN FRONT OF SOMEONE.

MY QUESTIONS:

1. WOULD YOU RATHER HAVE FEET FOR HANDS OR HANDS FOR FEET? I THINK I'D ROCK THE DOUBLE HAND SYNDROME. I DEFINITELY COULD GET MORE DONE.

2. WHEN DID YOU FIRST REALIZE YOUR PARENTS AREN'T PERFECT? I WAS TEN. I CAUGHT MY MOM CHEATING ON MY DAD. I TOLD MY DAD, AND EVERYTHING FELL APART. I REGRET SAYING ANYTHING. I OFTEN WONDER IF I HADN'T IF MY FAMILY WOULD STILL BE TOGETHER.

3. FAVORITE COLOR? MINE IS... OKAY, DON'T LAUGH, BUT I REALLY LOVE PURPLE. I MOSTLY WEAR BLACK, BUT IF I COULD PICK, IT WOULD BE PURPLE.

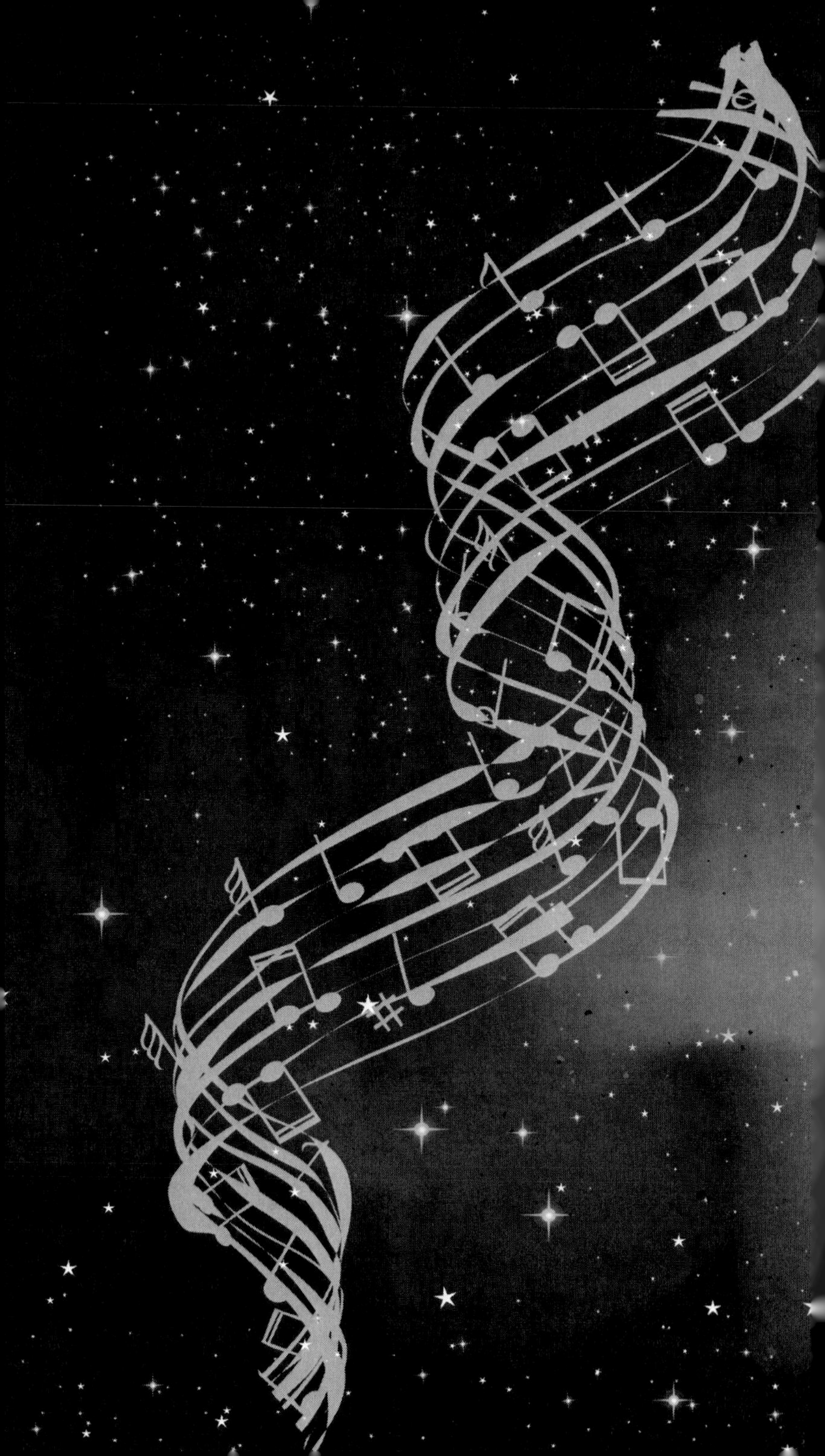

Chapter Eight

LENNOX

BED REST PASSED by agonizingly slowly, and death almost seemed preferable by the time the official all-clear came. It had been nice to spend time with Noah and my parents, but the constant questions and checking-in reminded me why I'd moved out. I loved my family, but preferably, in more of a few streets over and weekly dinners kind of thing.

Waving to my mom, I walked to my apartment building. After the appointment, we went to lunch and then went shopping. It was supposed to be a quick trip, but it turned into a few hours. Now, exhaustion coated me, and I was ready to be back in my space.

Unlocking my door, I was surprised when I didn't hear Simon. He typically had Sundays off, and we spent many of them binge-watching on the couch together. Walking through the whole place, I didn't find him in any of the rooms. Nothing looked out of place as I scanned it. Now that I thought about it, Simon had been quiet all weekend.

After dinner the other night, I hadn't seen or heard from him. Typically, we texted all day long about every mundane thing. Opening my phone, the last text I received from him was two days ago. *Fudge*! Dialing his number, it went straight to voicemail. Panic started to crawl up my chest, and I raced out of the apartment to find him.

Something was wrong, I just knew it.

When I got out to the parking lot, I remembered my car was still at the shop. I'd forgotten to make sure to drive it here. Except as I frantically searched for the Lyft app, I saw my car parked in its usual spot. Simon must've brought it back for me. Warmth filled my chest at the thought.

No time to get weepy about it, though, and I raced to it and flung open the door. The hinges creaked, and I started my ritual of praying my car would start. Smoothing my hands over the cracked leather of the steering wheel, I gave it a soft caress. Turning the car radio to 88.7 FM and the defroster on, I lifted the emergency brake, and turned the key halfway, then back, and then all the way.

It might sound ridiculous, but this combination of things never ceased to fail me. Betty roared to life just as expected, and I kissed my fingers and placed it on the rearview mirror.

Take good care of your girl, and she'll take good care of you.

Backing out, I tried to keep my anxiety away from my gas pedal to not disturb the acceleration. Making it over the last speed bump, I sighed in relief at making it this far. Typically, if Betty was going to break down, it was in the first five minutes. Her continued purr was a good sign for the drive.

Turning left, I started with all the usual places we hung out. This wasn't the first time Simon had gone off the rails, but last time, I'd at least been there and known. I felt like a horrible friend at the moment for having missed this, too wrapped up in my own head to pay attention.

The year I didn't like to think about, much less remember, was the last time Simon had disappeared for a few days, until I found him stranded in a Motel 6. He still hadn't told me what occurred, just that it hadn't been good, and they'd taken his money and phone. He was bruised and smelled of old trash, but I was just so happy to have found him, I gave in and dropped it.

Now, I was kicking myself for never asking more. Maybe he secretly had a gambling problem? Perhaps he had online hook-up orgies? Was he secretly training to be a drag queen? Or maybe, he was part of a weird cult? Fight club?

It really could be endless when it came to Simon, the man was unpredictable.

Driving by his parent's house, I didn't see his car, so I kept going. Next, I tried our favorite restaurant, park, and even the library. It had already been an hour, and I was running low on gas and ideas.

Attempting to try one more place, I turned around and prayed I'd make it there. It was about ten minutes later when the worst thing that could happen, happened.

"No, no, no, Betty. Come on, girl."

Despite my encouragement, the sputtering and deceleration of the car continued, and I soon found myself pulling over on the side of the road as the car died a slow death. Dropping my head to the wheel, I sucked in a few breaths as I attempted to reign in my emotions. The tears burned my sinuses as I kept them at bay.

"It's going to be okay. You can do this, Lennox. You can. You're tough and capable. You don't need a man to do this for you."

Feeling determined, I lifted my head, resolute in finding a solution. When I turned to open my door, I screamed, jumping back as I clutched my chest to slow my heart.

"Cheese on toast! You scared the crap out of me, you big meanie head."

His deep resounding chuckle filtered through the closed door, the sound determined to make me tingle where the sun didn't mingle. Narrowing my eyes, I tried to persuade my body to stop having a hay day and remember we hated him, for reasons unknown, but we did.

"Talk to yourself a lot there, James? Looks like you could use a hand."

"Sorry, what? I can't hear you."

I cupped my ear, attempting to fake not being able to hear, not wanting to admit anything to him. His smirk confirmed what I feared. He didn't buy it for a second. Sighing, I rolled the window down painstakingly slowly as I attempted to act put out by him being there. The squeak of the handle with each turn had the hair on my arms raising at the sound. I think dogs in the whole state of Kentucky heard the window whine.

"Peach, this car is a piece of shit, and I think it's finally decided to die. You need to put it out of its misery."

"What?" I couldn't even form words. My head was spinning as I tried to formulate a response back, fear crawling up my throat at the thought. "No! She's not. Betty just needs a rest. She's a good girl."

I caressed the wheel, attempting to soothe her hurt feelings, not caring that Tatzilla probably stared at me with ridicule. The crack of thunder overhead had me tensing, and I started to roll the window up as quickly as possible. My arm was cramping with each spin, but I managed to get it up.

He knocked on the window, causing me to jump again. My nerves were officially shot, and somehow, I kept forgetting he was there. How? No clue. I'd go with the brain injury again, despite being cleared by the doctor this morning.

"James. Come on."

"No."

Crossing my arms, I planned to stay in my car until I figured out a plan. He could go away and leave me to it. I'd think a lot clearer if he wasn't distracting me with his hot bod voodoo.

"James! You have two seconds to get out of the car before I grab you myself. The storm is coming and moving fast. We need to go, *now*."

Shaking my head, I kept staring at the front and decided to call my dad. It wasn't handling it entirely by myself, but it was better than asking Tatzilla for help any day. Leaning over, I went to grab my purse and phone when my door was wrenched open.

I was beginning to seriously think the doctor had gotten it wrong because, again, it took me a few seconds to realize what was happening. Which unfortunately, allowed Tatzilla to gain the upper hand as I just stared blankly at him like a clueless kitten.

Slade's head appeared in the open spot, his tattoos sharp against the grey interior. One second, I was staring at him, my mouth open, my phone and purse in hand, and the next, he was grabbing my keys, and then, well, me.

In one swift move, he'd grabbed me up by the legs and managed to bundle me in his arms as he pulled me out of the car. Squealing, I barely kept my balance and ahold of my purse as I went flying over his shoulder. He stomped off with a purpose, not wasting a second as I attempted to wrestle out of his grip.

Tatzilla sat me on the seat of his bike, tossed me a helmet, and straddled the beast in quick succession. When I felt the purr of the engine roar under me, I succumbed to my fate, not feeling brave enough to jump off. Quickly, I secured the helmet, threw my purse strap over my body, and shoved my phone in, just as he took off.

Grabbing a hold of him, I ignored how his body felt as I gripped him tightly. My body shook, the adrenaline and impending storm sending me into a tailspin. The crack of thunder had me huddling into his back, my face burrowing into his shirt, his smell invading my nostrils. I expected to be disgusted, but I found it soothing, like a warm blanket around a fire.

When we came to a stop at a stoplight, I felt him place his hands over mine for a brief second before we were taking off again. The small gesture comforted and confused me enough that my body stopped shaking the rest of the trip.

He pulled in somewhere and parked a moment later. Once his body moved out of my way, I realized we were at the shop. The sun was setting, and the sky had gone dark with the approaching storm. Taking off his helmet, Slade motioned for me to hurry and eventually, moved me off the bike himself. It didn't matter, though. Almost to the second, as soon as my foot touched the parking lot, big fat raindrops began to fall from the sky. At a run, we made it into the shop a few minutes later. It would've been quicker, but we'd been waylaid by the million locks as Slade attempted to unlock them. By the time we entered the store, we were both completely drenched.

"Bet you wish you didn't have as many locks now, huh?"

Slade turned to me, a retort on his lips, but when he looked at me, he stopped and stared for a long moment, and I couldn't figure out what was happening.

"Earth to bossnemy? Did you have a stroke or something?"

Waving my hand in front of his face, the movement captured his attention, earning me a scowl. It seemed my mere existence frustrated him today and it grated on me. I didn't want to admit it. It was much easier to pretend I didn't care, but it did. I acted like I didn't care what people thought of me, and for the most part, that was true.

But I also had this deep-seated desire to be liked, and when I hadn't done anything to my knowledge to earn his disdain, it hurt, *a lot.*

His lip turned up, and he scowled down at me. "Do you always have to wear dresses?"

Confused, I furrowed my brow. "I don't *have to,* but I like to. What's it to you anyway what I wear?"

Huffing, I crossed my arms, the dampness of the material reminding me I was soaking wet. My body started to shake, and I realized how chilled I was. Rubbing my arms to garner heat, I glanced down, and the color of my dress registered.

Mother of pearl! My dress was practically see-through! No wonder Tatzilla had stared.

Burrowing further into my arms as a protective shield, I debated on how to fix this situation. It was obvious Slade was disgusted by me. The dress was stuck to my body, offering a skin-tight look at every inch of me, the white highlighting each roll of chub. I embraced my body and had accepted it wasn't the same as the tall skinny Crystals of the world, but it didn't mean I didn't feel some self-consciousness every now and then. Especially when I stood practically naked in front of a man. Spinning, I took off for the back.

"James! Stop pouting and get back here."

I wanted to ignore him on principle, tired of his ordering me around. Plus, I was cold, and I hoped he had something in his office. Stomping as I went, I couldn't pass the opportunity to showcase my displeasure. The further back I ventured into the shop, the more I noticed how dark it was. The thunder rolled above, and a lightning streak lit up the window upfront, causing me to jump again. Crapola, the power was out, and the sun had set.

I couldn't see any further into the shop, and the thought of blindly walking in terrified me. I'd seen enough horror movies that started this way.

"Um, Slade? I can't see."

"Open your eyes, James."

His voice took on an ethereal quality, the deep timber rolling through me, and I almost moaned out loud at the way it affected me. I found myself shivering for an entirely different reason now. I hadn't realized I'd closed my eyes until I opened them and found him standing directly in front of me, his phone flashlight bright in front of my face.

"Here."

He shoved something into my hand, and I realized it was a shirt. Looking back up, he'd already walked off again, leaving me in darkness. Muttering under my breath, I picked up the pace to follow him, not wanting to be left alone in the stormy atmosphere a minute longer.

A soft glow emitted from where I assumed his office was, and I headed there. Just as I stepped in, I caught a brief glance of his naked body in the dim light before he pulled a pair of low-slung athletic shorts up.

Slade turned, finding me immobile in the doorway and a twisted smile tilted his lips, instantly cooling my arousal. Scowling myself, I stuck out my tongue as I stepped into the room. I twisted the shirt into my hands, unsure what to do now I was here. Slade propped himself against the desk, his gaze critical as he watched me.

"You're not shy, are you, *Peach*?"

The taunt was obvious, but I found myself falling into it regardless, as heat seared my skin. Embarrassment or arousal, I didn't know.

"Scared? Why would I be scared?"

His thumb brushed against his lower lip as he assessed me, and I found myself tracking its movement. He lowered his hand, shaking his head, disbelief etched in his features as I stayed frozen.

"Funny. You said 'scared' when I asked if you were shy." He smirked, pausing to let that sink in. I didn't have an answer for him. "I thought you were braver, that's all. Surely, a little nudity doesn't scare you?"

"Nudity? I'm not getting nude with you! What, you think because you rescued me, I now owe you a sexual favor or something?"

I was appreciative of the darkness, hiding the redness that had taken over my body and crept up my neck. Flustered beyond belief, I stammered all over the place as I tried to decrease my heart rate. My dream from the other night came to the forefront of my mind at the mention of nudity, and I had to hold myself back from jumping him to see if it was accurate.

*He hates you. In fact, he loathes yo*u, my inner voice chorused.

Tatzilla stood and sauntered toward me. I'd never

seen him appear so cocky before, at least not toward me. There was so much sexual swagger in his approach, I wondered if I'd just gotten pregnant from his walk alone.

If there was ever an appropriate time to cuss, it would be now, because dayum, the man dripped sexual innuendo. Or perhaps, the dripping was me, and for the second time in a week, I wondered if I'd squirted.

The familiarness of the thought had me pausing as a memory pushed to the surface between Simon and me. But as Slade drew nearer, I shoved it aside, unable to focus on it. The only thing in my vision was him.

Water dripped down my body, a puddle collecting at my feet. My hair was a sopping mess flat against my head, and yet under his gaze, I felt seen by him in a way I never had before.

"Peach, put on the damn shirt. I can see your nipples from across the room, and I only have so much restraint. Plus, if you catch a damn cold because you're too stubborn, no one will believe me that you chose to stay wet. I'll have Simon and Bubba so far up my ass over it, I won't be able to sit for a week. So, please, for the love of my ass, take off your clothes. If you're nervous, I'll turn my back."

He towered over me, breathing down at me, and I felt every hot caress of his breath as he spoke. I missed half of what he'd said, too focused on the energy surging between us, that underlying current now a blazing fire. Keeping his gaze, I dropped the shirt onto the chair and pushed off my straps.

I wanted to be seductive while doing it, but it came out

more angrily than I intended. My hackles had been raised, and it took everything in me not to be a stubborn donkey's butt and stay in the wet dress. The cold won out in the end, and I submitted to his demand, hating every second of it.

Pushing the wet material over my breasts, I slid it down, having to practically peel it off where it had molded to my skin. The slapping sound of the dress hitting the ground echoed in the small room. I was so angry, my breathing had increased, my thoughts dared me to put this guy in his place, to show him just how unaffected I was by him. His jaw ticked, his eyes never leaving mine, not even when I unhooked my bra and dropped it to the ground. Slade stayed zeroed in on me, his emotions hidden behind his wall.

My earlier self-consciousness had long fled now, and I stood practically naked in front of him, daring him to do something. Gathering my hair in one hand, I wrung it out, the water puddling on the floor. I didn't care that my tits were out on display. I wanted to push him over the edge like I had in my dream. I only needed to find the right button to push. I felt daring, a strong desire to punish Slade for hating me.

Slowly, I grabbed the shirt and slid it on over my head. His fresh woody smell encircled me, laying claim to my skin as I covered my body with him. I couldn't help it. I breathed it in, a shudder rolling through me at smelling him this close. It was bold and fresh, bringing a heat to my skin as the shirt kissed it. Once it was over, I pulled my hair from the collar and returned to staring at Slade. Except he was no longer in front of me.

Slade was bent over his desk, his arms braced on it as his back lifted, presumably taking deep breaths, in and out.

Rolling my eyes at his dramatics for having to be in a room with me, I scooped up my wet clothes and tip-toed out into the hall. I snagged one of the candles he had lit as I went, not wanting to be in the darkness alone. Hanging my wet clothes in the bathroom, I found a comb and managed to detangle my hair. It started to kink up as it dried, and I knew I'd have a frizzy mess once it finished.

Stepping out, I returned to the office and found Slade sitting on the floor, a bottle between his legs. Quirking an eyebrow, I set the candle down and sat on the floor opposite him.

"Playing spin-the-bottle with yourself?"

"I was thinking more truth or dare. You up for it, Peach? Or are you, what was the word you used? Too scared?"

The thunder cracked overhead again, making me jump, and I swallowed. "I'm not scared."

He chuckled, that rich tone hitting me straight on the clit, and I crossed my legs in a different direction as I tried to get some friction indiscreetly. He poured two shot glasses and pushed one over to me. I stared at the liquid for a moment, debating if I was about to do this. I hadn't drunk anything since that night. Slade's voice had me lifting my head.

"Truth or dare, James?" He smirked, his cockiness returning, and I found myself wanting to wipe it off his face. Perhaps, this could be my chance to get some answers and finally discover what I'd done to him.

"Fine. *Dare*."

His smile widened, his eyes lit with mischief, and I wondered briefly what the hell I'd just gotten myself into.

Blaze

I'll forgive you for your awful knock-knock joke. I want to sing "Purple Rain" now. I feel like it matches you. Your love of rain and the color purple. Maybe just Purple Blaze then.

What kind of music do you like? I love all kinds of music. It's a thing with me and my dad. We'll play around on his guitar and play 'Guess This Song.' I love to sing too. I'm always humming. I'd love to sing on stage one day, but I don't know if I'll ever get up the courage. Like you, I think it seems frightening. When you're up there for everyone to see, it's so raw. Is that why you won't?

If you could see me now. I just blew out a big breath making my hair flutter in front of my face because even though you're right and pen pals are perfect to share secrets with, it kind of feels too raw still. But maybe I need to get it out there. How about I give you pieces of it, and so each time, I'm a little step closer to the truth?

The first piece. Well, I thought I was in love with my best friend.

I've included a picture of my backyard. See? No cows. So, now you can say you've seen the sunset in Kentucky. While I don't have cows, there are a lot of farmlands around, though I'm partial to the horse farms. Horse racing is huge here and in Northern Kentucky, there are rolling acres of bluegrass and horses. If I stay here when I grow up, I think I'd move there.

I'M GLAD THE STARS WORKED FOR YOU. I DON'T KNOW WHAT TIME ZONE YOU'RE IN, BUT MAYBE ONE NIGHT WE CAN GO OUT AND LOOK AT THE STARS AT THE SAME TIME AND IT WILL BE LIKE WE'RE SHARING IT TOGETHER. MAYBE IT WON'T FEEL SO BAD? IT'S PROBABLY A CORNY THING TO SAY OR DO. SO, IF YOU DON'T DO IT, JUST DON'T TELL ME, OKAY? I'D RATHER BELIEVE IT INSTEAD OF FEELING LIKE AN IDIOT.

1. DOUBLE HANDS OR FEET? I THINK I WOULD RATHER HAVE HANDS AS WELL. IT MIGHT GET WEIRD, BUT HAVING TOES TO EAT JUST DOESN'T SOUND APPETIZING.

2. PARENTS NOT BEING PERFECT? MINE WAS TWO SUMMERS AGO WHEN NOAH WAS 6 MONTHS OLD. MY MOM HAD HER FIRST MANIC EPISODE THAT I WAS AWARE OF. IT WAS THE START OF THE BULLIES AND MEAN GIRLS. SHE GOT HELP AND IS BETTER NOW, BUT NO ONE LETS HER FORGET IT.

3. MY FAVORITE COLOR IS A TIE BETWEEN TURQUOISE AND PURPLE. I KIND OF LIKE THAT IT'S YOUR FAVORITE COLOR TOO.

MY QUESTIONS.

1. WOULD YOU EVER GET A TATTOO? I KIND OF HAVE AN OBSESSION WITH THEM, BUT I ALSO CAN'T DECIDE ON ANYTHING SIGNIFICANT ENOUGH TO COMMIT TO.

2. WOULD YOU RATHER SQUIRT MILK OUT YOUR NOSE EVERY TIME YOU LAUGHED OR OUT OF YOUR ARMPITS EVERY TIME YOU FARTED? OH WOW, I'M LAUGHING AT MYSELF FOR THIS ONE. UMM... NOSE?

3. WHAT SUPERPOWER WOULD YOU WANT? SO, I'VE THOUGHT ABOUT THIS ONE FOR A LONG TIME. SIMON AND I HAVE THIS DISCUSSION A LOT, AND I HONESTLY THINK I'M LANDING ON TELEPORTATION. BEING ABLE TO GET FROM ONE PLACE TO THE NEXT JUST BY BLINKING OR WHATEVER? SOUNDS AWESOME TO ME.

Chapter Nine
LENNOX

THE WORD DARE tumbled off my lips before I could snatch it back. Every encounter with Slade felt like a game of chicken, so ending up in this position shouldn't have been a surprise. Yet, as I pierced him with a challenge in my gaze, my heart beating erratically and my palms sweaty, I wondered what the fudge was wrong with me.

I was starting to think I enjoyed his torture.

"Peach, I dare you," he said, deliberately pausing to drag out the anticipation. "I dare you to let me tattoo you."

Rolling my eyes, I grabbed the shot glass and tossed one back, attempting not to think about the possible consequences. The tequila burned as it slid down my throat, my face scrunched up and my mouth let out a hiss as I swallowed. Sweet molasses, this was dangerous. I calmed my racing heart, subduing my fear that we weren't going anywhere in this storm, not to mention I didn't have a car, so we'd be relatively safe inside drinking.

And safety was very relative. The combination of the tension between us, the booze, and Tatzilla's inherent sex appeal, I didn't know how well that boded for me. This had 'bad decision' written all over it.

But I couldn't let him tattoo me. I couldn't. It had already been promised to someone else, even if that no longer mattered. A promise was a promise, and I held a sliver of hope that one day it would still happen.

It was stupid and naive, but I held onto that morsel, snuggling it close at night. It might've been a promise I made as a teenager, but it just didn't feel as special if I did it any other way. I wanted it to be special.

"You're impossible, James."

I could hear the hint of anger in his words, but I ignored them. He wouldn't understand the dream of a teenage girl. Wiping my mouth with the back of my hand. I sat the shot glass back down as I began to think of a question for him. I knew what I wanted to ask, but in order to actually make sure he answered it, I had to delicately build up to it. Which meant I needed a strategy. The simplest would be to get him to drink so he'd lower his inhibitions and hopefully, his ability to hide the truth.

"Truth or dare, bossnemy?"

"Dare," he scoffed, apparently offended I needed to clarify. Rolling my eyes, I smiled mischievously as I made eye contact.

"I dare *you* to let me pierce your junk."

There had never been a more perfect moment for me to wish I'd recorded his reaction. He sputtered, briefly shocked before his hard mask returned. Grabbing the bottle, he angrily poured a shot and threw it back, slamming it on the ground between us when he was done.

"As if I'd let you touch my cock, *Peaches*."

Quirking an eyebrow, I ignored him and the fact he'd made the nickname sound more seductive and waited him out. I'd given him two piercings over the three years I'd been here, his eyebrow and his tongue. He'd been an absolute baby about both of them. I knew he'd never go for the Prince Albert. I was playing the long game, but the way he denied wanting it had me itching to do it now.

Slade sneered at me, and I continued to look at him, determined to do the next one. I needed to stay on top of things and not be tipsy. The tequila was already coursing through me, I didn't need any more.

"Truth or dare?"

"Truth."

He grinned, and I worried I'd fallen into *his* trap. Though, I didn't have anything to hide, so it had to be the safer option. Right?

"How many sexual partners have you had?"

Relief washed over me at first, happy with the easy answer, but then the tendril of fear, the anxiety of the memory I ignored poked its ugly head up. Blinking, I pushed it back, knowing I didn't have to remember if I didn't want to. The pause, though, had Slade grinning in victory, thinking he'd won.

"Don't tell me you're a *virgin*, James?"

Rolling my eyes, I adjusted my legs, stretching them out in front of me as I leaned back on my arms. The shirt lifted up my thighs, getting closer to my bare pussy in the process. I held it, though, watching the way Slade's eyes tracked the material and the minuscule flare of his nostrils. He wanted to act unaffected and like he despised me, but I was beginning to expect it was all an act. His tiny ministrations gave him away. I didn't want to admit, I'd become an expert in them over three years.

The bomb ticked closer with each push and pull between us, the inevitable explosion on the horizon, and for the first time, I wondered if the collateral damage might be worth it.

"No, I'm not a virgin, *Evans*. It just took me a minute to count all my lovers," I winked. "But, you said sexual partners, so do you mean full-on intercourse or any sexual behavior?"

He stared blankly at me, shock on his face before he recovered. "Who the fuck says sexual intercourse? It's *fucking,* Peach. If you can't say it, I doubt you've ever done it." Slade's jaw ticked as he breathed in. "But I don't care about every blow job you've given, just how many cocks you've ridden. How many dicks have you wrapped your cunt around?"

Squishing up my nose, I leveled him with a look. I knew he was attempting to disarm me, but really, *cunt*? "Why do you have to be so crass? No one talks like that! Not in the south anyway. And I can say the f-word, I just chose not to. You bullying me isn't going to make me do it, either. I've dealt with far worse ones than you, *Evans*."

I hadn't meant to get so worked up over it, but the indignation coursed through me, and I found myself breathing rapidly. "So, for your information and the game only, I've slept with, bumped uglies, and done the horizontal tango with four people."

Leaning back on my arms, I wanted to give the look of nonchalant superiority, but the shifting of my legs probably diminished it. I didn't want to be affected by his words, but hearing him say it next to my name, and then describing it, aroused me. I wouldn't admit he was the one currently featured in my fantasy.

He observed me, almost as if he was assessing my honesty. Every now and then, his eyes would drop down to my legs, or more specifically, the area between my legs where the shirt hit. It was too dark to tell, but he seemed as affected as me by his words. It alleviated some of my own guilt, knowing my plight was reciprocated.

"Is my answer satisfactory, Evans?"

"Hmph," was the only response I got.

Twisting my legs sideways, I leaned forward as I prepared my next attack. "Truth or Dare?'

"Truth," he challenged. Ah, so was that how it was going to be? He'd do whatever I did? It gave me a whole new approach.

"Hmm, let's see. Oh, I know," I grinned. "Why won't you let me be an apprentice?"

He seared me with his espresso eyes, swallowing while he debated answering. Keeping my face neutral, I blinked my eyes slowly, offering my best puppy dog eyes. It did nothing, as usual.

"*Because* you're not ready."

That was it. The same darn answer he'd given me over and over. Huffing, I crossed my arms, forgetting I only had on a t-shirt. The movement drew it up under my breasts, the hem rising higher, barely covering me now. He swallowed, and hot fudge sundae, if that wasn't one of the sexiest gestures I'd ever seen.

"Truth or dare?"

I'd wanted to do another truth, but with the new knowledge I had, perhaps a dare would be better this round. Outside of tattooing, I didn't think there was anything I wouldn't do that we had access to. Being stranded and without power did give some restrictions.

"Dare."

"I dare you to sing for me."

I gasped, not expecting the request. It was on the tip of my tongue to decline it, but then I saw his smirk. Slade thought he had me again, he expected me to turn it down. My stubborn pride reared its ugly head, and I justified it was only him. I didn't care what he thought, so he couldn't be that scary. Or at least I tried to convince myself that. Without giving it much more thought, I started singing before I could change my mind.

It was weird. My voice came out strong, my confidence solid as I held eye contact. It was quiet all around us, the rain and thunder the only sound. None of the usual noises, the computers or equipment could be heard with the electricity out. So, my song filled the space, echoing off the walls almost, the acoustics almost ideal.

"Foolish Games" by Jewel, an old favorite, fell from my lips, the words hauntingly beautiful and oddly relatable to me and Slade. You know, if I was in love with him or something. Which I wasn't. Nope, not this girl.

As the last note rang out, I transported back down to the plane I'd been in. Slade looked slack-jawed, and I didn't know how to feel about it. Directing the attention off my emotional tune, I pounced. "Truth or dare?"

I hoped by not commenting, he'd drop it. He studied me, something shifting in his gaze, and he held it as he made his choice. "Dare."

"I dare you, to let me tattoo *you* and prove I deserve the apprenticeship."

If I had a dollar for every time I'd shocked Slade tonight, I'd be at least twenty dollars richer. I watched as he debated before pulling the bottle to him and swallowing. He was up to two shots now. I'd wanted him to drink on that one, but as the tequila slid down his throat, disappointment covered me.

"Truth or dare, James?"

"Truth."

"Who was the last person you hurt?"

I cocked my head, wondering the purpose of his statement, not missing the thinly veiled anger. When he didn't budge, I thought about my answer. "Do you mean physically or emotionally?"

Slade gritted his teeth, not wanting to give me direction. Rolling my eyes, I answered it both ways. "No one emotionally. But physically, Simon when I hit him with the door."

"You *sure* about that?"

"Yeah, I'm sure." Questions lined my brow, not understanding his tone.

"You might want to rethink that, or perhaps we have different definitions."

Rolling my eyes, I dropped it, not wanting to get into it. "Truth or dare, Evans?"

"Dare."

Feeling slightly happy he'd deviated and leaving my truth question for when he was a little more imbibed, I needed to think of a dare. Tapping my finger on my lips, I thought of the perfect one. "Let me dye your hair!"

"Why is every dare you give me have you doing things to me, James?"

He sneered, grabbing the bottle this time, and throwing it back for a long drawl before sitting it back down. I could see him starting to sway finally. Lifting my shoulders, I kept his weird back and forth to myself.

"Truth or dare, James?"

"Dare."

"I dare you to sit on my lap."

Laughing, I realized afterward it wasn't a joke. Shrugging, I crawled toward him and straddled his lap. I'd temporarily forgotten I didn't have any bottoms on. So, when my bare pussy settled on him, I sucked in a breath. Slade didn't touch me, but there was no denying he was stiff beneath me. As I relaxed, my hands bracing on his shoulders, I felt him grow even harder. A silent dare passed between us now, whether or not either of us would say anything about it.

This proximity was more intimate than I'd expected. All I could see were his eyes, the smoky dark espresso depths swirled with emotions. The light of the candles flickered over the walls, casting an eerie glow around us. We sat quietly for a few minutes while we drank one another in, and I wondered what was happening between us, this shift. Things were changing, and I didn't know how to process them.

"Truth or dare, Slade?" I whispered.

"Truth."

It was the moment I'd been preparing for, but now, I debated if I wanted the answer or not. This closeness made it feel like he was speaking to my soul, and I wasn't sure I could handle the information. Braving the recourse, I asked anyway, needing to know.

"Why do you hate me?"

He paused, the question familiar to me, a sense of deja vu washing over me causing my body to shiver as I waited, holding my breath. Slade regarded me, his jaw tight and his eyes searching, and I didn't think he would answer. I was about to move off him and grab the tequila when he answered.

"I don't hate you, James. I *should*, but I don't. It kills me how easily it is for you to pretend. I know it would be easier if I could too."

I started to follow up, confused by his response, when he placed his finger on my lips, halting me. "Nope. One question at a time. It's my turn."

Blowing out a breath, my tongue tasted his finger briefly as I did, and I waited for his response. The contact zinged through me, hitting my clit directly, and I found myself involuntarily rolling forward, brushing against the hardness below me. I managed to hold in the moan, but only barely. My breath stopped in my chest as I waited for his question.

Through gritted teeth, Slade managed to get out the words. "Truth or dare?"

"Truth." It came out so breathlessly, I was surprised he heard it.

"If I were to check right this second, would I find your pussy dripping wet, begging for my cock?"

Gasping, I found myself unable to answer as I stared at him with my mouth open.

"What's it going to be, James? Are you going to answer honestly or take the shot? Either way, we both know the real answer. I can feel you soaking through my shorts. *You want me, Peaches. Admit it.*"

His taunting had me biting my tongue, not wanting to give him the satisfaction of a response. Slade was right though, I was in a bind. If I took the shot, I basically admitted to it and made myself closer to the edge of losing control.

On the other hand, I was a notoriously horrible liar. Out of the options, I had to try it to see if I could get away with it. There was no way I could admit how true his statement was. He'd had a lot to drink at this point, so perhaps it would be easier.

"The only wetness you feel is your own snake charmer leaking. Don't pretend you weren't hard before I even sat on your lap. Don't project your attraction onto me, *Slade*."

I wanted to high-five myself for the snark I just delivered, even if my soul was dying a little at the lie.

The satisfaction was short lived though, as I started

to doubt myself and wondered if losing a part of me was worth not admitting my desire. This battle between us had gone on for so long, it was my knee-jerk reaction to deny everything. Still, as I saw the hurt flicker in his eyes and his question ringing around my head about hurting someone, I wondered if I was only deluding myself.

Before he could retaliate, I did the only thing I could think of to salvage the situation—I kissed him.

Sealing my lips to his, I rocked my hips forward as I waited to see what he would do. When he stayed frozen, I panicked and pulled back.

"Sorry, everything I said was a lie. You just bring out the stubborn side of me unlike anyone I've ever met before, and I can't help myself sometimes. I hate the fact that you hate me so much that I go out of my way to hate you first or act like I don't care."

He stared, and a tear fell from my eye at the vulnerability I expressed. I couldn't take it anymore, the silence and the tension had officially become too much.

On top of the secret I held for Simon, I couldn't do this one too. Too many secrets battled for space in my head, and the more I gained, the less I was able to ignore the things I'd rather forget. I needed to forget more than I needed to deny this.

Lifting up, I started to make my way to the bathroom, stumbling in the dark, my eyes blurred with tears. I needed to get out of there. I'd even brave heading out into the rain if I needed to, but first, I just needed to make it to the bathroom.

A hand clamped onto my wrist, stopping me in the

hallway. I stood, staring at the darkness, not willing to turn around just yet.

"Peach, I," he paused, his voice softer than I'd ever heard it. "I told you already, I *don't* hate you. It's just easier to keep my distance. I," he paused, presumably debating his words. "You were right about one thing."

I stayed staring into the shadows, waiting. I couldn't turn around until he revealed more. I couldn't afford the vulnerability if what he was going to say wasn't what I wanted to hear.

"What?"

"That I was projecting my attraction onto you. Every day, I see you wearing your dresses and looking all cute and shit and not even knowing it, it's harder and harder to deny you. I *want you* so much, Lennox, but I *can't*."

Turning, I no longer cared if he saw my tears. He couldn't just say something like that and then shut down.

"Why? I don't understand. If you like me, why do you push me away?" I cried, clutching onto his forearms.

"You know why, you just need to admit it to yourself," he gritted, hanging his head, taking a deep breath as my tears streamed down my face. He looked back up, an uncommon softness in his eyes now. "Ssh, don't cry, James. I *hate it* when you cry."

"Then why do I always cry because of you?"

He dropped his head onto the top of mine, and I could feel his breaths coming in deep as he inhaled. Slade's hands had migrated into my hair, trapping me in a cave of him. His scent swirled around me, making me intoxicated. When his breathing slowed, he pulled back, leaning down to peer into my eyes.

Slade started to say something but stopped, clenching his jaw, his nostrils flaring. His hands flexed in my hair as he stopped himself from saying something. A small amount of light flickered over his features, painting him in a dim shadow, his eyes almost glimmering.

"This can't be anything more than tonight."

He slammed his lips onto mine before I could respond, and I caved to his touch. My inner voice wanted to fight back, so used to the fight between us, it felt like a loss to give in. But when he made my toes curl with the way his tongue swirled around mine, his tongue ring sliding over my own, I felt literal shivers all the way down to my toes. I couldn't stop now. I wouldn't.

Grabbing my thighs, he lifted me up, my legs wrapping around his waist instinctively. My hands tugged and pulled on his hair, the buzzed parts creating slight sensations on my palms as the long locks threaded through my fingers. He dropped me on a surface, and I laid back as he continued to move forward, leaning over me. Once our lips had sealed together this time, it was like they refused to be apart. Who needed air when the man kissed you like the world might end if he didn't?

Slade was everything and more of the version I'd dreamed. He dominated the experience but was delicate, conscious of the force he used as he rocked into me. I cursed the darkness inhibiting me from seeing his face, the look of his desire as he ravished me. When he pulled back to catch his breath, I sucked in a lungful before he crashed back into me.

My lips were swollen from his kisses, but they missed him the second he was gone, and I knew it would never be enough. The voice that urged me to have caution, to realize his words of it only being one night, attempted to poke through, but I ignored it, not caring of my potential heartbreak. Slade's kisses were intoxicating, and I was drunk on him.

Rocking into me, my legs tightened around him, pulling him closer. I could feel his cock against my pussy, the fabric a thin barrier between us. The shirt had ridden up to my waist, my lower section completely open to him. His hands started to shift up my torso, his large palms warming my skin with each brush of them. I felt feminine in his grip, his hands encompassing my waist and torso in one handful, my usual bountiful hips feeling tiny in his large grip.

Pulling apart for air again, this time, he began to suck on my neck, his thumbs making circles on my skin as he kept his upward trek. They'd made it under my breasts now, his thumbs tracing the area, and I rocked, hoping to push him to where I wanted.

"Feeling greedy, *Peaches*?" Slade smirked into my neck as he broke away from the mark he was sure to have left. I wanted to yell at him for the inevitable hickey I had, but something about it made me feel smug. He claimed it was only one night, but he'd marked me. There was some part of him that wanted everyone to see his claim, even if no one knew it was him, I would.

"Touch me, *please,*" I begged.

He didn't reply, but he dived down, taking my nipple into his mouth, his tongue ring now swirling around me. The metal had warmed from our passionate kiss, giving me a zing as he traced the sensitive peak. I arched up into his mouth, my lower section thrusting forward as well, his cock hitting my magic button.

"Fuck it," he growled before biting me on the nip.

I'd never mixed pleasure and pain together before, my experiences having been pretty vanilla, but as Slade bit my swollen nipple, I came so hard, my orgasm ripped through me. My moan escaped me, echoing around the space as I shuddered beneath him.

"Jesus, James, that was the fucking hottest thing I've ever heard."

It was like a switch flipped, and he shoved my borrowed shirt over my head, pausing for a second to take in my naked body in the dim light before descending on me. His skin was warm, the hard planes rubbing against me, and I wish I had time to trace his tattoos with my tongue. Slade's body was an artist's wet dream, the muscles and art giving you so many things to drool over. I managed to shove his shorts down with my heels and felt his penis slap against me.

Reaching down, I wrapped my hand around him and squeezed. Slade dropped his head into my neck at the touch, breathing deeply as I ran my palm up and down his length. His breathing was ragged, and his chest rumbled as I pumped him. He felt long in my hand and girthy. I wondered if he would even fit. I must've paused, or perhaps made a sound, because he lifted his head, a cocksure smile on his lips.

"Don't worry, *Peaches*, it will fit."

He licked up my neck before he lifted his body off me. I cried out, thinking he was stopping, but when he bent down and captured my lips again, the kiss was full of heat and promises, and I melted. Slade nipped my bottom lip, holding it between his teeth. I opened my eyes and watched as he pulled back, slowly releasing it as he did. Slade had always oozed sex appeal, it was a known fact, but as he pulled back, his smile and brow in that cocky tilt, I didn't think I'd ever seen a sexier man.

He stepped back, and my eyes dropped to his dick, fully erect, so big, it swung, hitting his thigh with each step. I couldn't tell what he was doing in the dim light, but I tracked his steps. My hands wandered over my body as I waited for him to return.

He opened a drawer, and I heard him fiddling around in it before the crinkling sound and tearing could be heard. Once he had the condom rolled over himself, he walked back to me, stopping to watch me as I explored my body.

"Peaches, you're better than anything I imagined, and I've imagined you *naked* a lot."

I gasped at the honesty, while Slade lifted me, and the head of his snake charmer began its seductive dance toward me. My legs found their way around him like a magnet wanting to be there. Slade's hands anchored themselves on my hips, and I inhaled a breath, waiting.

He descended, attacking my lips again, his tongue battling with mine as we sealed our bodies together.

Staring me straight in the eyes, my breath caught in my throat as Slade, my Tatzilla and bossnemy, slid into me, and my whole body sang out in a chorus of "Hallelujah".

Nothing had ever felt this magnificent. Nothing.

The only one who might've had a chance at being this amazing was Simon, and we'd been inexperienced sixteen-year-olds with no skill to our name. Slade was an alpha male, full of masculinity and sex appeal. When he thrust into me, his long dick had me arching my back, my eyes rolling to the back of my head, seeing stars. It was the most magical penis I'd ever felt.

He never let go of my hips, flexing his fingers as he used them to lift me up and down on him. His pace was unrelenting, and I found my body in a constant state of shuddering and sensitive pressure points. Slade charmed my body like he equally hated and loved me, a thin line between the two as he pounded into me. His grip on my body bordered on possession, his thrusts of aggression, and his kiss of passion.

I was gone, too full of magical peen and stimulation overload to process what any of it meant.

I needed his hands, I needed his cock, and I needed *him*. And right at the second, I had it. It was all I could concentrate on.

When he pulled my body all the way up, my legs tightened, my arms wrapping around his neck, as our faces became flushed with one another. He kissed me, his eyelashes fluttering against my cheek as they closed.

Plunging into me deep one more time, he held me there as he emptied himself in me, the kiss a searing promise on my lips and heart, and I didn't know if I would ever be the same.

He laid us down on what I now realized was the tattoo table, and my body tingled from head to toe. I found myself curling into him and falling asleep to the beat of his heart beneath me.

I wished in my heart that he hadn't meant it. That it could be more.

Slade had marked himself on my skin, and I would never be the same. The walls were down, the gate was open, and I could no longer deny my feelings for him. I was a goner, and I prayed my curse wouldn't strike me down, breaking my heart into a million pieces once again.

NO, I'M NOT A FISH. ARE YOU A FIRE? IT'S A JOKE. MAYBE I'LL TELL YOU ONE DAY. I DON'T THINK I LOOK LIKE ONE EITHER.

I SUPPOSE IT'S GOOD TO HAVE A FRIEND LIKE LEMON. SHE BOTH FRUSTRATES AND INSPIRES ME.

DARK HORSE, YOU SAY? I'D LIKE TO THINK I WAS THAT COOL, BUT I'M A NERD WHO LIKES TO PRETEND HE'S AN EMO KID. OUR TOWN ISN'T THAT PROGRESSIVE, SO IT'S MOSTLY COUNTRY BOYS, PREPPY GUYS, OR JOCK ASSHATS. I DON'T REALLY FIT IN WITH ANY OF THEM. LEMON IS THE ONLY ONE WHO UNDERSTANDS ME.

WHAT HAPPENED WITH YOUR BROTHER? WHAT'S YOUR SECRET? I FEEL BOLD ASKING. I WOULDN'T NORMALLY DO THAT IN PERSON, BUT MAYBE YOU'RE RIGHT AND THIS PEN PAL THING CAN BE THAT. I'LL KEEP YOUR SECRETS SAFE, AND YOU KEEP MINE.

SO, CONFESSION TIME, I'VE BEEN IN LOVE WITH THE GIRL NEXT DOOR, MY BEST FRIEND FOR AS LONG AS I CAN REMEMBER. WHEN WE WERE YOUNGER, IT WAS THAT SWEET PUPPY LOVE, AND THEN ONE DAY, I REALIZED THE BEAUTIFUL WOMAN SHE'D BECOME, AND MY BODY TOOK NOTICE.

THE LOVE IN MY HEART SWITCHED FROM PUPPY LOVE TO DESIRE AND I COULD BARELY BE AROUND HER WITHOUT SPORTING A BONER. THEY WORK WELL TO COVER AN ILL-TIMED ERECTION, IN CASE YOU EVER FIND YOURSELF IN NEED.

SO WHY DON'T I TELL HER? I TRIED ONCE, BUT IT UTTERLY FAILED. THEN THE FEAR OF LOSING HER COMPLETELY OVERTOOK ME AND I SUCCUMBED TO BEING HER FRIEND FIGURING IT WILL BE BETTER THAN NOTHING.

THAT'S MY FIRST SECRET, BUT NOT MY ONLY.

GRAPHIC NOVEL... WELL, I JUST FINISHED GHOST WORLD AND IT WAS KIND OF AWESOME. WHAT DO YOU RECOMMEND? COMICS, I'M A CLASSIC MARVEL GUY.

I COULDN'T IMAGINE MOVING THAT MUCH, BUT I'M ALSO ENVIOUS OF ALL THE EXPERIENCES YOU MUST HAVE. I'VE LIVED IN THIS SMALL TOWN MY WHOLE LIFE WHERE EVERYONE KNOWS ALL YOUR BUSINESS. NOTHING IS A SURPRISE OR EXCITING, BUT IT ALSO SOUNDS LIKE A NIGHTMARE TO HAVE TO START OVER THAT MANY TIMES.

BURN, BURN, BLAZE.

Chapter Ten

LENNOX

I SHOULD'VE BEEN MORE prepared. I should've known it was inevitable. I should've protected my heart better. But as my Mama always said, you can 'should' all you want, but you'd be left standing in a pile of should's, shoulding on yourself. I always thought it was funny as a child, a genius way to get away with saying something similar to a cuss word. Not so in the moment when I found myself alone.

Waking, the first thing I noticed was how cold it was, my naked skin bare to the cool air. Rubbing my arms, I slid off the table, even more amazed we'd even both fit. Maybe if I was lucky, it would be only a manic dream, part of my head trauma, and manifestation from the other day. But as I looked around for something to put on, the soreness between my legs and the bite mark around my nipple told me otherwise.

I'd been ghosted.

It stung. In fact, it sucked a great big one, but I couldn't be angry. He'd warned me, told me upfront. I couldn't even be upset with him just because my heart had decided to get involved. Unfortunately, it meant my curse was indeed still alive and well.

Dressing in my clothes from the day before, I

readied myself to make my own escape. It was 6 am, so no one would be here any time soon, but I wanted to go home, put on some pajamas, and watch crappy TV while eating ice cream. At least it was my day off.

Wiping down the table, I had a momentarily crazy thought of leaving it, making Slade deal with it since it was his, but I couldn't stand the thought of someone else accidentally sitting on it. So, I tossed all the candles, put away the flashlights, and hid the half-drunk bottle of tequila. The shop looked normal again, and no one would know anything had occurred here.

I tried not to dwell on the fact that I could erase a night with me so easily. No one wanted to think of themselves as unmemorable, but my heart reminded me I was. Only one person had ever stayed, and in the end, he left me too. The pain was too heavy, and I didn't want to tumble down that dark abyss. Walking to the door, I remembered why I was stranded here in the first place.

Geez oh Pete, could anything go right this morning?

I laid my head against the door, exhaustion hitting me like a ton of bricks, as I stood there for a few minutes. Sucking it up, I walked over to my stool, and sat down, praying my phone still had some charge. Thankfully, it wasn't dead yet and I had messages from Simon. I didn't want to think about forgetting the whole reason I'd been out was to find him. Fudge, I was a crap friend. Maybe I did deserve to be left.

Si: Lenn, what's up? I saw your million calls. I'm headed home. Want Chinese?

Si: Lenn, it's getting bad out. Are you safe?
Si: Lenn, I'm getting worried. Please, call me back.
Si: Lenn, your dad said your car was abandoned on the side of the road. I'm officially past worry and headed straight to scared shitless. Call me.
Si: Lenn, please, come home. I need to know you're alright. I'm two seconds away from driving and looking for you.
Si: Slade called and said you were safe but stranded at the store. Call me in the morning if you need a ride. That's if you and Tatzilla don't kill one another by morning.

There were a few from my dad and mom too, but they all ended the same. *Slade had told my family I was safe*. I didn't know when he'd done it, but it was clear he'd taken the time to tell at least one person. I wanted to deny how it made me feel hopeful, even though it shouldn't have. He'd care enough to let people know I was alive. That had to mean something. Right?

Dialing Si, he answered after one ring. "Lenn? You there?"

"Hey. Yeah, I'm here. Where were you? I was worried."

"Uh, I went to a movie and had my phone off. When I left, I saw your call, but then you weren't answering. When it started to rain and storm, I was worried when you weren't home. Are you okay?"

I didn't want to admit the care in his voice had me on the verge of tears again, but I stuffed it down, swallowing. "Yeah, I'm fine. A bit stranded at the moment. Any chance you can pick me up at the shop?"

"I'm on my way, Lenn."

"Thanks, Si."

As I waited, I checked my blog and found a new message from B.E.R. An excited thrill raced through me, and I clicked on it. We'd been chatting almost daily since I was at my parents' house. It helped pass the time and gave me something to focus on.

Nox books,

I read the book you recommended, and you were right, it's fantastic. It had me on the edge of my seat the whole time. Do you think people are like that in real life? That focused on other people or deluded? It gave me some Gone Girl vibes. I think psychological thrillers are gripping. Do you read a lot of them? I know most of your posts are romance books.

Speaking of romance, have you ever heard of these books called Reverse Harem? I can't believe people read that filth. One man, one woman. That's how love should be.

What are you doing today? Reading a new book yet?

Hope to hear from you soon. I enjoy talking to you. It brings meaning to my day.

I'll be waiting.

Your B.E.R.

Scrunching my brow, I wasn't sure how to take his comments today. Everything had been superficial and light up to this point, but today's message had my stomach feeling weird. Maybe I was feeling guilty after my night with Slade, but that didn't feel right either. I hadn't heard of the books he talked about, though. Looking out the window, Simon wasn't here yet, so I opened my kindle app.

Typing Reverse Harem into the search bar, I was amazed when over 14,000 books appeared. Wow! There was a whole genre I knew nothing about. Clicking on a random book, I read the description and noticed at the bottom it said, 'why choose'. The words wormed their way into my head, and I found myself rolling them around. *Why choose*? Did that mean what I thought it meant?

Deciding to educate myself to fully respond back to my blog posts, not for any other reason of course, I clicked on the book. I'd already read through the first two chapters when I heard Simon pull up. Needless to say, I still hadn't figured out what 'why choose' was about, but I was digging the storyline so far of an ice skater flying across the country for a job.

Marking my spot, I left the shop after securing the million and one locks on the door and ran to Simon's car. Jumping in, I vaulted myself over the middle and hugged him hard. Simon's arms wrapped around me just as quick, and I felt him sigh into my hair. His scruffy jawline brushed against my cheek, his intoxicating scent that was all Simon flooding me. He was always a unique mixture of shampoo and shaving cream that worked for him. I ignored the way my toes curled or how the smell alone made my heart race.

"Everything okay, Lenn?"

"Yeah, I just missed you," I mumbled into his neck,

not ready to let go. "I got home, and you weren't there, and I was worried. I don't know what I'd do without you, Si. You're my everything."

I hadn't meant to be so vulnerable, but apparently, it all flowed out anyway. I felt him tense, so I pulled back, pretending I hadn't felt it. The hurt slashing against my already wounded heart. I shakily clicked my seatbelt in, my hands wobbling the whole time. Turning, I stared at the window, my lip trembling, but I held it all at bay.

"Lenn, look at me, please?"

Simon's voice was soft, and I found myself turning despite myself. I couldn't deny him anything, even if it tore my heart into pieces.

"What's up, Si?"

Shaking his head, he reached over and wiped a tear off my face. "Why the tears, pretty girl?"

Shrugging my shoulder, I didn't think I could answer. The last twenty-four hours had been a whirlwind. "It's just Betty. She's officially bit the dust. And then you know, I had to spend the night with Slade, and he left this morning, leaving me all alone," I huffed.

Simon watched my features, surveying them for truth as I rambled. He gently wiped the tear from my face, a crooked smile appearing. "Well, I might have something to make you happy. I found something. Do you want to check it out now?"

"Sure, sounds good. But could we maybe get some food first? I haven't eaten since lunch yesterday."

"Mama's or Wild Eggs?"

"Oh, we gotta go to Mama's. This early, she'll still have fresh biscuits!"

"Sure thing, Lenn."

Sitting back, I stayed twisted, so I could watch Simon as he drove. He was just so beautiful. A sigh escaped me at the thought, and I tried to hide it by closing my eyes and pretending I was sleeping. My face heated, but I ignored it and kept my eyes closed the rest of the way.

AFTER A GLORIOUS BREAKFAST, Simon took Nashville Rd past Lost River Cave, and I turned and looked at him. This wasn't an area of town we spent a lot of time in. He kept smiling, staying mum on the topic of where we were headed. When we pulled up into a long driveway twenty minutes later, I was even more confused. Following up the steps to the classic ranch house, I waited while he knocked on the door. An older man answered, a broad grin on his face at the recognition of Simon.

"Simon! So good to see you, boy! Is this your girl? You're here for the surprise, aren't you?"

"Yep. Can I take her around back?"

"Go on, you know the way."

"Thanks, Horace. I'll stop by before we leave."

"Make sure you do. Gladys will have some tea and cookies, I'll bet."

Simon grabbed my hand and pulled me down the steps and around the house. He walked so exuberantly, I couldn't even ask him questions. I began to wonder if maybe I was in an alternative universe, or a case of the body snatchers, and now Si was taking me out to be killed in a shed. I tried to lock my heels into the dirt to slow him down, but I didn't have much luck as his 6 ft frame kept dragging me to the shed of terror.

"Si, I don't think this is such a great idea. I still have plans and things I want to do. You don't need to do this. We can figure something out, but *murder* is never the answer."

He finally stopped, turning to look at me in confusion, his brow raised as he tried to figure out what I'd said. Sadly, I said crazy stuff all the time, so he didn't pause long before opening the door. "What are you talking about, Lenn? I'm not going to kill you. Here," he tugged again, "what I have to show you is in here."

Simon pulled me in further, as light filtered through the dust particles floating in the space. Shielding my eyes from the reflection, I tried to figure out what it was he was being so secretive about. When my eyes adjusted, I saw a giant blob in the center with a black tarp over it.

"Wow, a black tarp, you *shouldn't* have."

"Lenn, it's what's *under* it." Simon shook his head in exasperation, frustrated I didn't appreciate his secretive game or show him proper enthusiasm.

He pulled the tarp back, and I stood staring for a second as I took in what had been hidden under it. A high-pitched squeal left me before I knew what my body was doing. Launching myself at Simon again, I threw my arms around his neck. Apparently, it had become my thing. Unfortunately, my inertia, thank you, eighth-grade physics teacher, was too much this time and the force created knocked us both down, landing in a heap on the hay-covered floor. I started to kiss him all over his face in happiness, not caring my body was spread across his. Simon's arms wrapped around me, his hands falling to my bum as I attacked him, not even trying to stop me. He laughed, the chuckle rumbling through me, and I pulled back, a massive grin on my face as I peered down at my best friend.

"I don't even know what to say."

"So, you like it, Lenn?"

Pulling a face, I give Simon a look of incredulous. "Si, it's only been the car I've wanted since I could drive! Of course, I love it! How did you find one?"

He leveled me with a smirk, and I swallowed, not used to seeing the cocky assurance on his face. It did things to me, and it wasn't the best time to remember I didn't have on underwear. My breath caught in my throat as I stared down at his beautiful face, his grey eyes sparkled in the light. The hay had fallen all around us from our fall, and suddenly, my body realized it was in the perfect position for my teen fantasy to come to life, the setting even a sweet romantic one.

Clambering back, I quickly climbed off my best friend and smoothed down the skirt of my dress, dusting off some hay. Turning swiftly, I hoped to hide my red face as I walked around the car. It was sunshine yellow, and there didn't appear to be any dents or scratches on its finish. When I rounded the bumper, I peeked out of the corner of my eye as I watched Simon sit up. Taking a step further, I found I could see him in the side mirror. Bending down, I pretended to inspect something as I watched him. He brushed hay off, shaking it out of his hair as the silver locks fell against his face.

I was about to step back when I saw it. As he started to stand, his lower section came into view, and in his skinny jeans, I could see everything. Including the outline of his *donkey kong*. Gulping, I watched as his hand brushed over it, positioning it as he stood. When he began to lift his head, I dropped my eyes and bent further down to inspect the imaginary thing I focused on. His strangled voice had me spinning a few seconds later, almost hitting my head on the mirror.

"*Lenn*, are you not wearing panties?"

Smoothing my skirt down, I walked quickly to the driver's side and opened the door. "It's not nice to look, Si. Now, are we taking this for a test drive or what?"

I peeked over when he didn't answer. He swallowed, a look of torture on his face. Sliding in, I tried to calm my racing heart. Something about the look had me recalling a memory, something from the morning I hit my head.

I'd spilled my cheerios, and he'd come over to help me clean it up. His face looked similar then. My heart dropped. *I was losing him.* It was obvious now. He was preparing to leave me too.

When he finally got into the car, I realized it was a stick shift, and I dropped my head. *Shiitake mushrooms!*

"Um, Si. I don't know how to drive a stick. We'll have to go tell— "

His hand covered mine, stopping me mid rant. "I'm going to teach you, Lenn."

Shaking my head, I braved it and looked up. "You said never again after last time."

Simon laughed, his thumb casually tracing over my hand and holy chocolate balls if it wasn't sending me shivers that made me quiver below. "You're not sixteen anymore. I think it will be different this time."

"Are you sure?"

"Yeah."

"Well, okay. Let's take it for a spin. Eek! I can't believe I'm finally in my dream car."

"Why in the world a 1975 Volkswagen Beetle is your dream car, I've never understood."

"Duh, movies!"

"Movies?"

"Yeah, it's the car of my childhood. Herbie, Footloose, even Mad Love! This car promises good times! Plus, it's just so cute, I could pinch it!"

"Well, how about you start it up there first?" Simon laughed and motioned with his eyes toward the ignition. Turning the keys, I felt guilty for feeling relieved when I didn't have to go through a whole routine to get her going. RIP Betty!

The car purred to life, and my heart sang out in joy at the sound. Placing my foot on the clutch, the only thing I remembered, I turned to Simon for further instruction.

"Okay, put the car in neutral, and press your foot down on the brake pedal."

"Um, which one?" I asked, looking at three pedals.

"The center one and move the gear shift into first position once you do."

Pushing down on the pedal, I moved the gear and looked back to Simon. He smiled, a twinkle in his eye I hadn't noticed before. "Now, release your foot from the brake. Now comes the part you always struggled with. It's a dance of perfect balance as you release pressure from the clutch, you press down on the acceleration. Nothing more, nothing less, just listen for the sound. Once your foot is off the clutch, you'll move forward. Think you got it?"

"Uh, yeah. Sure, it seems easy enough."

Turning, I did as Simon instructed and did the clutch dance, and I found myself moving forward. Doing a happy dance in my seat, I forgot I had to keep my feet on the pedal making the car stall. Banging my head on the steering wheel, I sat back and tried again. The second time, I remembered to keep it pressed, and made it further out of the shed and down the dirt road. I cringed at the dust getting on the clean yellow but knew I could wash it later. The dreaded hill approached, and the car started to make the grinding sound, and I panicked, turning to Simon for help.

"Now, when you hear that sound, it's like the gears are shouting at you 'change me, change me'. So, change them. Engage the clutch and move the gear into the next position."

Gulping, I nodded and did as he suggested. I stalled the first time, but I managed to get it the second time, and I was careening over the hill, a smile on my face. We drove around the country roads, the windows down, and I knew this car was meant to be mine. Whatever I needed to do to make it happen, I would do it.

We pulled back into the farmhouse twenty minutes later, and I parked next to Simon's.

The old man sat on the porch swing and waved at us as we approached.

"Well, did your friend do a good job or what, missy? You gotta name picked out? A good car needs a name."

"Wait? I thought it was your car?"

"Oh, no. Simon's been searching for this car for a few years now. I run a dealership in town, and when I saw one come across an auction site, I called him up. He's been out here fixing it up for a few weeks. He did a good job, huh?"

I turned, my mouth open as I processed the news. Simon sheepishly rubbed the back of his head, his cheeks a crimson red I didn't often see on him. "You did this? Why?"

"I knew you wanted one. It wasn't a big deal. How about those cookies while we think of a name?"

Simon changed the subject, and I let him as I walked into the house behind him. My mind swirled about what this meant. An hour later, I'd signed some forms, had a credit check, and wrangled a deal for Betty with the old man. He'd been a shrewd businessman, but fair, and I felt good about the price of the car. It wouldn't drain me too much, and I'd be able to pay it off in two years.

Simon walked out the back, leaving me with Gladys as he went to retrieve the last of his stuff he'd stored in the shed. Picking up our glasses, I took them over to the sink.

"That boy of yours sure is sweet on you. I remember when Horace used to look at me that way."

"Oh, no. It's not like that. We're just friends. He, uh, likes *boys*."

"Well, that might be true sugar, but he likes you too. He's been friends with Horace for quite some time now, and I've gotten to know the young man myself. You're the only person he talks about. Well, you and the one other, the angry one, but I can't remember his name," she paused, looking up to think before starting again. "But you're the feature. He's sweet on you, sugar. The amount of time he's spent searching and making it presentable, that isn't someone who just sees you as a friend."

She nodded toward the door where the men stood, Simon, looking back at me a couple of times, a smile on his face as they talked. I thanked her and grabbed my stuff as I headed out the door. When the men saw me approach, they shook hands, and Horace clapped me on the shoulder as he walked by.

"You take care of Sunny. She's a real beaut', that car."

"Will do, sir."

I smiled at the mention of the name. We'd landed on Sunshine, Sunny for short. Simon walked beside me as we made our way to the cars. "I'll follow you home in case you get stuck or whatever, but I think you'll be fine, Lenn."

Nodding, I slipped into the car, putting it into first and heading toward our apartment. Amazingly, I managed to switch the gears without too much grinding or stalling. The road was open and flat, allowing me to coast at times as my mind whirled. Maybe things have changed with Si? It was the second time in a few days that someone had mentioned something. Perhaps I'd gotten so used to seeing Simon one way, I hadn't allowed myself to hope for more out of protection. I knew I'd guarded my heart, not wanting to be crushed again, but had I closed it off instead?

Maybe my curse all along had been my own fault?

I'd geared myself up to talk to him about when we got home, but he called as we were pulling in that his mom needed him to fix a hair disaster, so he was heading over there and would see me later. I laid in bed that night reading my new book, and I began to open my mind to all kinds of possibilities. Maybe, I didn't have to choose either.

Pulling out my laptop, I wrote back to B.E.R before crawling into bed, needing to say my piece before sleeping. After I submitted, I pulled the covers up and hoped I'd be able to talk to Simon soon. Slade hadn't answered any of my messages either, but I wouldn't let him ghost me.

If the curse had been me closing myself off, then I'd open myself up, be damned with the consequences. I was stronger now; I could handle it I hoped. I wanted to believe in a world where love was worth it instead of hiding from it.

Dear B.E.R,

I'm glad you enjoyed the book. There are probably people who think and do those things.

I hadn't heard of reverse harem until you mentioned it, so I looked it up and downloaded a book. I want to thank you for introducing me to the new genre. I disagree with your assessment, though. To me, love is love, and if you find that with more than one person, why not? Two men can love each other, and two women, and even two men and one woman. Love is never wrong.

Noxbooks

Starry Nox,

TODAY WAS A ROUGH DAY. IT WAS ONE OF THOSE WHERE EVERYTHING FELT LIKE IT WENT WRONG FROM THE MINUTE I WOKE UP. MY PHONE DIDN'T CHARGE, SO MY ALARM DIDN'T GO OFF, WHICH MEANT I WOKE UP LATE. THEN MY BROTHER USED UP ALL THE HOT WATER AND MY SHOWER WAS COLD. THE LAST OF THE COFFEE SPILLED ON MY SHIRT, AND I MISSED THE BUS. WELL, I HAD TO TAKE THE BUS BECAUSE MY CAR WAS OUT OF GAS. IT WAS A PRETTY SHITTY START.

I WENT TO MY FIRST CLASS, AND I ZONED OUT, NOT WANTING TO BOTHER. I WAS DOODLING IN MY NOTEBOOK WHEN I REALIZED I'D DRAWN A CONSTELLATION. THE SIGHT OF THE FAMILIAR CASSIOPEIA CALMED SOMETHING IN ME AND DESPITE NEVER HEARING YOUR VOICE, I HEARD IT IN MY HEAD. NOW, I IMAGINE YOU AS A VERY SOUTHERN OLD LADY IN MY HEAD, SO DON'T HATE ON MY PRONUNCIATION.

"NOW LISTEN HERE, BLAZE. DON'T BE THROWIN' NO HISSY FIT JUST BECAUSE YOU AIN'T GETTIN' YOUR WAY. THE SUN DIDN'T RISE JUST TO HEAR YOU CROW, SO DON'T BE GETTIN' MAD WHEN NO ONE LISTENS. YOU WANT PEOPLE TO NOTICE YOU? THEN YOU GOTTA GET OFF YOUR HIGH HORSE AND MAKE AN EFFORT. NOW, GO AND MAKE A FRIEND."

REGARDLESS OF IF YOU WOULD'VE SAID THAT, IT WAS HELPFUL JUST KNOWING YOU WERE ON THE OTHER SIDE OF THE WORLD AND CARED. OR AT LEAST I HOPE YOU DO.

I PAID ATTENTION AFTER THAT AND DIDN'T FAIL MY TEST. THE DAY DIDN'T MAGICALLY GET BETTER, BUT IT WASN'T ANY WORSE EITHER. SO,

1. TATTOOS? YES, I WOULD GET A TATTOO. I ALREADY HAVE ONE ACTUALLY. SOMETHING ABOUT THEM DRAWS ME IN. I SEE MYSELF GETTING A LOT. MAYBE ONE DAY I'LL TELL YOU WHAT MY FIRST ONE IS. IT'S KIND OF PRIVATE. YOU DEFINITELY SHOULD MAKE IT MEAN SOMETHING. IT'S AN IMPORTANT STEP.

2. MILK PITS VS. BURP FARTS? I LAUGHED FOR TEN MINUTES STRAIGHT WHEN I READ THIS ONE. MY BROTHER LOOKED AT ME WEIRDLY AND DEMANDED I TELL HIM WHAT WAS SO FUNNY. HE CHOSE FARTED, BUT I'M WITH YOU, NOSE ALL THE WAY.

3. SUPERPOWER? SOME DAYS, I WANT THE ABILITY TO FLY SO I CAN FLY AWAY FROM ALL THE THINGS THAT I DON'T LIKE. OTHER DAYS, THE ABILITY TO STOP TIME SO I CAN UNSCREW UP MY LIFE. I'M CONSTANTLY FUCKING THINGS UP. IT WOULD BE NICE TO HAVE A REDO BUTTON.

MY QUESTIONS

1. WHAT'S YOUR FAVORITE FOOD? MINE IS TACOS. THERE'S THIS AMAZING TACO TRUCK ON THE BEACH THAT HAS THE BEST TACOS EVER.

2. WHAT IS THE WORST THING YOU'VE EVER DONE? MINE WAS BREAKING UP MY FAMILY. I REGRET THAT DECISION EVERY DAY. OUTSIDE OF IT, I STOLE MY BROTHER'S FAVORITE BASEBALL CARD ONCE AND HID IT. I DON'T KNOW WHY I TOOK IT. I JUST DID. I NEVER TOLD HIM, AND I STILL HAVE IT.

3. WOULD IT BE BETTER TO NEVER BE ALONE BUT HATE EVERYONE YOU'RE WITH, OR FOREVER BE ALONE, BUT HAVE LOVED ONCE? I THINK I'D RATHER BE ALONE THAN LIVE A LIFE THAT'S A LIE.

I TRIED NOT TO BRING THE MOOD DOWN, BUT I THINK I DID ANYWAY. I HOPE YOU'RE HAVING A BETTER DAY THAN I AM. THE STARS ARE PRETTY TONIGHT.

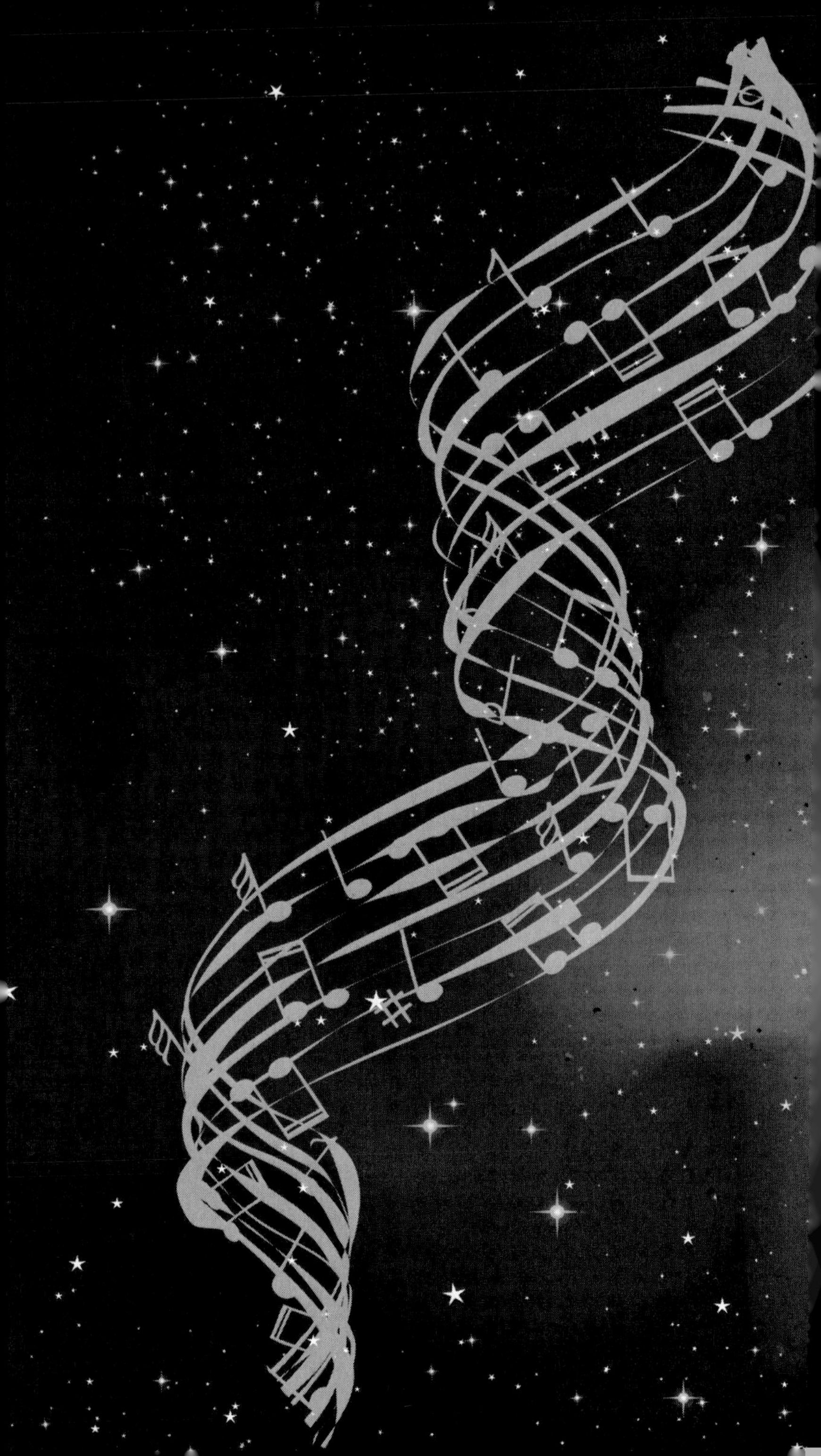

Chapter Eleven
LENNOX

TAPPING my fingers on the counter, I clicked a pen in the other as I stared at the door, waiting for Slade to arrive. I was determined to corner him today and discuss what happened two days ago. He still hadn't responded to any of my text messages. He even had the nerve to leave it on *read*. The more I thought about it, my irritation grew, and I was a raging ball of fury an hour after we'd opened.

Yet, there was still no sign of the bossnemy.

"Why do you look madder than a wet hen, Lennox?" Bubba asked, sidling up to me as he leaned against the counter.

"I have a bone to pick with Slade. I'm just waiting for him to show his face."

"Well, that might be a while."

Turning my head in his direction, I almost took him out with my hair as it whipped around. "What do you mean it might be *a while*? What in the Sam Hill are you talking about, Bubba? Start. Talking."

He raised his hands, catching the fire in my eyes. Southern men knew all southern women had a scale, and the wise ones were quick to learn the limit and not push a mad one. It *never* ended well for them.

"Slade called me early Monday morning, saying he had something to take care of out of town and wouldn't be back until later this week. Asked me to open the shop and mind things while he was away."

"Did he say anything else?" My jaw was clenched tight, and I worried the pen in my hand was about to snap.

"Nope. Was he meant to?"

"Nope."

Turning back, I started clicking the pen more aggressively, and I knew I was about to explode. Bubba backing away slowly, only confirmed it.

"We're slow this morning, sweetie. How about taking an early lunch? I don't need you back until about 2 pm anyway." I was nodding before I even spoke.

"Yeah, thanks. That's a great idea."

I inhaled and exhaled briefly and gave him a reassuring smile. Bubba didn't seem sure, though, and watched me as I grabbed my purse and headed out of the store. When I spotted my car in the parking lot, I instantly smiled. Sunny brought a feeling of euphoria, and I knew what I needed to do. I'd go and practice driving. It would be a good use of my time and keep me calm in the process.

Checking my phone, I decided to see if Simon was free. His schedule varied like mine, and some days, he could take a long lunch too. I hadn't seen him since we picked up Sunny yesterday, and I still wanted to talk with him. It was bugging me that I didn't know where we stood. Everyone was getting in my head and changing how I saw things. Nothing was safe anymore.

Me: I'm taking an early lunch and going driving to practice. You wanna join?

Thankfully, the bubbles started to move, and I was relieved when he responded back immediately.

Si: Can't, perm. Can we grab dinner together tonight, though? There's something I wanted to talk to you about.
Me: Yeah, that sounds great. There's something I want to talk to you about too.
Si: Cool beans. I'll pick up Mancino's. Your usual?
Me: Yep! You know me.
Si: Yeah, I do, babe.
Si: I'll see you tonight. Mrs. Fleming is getting antsy.
Me: Can't wait!

Okay, so maybe one conversation would finally happen. Feeling a little more settled, I got into my car and drove out to a country road I knew had a lot of hills but wasn't heavily traveled.

On my third pass-through, I felt more confident with shifting gears and started to head back to the shop. I was feeling better as I cruised along and even had the radio blaring. A classic country song played, and I skated my arm on the wind as I sang along with the lyrics. I was close to town when it happened.

A cat ran out in front of me, and in my panic, I forgot all about the clutch, and I skidded as I attempted to stop. The thump I felt didn't bode well. Throwing my door open, I hurriedly climbed out of Sunny and rounded the bumper.

"No, no, no, no, no. Please, be okay," I mumbled in fear.

Kneeling, I placed my hands on the cat and felt reassured when I felt its chest rising. A car door slammed behind me, and I exhaled, relieved I wouldn't have to make any decisions on my own. The only thing that scared me as much as storms was having to make decisions. Like, ew.

"Everything okay?"

The voice sounded familiar, but I didn't turn to look, focused on the cat.

"I'm not sure. He came out of nowhere, and I'm still learning how to drive with a clutch, and I skidded. I think I just bumped him, but he's not moving too much."

The stranger knelt down next to me, and when I looked up, tears I didn't realize were in my eyes fell down my face. The water blotches inhibited my gaze, and I had to blink a few times to see. His blonde hair fell over his forehead as he bent down examining the cat with gentle fingers.

"What should I do? Do you think it's going to make it?"

"Yeah, I think the cat will be fine. We can take it to the vet up the street. I know him, and we can just make sure. Okay?"

When he looked up, I found myself mesmerized by soft blue eyes. I didn't realize he was saying my name until he snapped his fingers in front of me. I'd gone a little goo-goo there for a second.

"Huh?"

"Lennox?"

"Yeah. What's up?"

He chuckled, and I liked the sound. A memory tugged at me, but I couldn't grab on to it. I shook my head trying to shake it loose, but he interpreted it as a no.

"Wow, I didn't think I was that unmemorable. It's me, Thane. We met at Rookies last week? Shared a pickle appetizer and strawberry lemonade?"

"Thane," I mumbled, trying to put the pieces together. Suddenly, a sharp pain could be felt behind my eyes. "Ouch," I groaned, grabbing onto my head, and standing. Unfortunately, that turned out to be a horrible idea as I wobbled, light-headed from the sudden movement. His warm palm settled on my forearm, steadying me.

"Careful, Cherry."

The kind gesture and touch brought back the memory, and I found myself blinking up at Thane, remembering our date. "Oh my God! Thane!"

I hugged him, recalling the amazing kiss we had. In the chaos of everything that unfolded it had gotten pushed to the back burner of my mind. Pulling back, I began to talk a mile a minute. "I'm so sorry. I hit my head the next day, had a bit of memory loss, and then life kind of blew up in my face and I just forgot, pushing our date aside."

"Wow, that's kind of the most unique way I've ever

been told a girl isn't into me, and in person," he smirked.

"No, no, it's true, I promise. I can prove it. Here." Lifting up the side of my hair, I showed him the place I had stitches, and he winced.

"Okay, I might believe you. That's pretty extreme just to reject me."

"I promise, it's not. A lot has happened since then and I have a tendency to only focus on the things right in front of me. Sorry, character flaw," I cringed, scrunching my nose. "When you touched me, it all came flooding back."

"I think it's cute you have a flaw, you're pretty perfect otherwise. And I guess, it's a bit romantic, kind of like Sleeping Beauty I suppose."

"Um, how so?"

Unfortunately, he didn't get a chance to answer as a loud semi blared their horn at us. We'd been in the middle of the road, holding each other as we talked, forgetting where we were. Shrieking, I pulled him over to the side of the road, getting out of the way of the truck. The driver pulled his horn as he sped by, the loud sound reverberating around me, making my head hurt even more.

"Dagnabit! That hurts!"

Bending over, I tried to get the sound to stop ringing around in circles. Once it settled down, I looked up, remembering the cat I'd hit. The middle of the road was clear, so I chose to believe he ran off, the air only being knocked out of him. He was fine, I told myself.

"The cat…"

"Yeah, he's fine. Got up and ran off before the big truck went by."

"Oh, thank goodness. I doubt I could live with the guilt."

"How about we take this conversation to a more suitable location than the side of the road?"

"I'd love to, but I gotta get back to work." I bit my lip, uncertainty filling me now. I remembered liking Thane that night, but what if things with Simon were changing? What then? Was it fair to either of them to start something? Not to mention Slade. How did he fit into all of this? As much as I wished life was like my books, I didn't think I'd get to have three boyfriends like Sawyer in the book I devoured last night. Though, that lucky girl had five, possibly six if the one ever got the stick out of his rear. He had some similarities to Slade. Maybe I'd needed to finish this series so I'd know how to handle him. It could be research!

"Oh, well, that's too bad. I'd like to see you again if possible. Do you still have my number?"

"I uh, don't know. Here, give me your phone."

Thane pulled it out of his pocket and handed it to me. Entering my number, I sent myself a message, so I'd know it was him. Handing it back, I felt some butterflies as our fingers crossed paths, but it didn't feel as exciting as before. Maybe it was more of the memory loss, and I was forgetting how it felt.

"I uh, gotta go, but I'll text you."

Turning, I walked back to my car quickly, peeking

over my shoulder as I did. Thane looked a little sad, and I hated to think I was the one who made him feel that way, but I was just as confused. Waving over my shoulder, I hoped to bring back the fun-loving guy I think I remembered meeting. His smile lifted some, but his blue eyes still held a lot of doubt. Once I was in my car, I watched as he walked back to his.

I thought about him the whole way back, wondering if I'd just made a huge mistake not taking a chance with him. A huge pit formed in my belly, and I chewed on my lip, doubt creeping in.

I'D BEEN HOME for about thirty minutes after finishing my shift and was becoming antsier with every passing minute. I'd sent a text to Thane, but I hadn't heard back from him yet. There was another message alert on the blog, but I still didn't feel like dealing with B.E.R.

Twisting my hair up, I turned my head in the mirror, trying to determine if I liked it better one way or the other just to pass the time. When I heard keys in the lock turning, I dropped it, running to the couch, and flopping on it, smoothing my skirt down like I'd been there the whole time.

Never mind that I was now panting from the run and dive I'd done. When the door opened, I turned the expression of innocence at Simon.

"Oh, hey. You're here. Do you need any help?"

"Hey," he paused, smiling at me. He appeared hesitant, though, and apprehension filled me. Shaking his head, Simon dispelled himself from whatever spell he'd been under. "No, I'm good. Thanks, though."

"Yeah, no problem."

He busied himself in the kitchen, and I watched from the back of the couch, my head resting on my arms as he unloaded the bags he had. Simon was elegant in his movements, and I'd always admired his ability to make everything he did look flawless. He took out our sandwiches and placed them on plates, grabbing silverware and napkins in the process, before placing it all on the table. I sat stunned for a moment, not used to sitting there. When he put two drinks down as well, I finally pulled myself out of the stupor and got off the couch.

"Oh, wow. An actual dinner at the table. This *must* be important."

"Yeah, I think it is."

"Okay," I gulped, suddenly filled with dread. My history with romantic entanglements never ended well —my virginity, my first kiss, my first long-distance crush, my first job, my first serious boyfriend. Basically, I sucked at firsts. Realizing this couldn't be a first in any category, I calmed and took my seat.

"So, how was your day?"

Okay, so apparently, we were going to do small talk first. Swallowing a bite of my sandwich, I wiped my mouth before speaking. "It was okay. I practiced some and feel like I'm making progress. But then I hit a cat, and," I stopped, my lip trembling as I recalled everything.

"Oh my God, Lenn. Are you okay?"

Reaching across, I grabbed his hand, needing his comfort. "I love that you ask how I am first instead of the cat." I laughed as I wiped my eyes. "Yeah, I'm okay. I guess I hadn't realized the intensity of everything I've been feeling since last week. Ugh, so yeah, I hit a cat, and while I was checking on it, a person stopped. And um, I didn't tell you something."

I didn't know why I was bringing this up now, but it was like my mouth wouldn't stop. Lifting my eyes, I took in Simon and wondered how this would affect things. Was I sabotaging? Was I doing this now so he couldn't tell me?

"You know what, it doesn't matter. I'm okay, the cat was okay, and Sunny is okay." Blowing out a breath, I smiled a bit watery but forced it anyway. "I'm glad we're doing this, though. I've missed you and wanted to spend time with you."

"Me too, Lenn. Me too."

"So, what did you want to tell me?"

"Oh, um, it's nothing. Don't mind me."

"Oh, well, it just seemed kind of important."

He wouldn't look at me, shaking his head as he ate. Picking apart my sandwich, I stared at it, hoping it would give me the answer I sought.

"Are you not hungry?"

"No, not really. I might just go to bed."

Standing, I picked up my plate and took it into the kitchen. Standing at the sink, I tried to stop the tears, but everything inside of me had crumbled. The day had been a lot; from my rage, then fear, all of it bringing back memories. So, I stood at the sink and cried, hoping to get it out of my system. I'd thought my tears were silent, but a few seconds later, Simon turned me into his arms, and I completely fell apart sobbing.

I wanted to be strong and not need Simon or his comforting embrace, but he felt so warm and safe, so I gripped onto his shirt tighter and buried my head into his chest. I felt Simon's hand rub the back of my head, soothing sounds leaving his mouth. When I started to hiccup, he pulled me back, wiping the tears with his thumbs.

"What's going on, Lenn?"

Shaking my head, I let my hair fall forward, covering my face. I couldn't take it. I couldn't be rejected again. Not with how I was feeling, all the emotions on the surface.

"Do you want to play a game or something?"

"No, I do want to go to bed. I'm exhausted. Thank you for being my Kleenex."

"Anytime, pretty girl. I'm always here for you."

Nodding, I tried not to dismiss his statement. He might think that, but he wasn't. Or maybe, it was more he couldn't be. Not the way I wanted him to be right now anyway.

Shutting my door, I climbed onto my bed and curled up with my pillows and stuffed animals. I didn't care that I was twenty-five. I slept with them every night. You only have to feel bad about things if you let yourself. I'd decided a long time ago not to.

An hour later, I'd calmed down, and had soft music playing as I tried to sleep now. I'd changed into some sleep shorts and a tank top, and I laid in bed, my star galaxy light shining on the ceiling.

Unfortunately, it didn't seem to matter how tired I was, I couldn't shut my brain off. So, I laid there staring at the stars hoping they'd bring me comfort like they had so many times before. It was hard when so many of my heartbreaks were also wrapped up in them. The sad song in the background played on, an accurate description of how I felt. Music usually brought me comfort, but today, it just reminded me of all the things I didn't have.

A soft knock sounded on my door, and I waited to see if Simon would let himself in or not. When nothing happened, I got up and walked to the door, my bare feet padding on the hardwood. When I opened it, I was surprised to find no one there, only a note. Picking it up, I opened it to find a card.

Lenn,

I'm an idiot, but mostly a coward. Since I can never find the words to say to your face, maybe I can show you. Follow the pieces.

Simon

A few feet in front of me was a white square. Picking it up, I realized it was like a comic book square. Inside it was a drawing of a boy and girl lying on a bed, reading.

"You're my best friend."

"You're my best friend."

"Let's be best friends forever."

"Deal."

I smiled, realizing it was us, a moment from our history when we sealed the friendship with pinky promises and Ring Pops.

Walking a few steps more, I found the next one. It was two people under the stars, sleeping in a tent. And I knew it had to be from our first time. The girl was asleep, but the boy watched her, hearts in his eyes.

"I'll love you forever."

A tear escaped at the words, and I kept going, needing to know what they all said. The following picture was the next morning, a girl on a table talking on a phone, a boy half out of the tent, a look of pain on his face.

"I think it's best we just be friends."

Oh no. Simon must've overheard my conversation and assumed it was about him. My heart picked up, and I ran to the next one.

The girl had a look of pain on her face as she faced the boy.

"Lennox, I like boys."

Quickly, I kept walking, grabbing them up. Hope wanted to fill my heart at what this could mean, but uncertainty and fear warred within making me squash it. The following picture had two blocks of when we were older, and I was going on a date in one.

"I hope he likes me."

"He will. You're the best, Lenn."

The second one was Simon supposedly talking to my date. Si had his hand on his shirt, threatening him up against a wall.

"If you can't give her everything, you better walk away now, or you'll not like it when my fists meet your face."

That cheeky little son of a bee sting! He'd threatened them away! A heat rose up as well as I thought about how sexy it was at the same time.

Walking to the next, I found a picture of Simon looking at me, heart emojis coming out of his eyes again, but I was oblivious as we did our everyday things.

There was one more, and I grabbed it, hoping it would be the answer. But this one wasn't a picture. Just a note.

Lenn,

I thought I could handle just being your friend, that I would get over it. I haven't. I don't think I can. I think of telling you a thousand times a day. But I don't. If you want me to leave, I will, but I couldn't spend another moment without you knowing the truth. I do like boys, Lenn. But not only boys, I like girls too, or well, one girl. If you can deal with this, I'm waiting in my room.

Simon.

Dropping it all, the papers scattered to the floor, and I rushed to his door. I was prepared to bust in and throw myself at him, but something halted me, insecurity most likely, and I paused instead. Knocking softly, I waited for him to answer. When the door swung open, my doubt left me as I took in Simon. My Simon, the one of my childhood, his face open, yearning, and hopeful. I hadn't realized how much he'd hidden, and I hated myself a little bit for not realizing it sooner. How many years had we missed out on due to misunderstanding and miscommunication? On fear?

Words were no longer needed as we crashed into one another, the longing and hope reflected on both of our faces now. Our barriers were gone, and we finally saw each other fully. It was the very epitome of a kiss scene from all my favorite movies wrapped into one.

Simon grabbed my face and kissed me, and I practically swooned at the magnetism we shared. It hadn't felt like this before. Then it had been the kiss of two kids, inexperienced and unsure. Now, Simon kissed me like a man possessed, like a man who'd been denied his favorite thing for over ten years. His tongue tangled with mine, swirling in tandem as we danced. It was sweet and sexy, the perfect combination of Simon.

I started pushing him forward, no longer wanting to be standing. He went willingly, his legs hitting the bed, and he stumbled down. Taking the opportunity, he pulled back and glanced at me.

"Does this mean what I want it to mean?"

"If you're asking if I love you forever too, then yes, all the yeses. But you gotta know one thing, Si. I wasn't talking about you on the phone."

"You weren't? But I thought?" He laughed, shaking his head. "You know what, I don't even care anymore. I have you in my arms, and that's what I want to focus on."

Kissing him again, I pushed him back on the bed, forcing him to scoot back. Straddling his waist, I let myself sink onto his lap, feeling the evidence of his arousal now. I rocked forward, not able to help myself. Letting go of his lips, I remembered what I wanted to ask him.

"Did you really threaten my date to Homecoming?"

Simon wore a sheepish look and slowly nodded. "I'm afraid it wasn't just your Homecoming date. I kind of threatened *all* your dates. I couldn't help it. If I didn't get to be with you, then I wanted only the best. I'm afraid I'm partially responsible for your curse. Do you hate me?"

"Never. It makes me feel a little better. At least, it wasn't completely all my fault."

"Are you kidding, Lenn? I had to fight the guys off in high school. You have no idea how sexy you are, do you, pretty girl?"

"I mean, I think I'm pretty, but nothing crazy. I feel I have an accurate reflection of my self-esteem."

"Oh, Lenn. That's where you're wrong. No man can

come into contact with you without flirting. You just don't realize it. Which has saved me from having to beat up half the population."

Laughing, I shook my head, unable to believe him. "So, have you been with any other girls since then?"

"No. I tried once, but it didn't feel right, and I stopped. I've been with guys, though."

Nodding, I kept running my fingers through his hair, happy to just be free to touch it. "I want to shake us both for not saying anything sooner, but I'm not sad we ended up here. I like it. What does this mean now?"

Simon laid us down, pulling me close, but kept us on our sides, looking at one another. "It means whatever we want it to mean. I know I don't see a future without you in it."

"Maybe," I hesitated, tracing my fingers on his chest. Peeking up, I stopped, briefly mesmerized by his grey eyes staring at me. He kissed my nose, smiling, and pulled back.

"Yes, Lenn?"

"Maybe we just keep it between us for a bit, so we can figure it out without everyone weighing in on our relationship."

"If that's what you want, we can do that."

"I think I'd like that. Keep it perfect and between us for some time. No curse involvement. I don't feel like dealing with the looks either."

"There's not really a curse, Lenn," he paused, understanding what I was really saying. "But we can keep it between us until you feel ready."

He pulled me closer to his chest, and I laid my head

there. My eyelids fluttered, and I knew sleep was coming now. I wanted to believe him on the curse, but something in the back of my mind told me not to trust it. He kissed my forehead, and I heard him whisper before I fell under, "Love you, my Lemon Drop."

Purple Blaze

While I don't relish you having a bad day, it did make me feel good that I was the one making you happy. Though, I do not sound like that! The audacity! Seriously, I'm not my mamaw. She'd tell me to stop being ugly right now, but yeah, I'm not an eighty-year-old woman for crying out loud!

I went on a date this week. It was horrible. The guy kept trying to look down my shirt! I hope not all guys are like that. My best friend isn't, so I guess there's hope for mankind. I think I'm cursed though. It's the third person I've gone out with, but I never get a second date. Granted, I didn't want one with this loser, but I'm starting to think something is wrong with me. Maybe I should ask Simon?

My mom had another episode today. It wasn't as bad as the one last year, but it makes me worried. What if I hadn't been here? What if something had happened to Noah? Or her? I'm going to do whatever I can to make sure it doesn't happen. I came home to find the house in complete disarray. The burners were on, and the house was filling with gas. Mom had just left, and it took a few hours before Dad found her. The scary part was that she'd left Noah. He was safe in his crib, but he'd been crying when I came in. I don't know how long she'd left for, but it worries me.

Dad said he's going to get her a new therapist here so she can see them each week and not have to go back to the facility. I just hope it helps. I complain about my brother, but he's my loveable turd. I don't want anything to happen to him. Apparently, they were weaning her off her meds to start a new trial and it had been going well until it wasn't. I hate that one little thing can flip it for her. I'm sure it's very

INSTEAD, THEY JUST THINK SHE'S CRAZY OR IRRESPONSIBLE. ANYWAY, ENOUGH SADNESS FOR TODAY. I'M GLAD I HAVE YOU TO SHARE IT WITH THOUGH. AT LEAST YOU WONT TURN ON ME FOR STAYING BY MY MOM.

1. MY FAVORITE FOOD? WELL, IT'S CHEESECAKE BUT LASAGNA IS A CLOSE SECOND. TACOS ARE GOOD TOO, BUT I DOUBT WE HAVE THE QUALITY YOU DO. I'LL HAVE TO TRY ONE ON THE BEACH ONE DAY TO KNOW THE GLORIOUSNESS YOU SPEAK OF.

2. I THINK THE WORST THING I'VE DONE, WELL, AT FIRST, I DIDN'T STAND UP FOR MY MOM. I LET THE KIDS SAY WHATEVER THEY WANTED. I WANTED THEM TO LIKE ME AND TO FIT IN. ONE DAY, AFTER HEARING SHELLEY CALL MY MOM "FREAK BABY KILLER" I BLEW IT. I SLAPPED HER AND WAS SENT TO THE PRINCIPAL. I FELT BAD ON TWO FRONTS THEN. I HATED LETTING MY EMOTIONS OVERCOME ME AND I HATED THAT IT TOOK THAT LONG FOR ME TO DO WHAT WAS RIGHT. WHEN I TOLD MY DAD WHAT HAPPENED, HE TOOK ME OUT FOR ICE CREAM AND DIDN'T PUNISH ME. WHEN I ASKED HIM WHY, HE TOLD ME I'D ALREADY LEARNED MY LESSON AND NOTHING HE DID WOULD PROVE AS EFFECTIVE AND BE OVERKILL. BESIDES, HE WAS PROUD OF ME FOR STANDING UP TO THE BULLY. HE TAUGHT ME HOW TO THROW A PUNCH THAT DAY TOO.

3. THIS ONE IS HARD FOR ME. I DON'T KNOW. BOTH OPTIONS SOUND LIKE A NIGHTMARE. I'M NOT GOOD AT BEING ALONE SO I GUESS, SURROUNDED BY PEOPLE.

4. WHAT'S YOUR DREAM JOB? MINE IS TO BE AN ART TEACHER. I LOVE ART AND I THINK I'D BE GOOD AT TEACHING IT TO KIDS. THOUGH, IF I COULD BE ANYTHING, IT WOULD BE A COUNTRY SINGER, BUT THAT WILL NEVER HAPPEN. MY PARENTS THINK I SHOULD DO SOMETHING WITH MATH THOUGH. SOUNDS BORING.

5. WOULD YOU RATHER HAVE TO HOPSCOTCH EVERYWHERE YOU WALK OR JUMP ROPE? LAME ONE, MY CREATIVITY IS SHOT TODAY. I'D RATHER HOPSCOTCH. I'D END UP KILLING MYSELF TRIPPING OVER A JUMP ROP

6. HOW DO YOU KNOW IF YOU'RE A GOOD PERSON? I WONDER ABOUT THIS EVERY DAY.

YOUR SHINING STAR, Nox ♡

Chapter Twelve

SLADE

I THREW THE WHISKEY BACK, the liquid burning my throat, making me grimace. I didn't particularly like the stuff, but it was one sure fire way to get drunk. And I *needed* to be drunk. It was the only thing that would dull the memories. But even as I sat here, three whiskeys deep, I couldn't dampen them.

Peach's moans, the feel of her skin, the way I felt inside her, and the way she smelled, all rolled around in my head on a constant loop punishing me. I'd woken up the happiest I'd felt in forever before reality crashed down around me at my circumstances.

It'd been a horrible mistake. I shouldn't have given in to her.

Once again, I'd been sucker punched by Lennox James' charm, making me crave her even more desperately and despise her all the same for it. I needed to remind myself of all the pain she caused me instead of the immense amount of pleasure the other night had been.

"You want anything else, mister?"

Grunting, I ignored the friendly bartender and threw some bills down as I stumbled out the door. *Shit*. I guess the whiskey had done its job after all. Bracing a hand against the wall, I waited until the floor quit spinning and kept going on my journey out of the Honkey Tonk bar.

The sounds of downtown Nashville hit me as I stumbled out onto the sidewalk. The street was packed with people, a constant traffic flow of cars sped by as the city started to come to life. It was only 9 pm, but I was drunk as a skunk. I started down the familiar block, shoving my hands in my pocket to appear aloof until I came to the brightly lit shop. *Equinox Ink.*

Walking in, Post Malone's newest song greeted me, a drastic change from the country on the street. The chatter of the people filled the space, creating a lively environment. I always loved that this shop was a full social experience being located where it was. When Adam noticed me, he perked up and walked over, grinning wide as he greeted me. His cheery nature wasn't what I wanted tonight, and it only made me scowl harder.

"Slade, my man, what brings you in?"

He went to grab my hand, preparing for one of those man slaps, but I kept mine in my pockets, not wanting to touch him. He'd worked for me for four years, and I'd known him a little longer than that, having roomed with the guy when I first moved to the city. He'd been a bartender back then and I stayed in his spare room before I bought this place. But I'd never really liked him.

Something about him creeped me out, his over friendly demeanor was too much for my sourpuss one, and he was just *too pretty*. I found myself wanting to mess up his face with my fist. Adam had proven himself, though, and in the end, I had to put my preference aside and do what was best business wise. He'd hung around the shop when it first opened, begging for a chance to apprentice, and he turned out to be a hard worker and a talented artist. So, I gave him one, unable to deny his skills. Eventually, I'd made him manager of the place when I opened the second shop. I didn't have to like him for him to run the place thankfully.

Grunting, I forced myself to answer him, despite wanting to do nothing but find a flat surface. "I'll talk to you about it tomorrow." Well, it hadn't been a full answer, but it would suffice for now.

His face fell, and I noticed how his eyes hardened for a second before his usual smile reappeared. Mr. Good Guy didn't like being dismissed. The part of me that liked misery relished in the fact he was angry.

"Right-o, man. I'm assuming you'll be in the apartment?"

Nodding, I didn't expand on my plans. I was the boss, I could do whatever the fuck I wanted.

"Cool, cool. I'll make sure no one uses it tonight, then. Got anyone joining you?" He winked like we were in on something, but this idle chit chat was the bane of my existence. It was the last thing I could tolerate right now, and I knew I'd hit my threshold for bullshit today. Ignoring him, I moved past, nodding at the other guys who shouted out a greeting as I passed. This place had been my first shop, and then I'd expanded in Bowling Green. It sounded backward, but I'd had a dream at one time.

Now, it was a reminder. *Everyone lies.* No one was who they said they were.

Every day I asked myself why I stayed, why I endured the torture, why I continued to slice my heart open and pour salt on it. It was always the same answer. Because I deserved it. Because of *Peach*.

Unlocking the door to the apartment, I stumbled in, hitting the light switch. The place reeked, and trash littered the floor, dishes flowing over in the sink. I scowled, annoyed at the disaster the crew had left it in. I'd need to talk to them tomorrow about common decency and cleaning up after themselves. I didn't care if they used the place for hookups or sleeping during off times, but this was unacceptable.

James would've never let Emblazed Tats get this way.

The thought had been simple, a recognition of how she added to the shop, and yet, it was the last bit of pressure needed to crack me open. Falling face forward on the bed, I prayed the sheets were clean as I tumbled into the past, my drunkenness finally dragging my ass under.

"You know this is stupid, don't you?"

"No, Thane, it's not. It's stupid not to try. I've been talking to Nox for years. I want to meet her."

"How are you going to explain your personality change, huh?" He lifted his eyebrow, his perfect golden retriever expression annoying me.

"I didn't ask you to do that. You took it upon yourself, so as far as I'm concerned, I'm the innocent one here."

"Yeah, I doubt she'll see it that way. Besides, you don't know she's who she says she is. Haven't you seen Catfish?"

"How can someone catfish me for eight years? You're just mad I'm not inviting you. Admit it, you're jealous."

Thane rolled his eyes, his perfect exterior cracking for a second. "Whatever. It's your funeral."

He stalked down the stairs of the apartment, slamming the door that led into the shop, his words echoing out around the place. I smirked, not caring he was pissed. He should just be glad I was talking to him. I'd been living in Nashville for over a year now, and I'd been tempted to reach out to Nox or even Fish the entire time. I knew they were only an hour's drive north, but I hadn't ever spilled my secret.

I hadn't meant to keep it, but after a time, it became second nature not to talk about some things. I only knew her address after the program had stopped, and we sent letters to one another for another year before switching to email. Occasionally, I would still send her things in the mail, but I'd use my old address. I knew it was deceitful, but it was nice not feeling pressured to disclose everything to someone unless I wanted to.

Everything with Nox had been easy. I shared more with her, and even Fish at times, than I'd told anyone in my life. I didn't want to lose that by meeting. The mystery would be gone, the facade broken, and I'd lose my best friend and confidant. There was no denying she was my best friend. You couldn't share everything that mattered with a person and not grow close to them.

The thing I wanted to deny was that I was in love with her. Because how could you be in love with someone you've never met? Someone you've never even heard the voice of but whose song was the lyrics in your heart?

But did you need to when you knew the outline of their soul? The way their words brushed against your mind like a lover's caress, or how they seemed to be the needle, threading your heart to theirs.

I'd never thought of myself as a romantic, but when I faced it, Nox and I had been writing love letters for years. It was an age-old tale, a long-distance romance, one found between the pages of scribbles of ink leaving smudges on my heart.

I'd tried dating in the beginning. I'd even tried just casual fucking. But no one ever measured up to the girl who owned my soul. Her words were rooted in me, a layer on my skin, our story told forever in ink. I'd just been too scared, or naive, to admit it.

She'd dated too, and while I denied how it felt every time she told me, that spark of jealousy flaring in me each time, I pretended it didn't. The relief I felt when they never panned out, I ignored as well. I was lying to myself, but it felt safer at the time.

Somewhere over the years, the truth between the lies had gotten so twisted, and I found myself wrapped up in two people. I'd never been ready to make a choice, knowing I'd hurt someone and lose part of me in the process.

It was almost losing her that finally pushed me to take the step. Walking out the door, my heart was happy as I headed to Layla's to meet my girl, my Starry Nox.

The sun blinded me, the pounding in my head a reminder of the ache I felt in my chest. It felt deserved. I rolled over, sitting on the edge of the bed as I tried to get the ringing in my ears to stop. Why were they ringing, anyway?

"Here."

A hand thrust a glass of water at me, the voice tired and frustrated. I knew it was Thane before I even saw his perfectly polished shoes. Lifting my head, I squinted as I tried to make him come into focus. When I could make out his shape, I reached out to take the glass. The coldness of it comforted me as I grasped onto it.

Bringing it to my lips, the cold liquid felt nice as it slid down my throat. Coughing, I drew back, having tried to drown myself in the liquid too quickly. Wiping my mouth, I took in my brother now that my eyes had focused on the room.

"What's your problem?"

I didn't mean to sneer, it seemed to naturally come out anytime I spoke nowadays, and Thane had become an easy target. He exhaled, hanging his head before taking a seat next to me. His dress pants were wrinkle-free, his shirt crisp as he sat down.

Thane was the complete opposite of me. He was clean-cut, all-American, with his dirty blonde hair and blue eyes, and I was as bad boy as you got. I was covered almost entirely from head to toe in tattoos, had a handful of piercings, and a scowl to make anyone's grandmother cry. My black hair and dark eyes made me appear like a dark horse, and I used them to my advantage.

We were fraternal twins, but most wouldn't even paint us as brothers. There had been a time when we were more alike, but like most things in high school, that had changed as well. After one too many moves, I gave up trying to be likable and succumbed to the shadows his golden light had cast, the obscurity a blanket for my insecurities.

"What are you doing to yourself, Slade?"

"Why do you care?"

"Despite your belief, I care about you a great deal. You're my brother, my twin. I thought we'd gotten past this mistrust, and we're friends, now?"

"Pfft, well, unless you can erase time, I don't see that happening."

Thane exhaled, something he did around me a lot. "I'm sorry, Slade. I screwed up, and the things that happened that night… Well, it sucked. No one denies that, but you can't let it eat away at everything in your life."

"That's easy for you to say. You weren't there, you don't have to live with the guilt."

"No… I wasn't," he paused, and for the first time, I noticed his own remorse, but he shoved it away, continuing his good guy routine. "It doesn't mean I don't think about it. But you can't live your life in the past. Not if you want anything in your future. You gotta stop chasing ghosts and let that shit go."

Gritting my teeth, my knuckles strained on the glass in my hand as I tried to calm my heart. He had no right to tell me how to feel. He wasn't there. He didn't know what really happened, only the version I'd told him. The guilt of that one moment haunted me, and I didn't know if I would ever forgive myself. How could you when you were responsible for stopping your own happiness and the demise of someone else's?

"I don't need any of your positive juju."

"Yeah, what fun would it be to believe in good things? It'd totally wreck the whole bad boy vibe you've perfected."

Laughing, I tilted my head and peeked up at my brother. "I like it when you drop the good guy routine."

"No, you just like it when I give you shit, so then it doesn't make you feel like such an asshole to me."

"Maybe," I shrugged.

Thane rolled his eyes, sighing before he stood. "Despite your belief, it's not an act. *I am a good guy*. It doesn't make me perfect, and we both know I've had my fair share of questionable behavior, but it's the choices you make each day, brother, that matter. I have to head to the office. Want to grab lunch later? Maybe tell me about what brought you back down here in the middle of the week? Hmm?"

"Yeah, okay. Thanks for the water."

He nodded, a slight smile on his face as he made his way out of the apartment. The door closing made the quiet in the place louder, and I couldn't handle it. Heading to the shower, I hoped to wipe the memory from my brain once and for all. It was a deluded fantasy, but as the water rushed over my tattoos, my pain inked into me, I knew I'd never escape it.

The bass boomed throughout the Honkey Tonk bar my roommate worked at, the windows shaking with the racket. I tuned it all out, my mission and focused on getting drunk as fast as possible. Today had been a shit show of epic proportions and I wanted to forget it. A cute girl bumped into me, a shy smile on her face, and for a second, everything else disappeared as I fell into her hazel eyes.

"Oops, I'm sorry," she giggled, her hand landing on my arm. It wasn't one of those fake laughs either, she was just past the tipsy side of drunk, and it was genuine. I liked how it sounded. "You'd think I'd have learned how to walk in these things by now. You haven't seen a tallish guy, crazy rainbow hair around, have you?"

"No."

"Oh, okay. Well, thanks anyway. You, at least, saved me from face planting."

"No problem. Do you need, um, help?" I didn't know why I was asking. The last thing I wanted to do was help her find her boyfriend, but I didn't want her to leave either.

"Oh, no. It's fine. I'm sure he's around somewhere. Thanks, though." She turned to go but stopped, her head looking over her shoulder. "Whoever did your ink is a legend. They're probably the most beautiful pieces I've ever seen." I was so lost in her words, I missed when she disappeared.

She liked my art.

Mine.

It was a mundane thing to think, but I'd been feeling hopeless today, like maybe I was on the wrong path, and then this Southern Angel reminded me of how influential art could be, even if just on my skin. Smiling, I didn't need the drink as bad anymore, but I still made my way there, my goal to drink only one now before leaving.

I found myself watching for her the rest of the night,

and when I saw some guy hitting on her, my protective nature rose up and I swooped in to save her.

"I think you should leave her alone." I stared down at the asshat, my stare lasering into him. He backed up, leaving her alone. She turned, and it felt like everything else disappeared. "Looks like you saved me again."

"Looks like it. Can I buy you a drink?"

"Sure, that'd be great."

Motioning for Adam, I ordered two drink specials before turning back to her. I found myself floundering for words as I stared at her. "So, come here often?"

She sucked on a straw, and I was immediately jealous of the damn thing as her tongue swirled around it. "Did you seriously just ask me that? Wow! That's almost as bad as knock-knock jokes."

"Hey! I happen to like knock-knock jokes."

Several drinks were placed down in front of us as Adam walked away in a rush, I wasn't sure which was ours and as hands began reaching for them, I grabbed two, hoping it didn't matter. Handing the cup to the girl, I watched as she drank a large portion down in a big gulp, and I lifted my eyebrows in surprise.

"Oh yum, peaches." She licked her lips, and I decided right then peaches were my new favorite fruit and I wanted to taste them on her.

"Lenn! There you are, I've been looking for you everywhere."

She turned to the guy, and I felt a pit form in my stomach. Seems like the guy she'd been looking for found her. Figures she was with someone. The guy was cute and the arousal I hid surged forward taking me by surprise. He caught me staring, a blush forming on his cheeks.

"I'm not talking to you, Simon."

"Lenn, come on. I'll buy you a drink and we can talk. It's important." He grabbed one off the tray of the waitress passing, handing her some bills, and giving it to the girl who's name I still didn't know. I went to stop him, afraid she'd had too much now after seeing her drink almost two back to back.

"I don't think—" but before I could finish, she tossed it down and took off leaving me and the cute guy there. He hung his head before looking at me.

"Sorry, I didn't realize you were talking. How many of those has she had?"

"Um, at least three in the last ten minutes, or so."

"Shit," he swore under his breath. "Uh, it was nice meeting you, I guess, but I better go find her before she gets herself into trouble. She doesn't drink much."

"Sure. Good luck."

I caught a glimpse of her raven hair whip around the corner a while later, and I followed, wondering if her friend had ever found her. It was idiotic of me to keep following her, she clearly had enough guys chasing her around. But something in me propelled me forward. When I came around the corner, though, I found her up against the wall, a guy standing over her. Something about it bugged me, and despite not wanting to interrupt an intimate moment, I found myself watching.

Okay, so maybe our moment had been one-sided, but when he put his hand around her throat and she thrashed, I couldn't stand by and let her be assaulted. Before I could step in, some guy stepped in from the shadows and the douche stalked off, practically running into me. He saw where I was looking and rolled his eyes, laughing at me.

"She's all yours, dude. Get in while you can, but beware of the lies she spews. She's a whore and a liar. I heard she's been playing guys all over Nashville. I'd stay away from Lennox James if I were you."

Something about what he said clicked in my head, penetrating the alcohol, and I grabbed his arm. "Wait. What did you say her name was?"

"Lennox James. Why? You heard of her?"

"No," I lied, bile crawling up my throat. "I just wanted to be sure I didn't sleep with her and get trapped, you know."

"Right, man. Yeah, stay away from that one. She's a mental case waiting to happen."

He clapped my shoulder like we were friends and left. A ton of bricks sat heavy on my chest as I realized the girl I'd fallen in love with was nothing but a liar. The name the girl at Layla's had given me earlier echoed around my head, and in some weird twist of events, I'd casually ran into my pen pal. It couldn't be that coincidental, could it? Only one way to find out.

Walking around the corner, the guy was gone, and I found her on the ground. Tilting her head up, I smacked her cheek to get her to wake up. She blinked, a smile lifting as she caught me.

"Tattoo man. Ow, that hurt. You're not very nice, but you're really hot," she slurred, touching my face.

I hated how my body responded to her touch, wanting to lean into it. How could this be the same person who'd stolen my heart? The same person who'd sent someone else to meet me at Layla's? Had everything we had really been a joke? Only one sure way to find out.

"Starry Nox?"

I held my breath as I waited to see if my heart would be crushed.

That was the moment I quit believing in love.

Fish,

YOU MAKE A GOOD POINT. I SHOULDN'T ASSUME YOU'RE A FISH. I CHOSE BLAZE BECAUSE SOMETIMES, I FEEL LIKE MY LIGHT MIGHT BE SNUFFED OUT IF I DON'T COME IN LIKE AN INFERNO AND SET ABLAZE ALL MY ENEMIES. MY BROTHER SAYS MY NEED TO PUSH PEOPLE AWAY IS A DEFENSE MECHANISM, BUT I DON'T CARE. HE MAKES FRIENDS EASILY, WHEREAS I'VE ALWAYS BEEN SEEN AS THE PROBLEMATIC KID. AFTER A WHILE, I JUST GAVE INTO THE STEREOTYPE. IT WAS EASIER THAN TRYING TO FIGHT IT, SADLY.

I'D LIKE TO SAY I'M STRONG AND ABLE TO STAND UP, BUT MOST DAYS, I'M JUST HAPPY TO MAKE IT THROUGH WITHOUT BEING NOTICED. I WISH I WENT TO SCHOOL WITH A FRIEND LIKE YOU, IT WOULD HAVE TO BE BETTER.

AH, MY SECRET. WELL, THAT'S A BIT LOADED. I FEEL LIKE I HAVE A LOT. THE ONE FROM THE OTHER DAY, WELL, I'M NOT SURE IF I'M H ETEROSEXUAL. WELL, JUST HETEROSEXUAL. I LIKE GIRLS, BUT I THINK I LIKE GUYS TOO. IT'S PART OF WHY I AVOID EVERYONE. EVEN IN CALIFORNIA, NO ONE LIKES A GAY BAD BOY.

I'VE JUST STARTED NOTICING MY ATTRACTION TO BOTH SEXES. I TRIED TO TELL MY BROTHER, BUT I FAILED. WE GOT INTO IT ABOUT OUR PARENTS AGAIN AND AS EVERYTHING WITH THEM, IT ENDED IN A FIGHT.

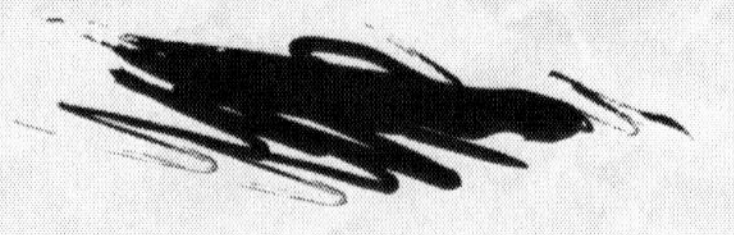

He more I hear of this Lemon, the more intriguing I find her. You're really lucky to have such a good friend, even if it doesn't develop into anything else, you at least have that person. I think you should tell her how you feel. Though, I'm the wrong person to take advice from since I hide from the world myself.

Will you tell me more of your secrets? I kind of like the idea of scribbled confessions, our ink whispers flying across the country.

I've just finished Ghost World and loved it. I'm also a Marvel fan. Which is your favorite? Would it be okay if I sent you one? It's really hard to find, but it's my favorite.

Thanks for listening, Fish.

Chapter Thirteen

LENNOX

IT HAD BEEN three days since I'd slept with Slade, two days since I kissed Simon, and one day since I realized I had no clue what the heck I was doing.

Sighing, I flipped the magazine, a scowl on my face as I glared at the beautiful couples in it. All it did was make me angry. I tossed it to the side and pulled out my kindle instead. Some more of that juicy book would be what the doctor ordered.

The door chimed a few minutes later, and I groaned, having gotten to a good scene. When I looked up, though, it was to find my mother standing in front of me.

"Mom? What are you doing here?"

Hopping off my stool, I rushed around the counter to give her a hug. It had been a few days since I'd seen her, so it was nice she'd stopped by. Even if it was a little suspicious.

"I just came to see how you were doing. Nothing nefarious, I promise."

"Well, I'm good. How's Noah? Dad?"

"They're both fine, sweetie. In fact, I'm inviting you over for dinner. Noah's dying to check out your new ride by the way. Sounds like Simon did well. I like it."

"Yeah?" I smiled. "He did, didn't he?" I couldn't stop the blush that spread, but thankfully my mother didn't appear to notice. "So, dinner, hmm? Yeah, I think I can fit you into my schedule," I laughed. "I'll stop by after work. Though, you know, there is this thing called a telephone, you could've just called."

"What's the fun in that?" She grinned, clearly up to something. "Besides, Simon has some products for me next door, so it was a win-win for me. I get to see my daughter and get some goodies. Plus, I made some muffins for Mr. Evans to thank him for helping me last week."

"I never understood why you liked him so much. He's always so mean to me."

"Now, honey. I know that's not true. He gave you this job and is always willing to help. He's a little prickly around the edges, but he has a good heart. I can tell these things, you know."

"Uh, huh. Your superhuman lie detector," I snarked, rolling my eyes. My mom claimed she could tell when people lied and whether or not they were good people. "It's nice of you to do that, but he's not here."

"Oh, it's not a problem. I'll just leave them on his desk. He told me he'd be back soon."

"Shut the front door! He answered you? Well, that's so nice of him to call *you* when he's avoiding me," I groused.

Crossing my arms, I walked back around to the counter, annoyed now that my mom was considered more important to Slade than *me*. Guess I needed to accept all the signals he was throwing me. It really had meant *nothing*.

I retreated back to my book while my mom patted me on the shoulder before walking to the back. The door chimed again, and I decided to wait this time to engage. I was at a crucial part in the story, and I didn't want to lose the rhythm of the scene getting pulled out of it again. Besides, if one more person annoyed me today, I might just lose it, my southern hospitality be damned.

Yeah, if my brain was cussing, everyone should steer clear of me today.

A throat clearing a moment later had me rolling my eyes. Sighing loudly, I groaned as I made a dramatic move to bookmark my page and shut my case before lifting my head. The words, "How can I help you?" were on the tip of my tongue, but as I came eye to eye with the person, I lost them.

"Good to see you too, Lennox."

This man was so beautiful, I found myself going speechless in his vicinity. His smile was radiant as he grinned down at me, and I found myself blushing. Pushing my hair behind my ears, I casually smoothed my blue flower dress, my nerves skyrocketing.

"Hey, Thane. What brings you here? You're not like, stalking me, or something?" I joked, laughing awkwardly at my attempt.

His face screwed up at the word. "No, of course not. I was stopping by to see my brother, actually. I didn't even know you worked here. This is the shop you were talking about?"

"Yep, the one and only."

He walked closer, leaning against the counter, bringing him even closer to me. His citrusy scent washed over me, transporting back to the night we kissed against his Jeep. "So, what's it like working here?"

Leaning forward conspiringly, I whispered, "It's great. Well, everyone but the owner. He's a bit of a prickly pear that I want to squash on a daily basis."

"Oh, *really*?"

"Mmhm."

He moved closer, and I found myself moving closer as well, drawn in by his magnetism. There was just something about Thane that both scared and excited me, making me lose focus of everything else.

"Lenn?"

Simon's voice sounded behind me and had me jumping back, knocking my knee against the counter. "Ow! Oh hey, Si. What brings you here?"

My face flamed, the position he found me in not looking well, despite how quasi-innocent it was.

"I was coming to bring your mom's goodies when I saw her car out front and see if I could persuade you to go to lunch." He had an odd expression on his face, and I knew I needed to fix this quickly. "But I guess you're busy."

"Nope, I'm not busy. This is Thane. We, uh, met the other night at the bar. He's here to see his brother. So, let me get him, and then we can go. Sound good? Perfect," I practically shouted in my need to say it quickly, I didn't even wait for him to respond. Turning, I addressed Thane this time. "So, what's your brother's name?"

As I asked this, my mom walked up and noticed Simon, giving him a hug before taking the bag he had for her. The distraction caused me to miss what Thane said.

"Oh, sorry. Who did you say?"

I focused back on Thane, the smirk he had throwing me. "Slade's my brother. He in?"

Everything went quiet as I stared at him, my mouth frozen in a shocked expression. Words weren't making sense today because I could've sworn he'd said Slade. Perhaps it was a lame joke.

"Ha, ha. Very funny. Slade doesn't have a brother."

"Uh, yeah, he does. It's me."

"Well, it's nice to meet you, Thane," my mom stepped in, her Southern hospitality ringing through. "I'm Robin, and this is Simon. But I'm afraid Slade isn't here."

"He's not? Oh, well, dang it. I came into town and wanted to surprise him. I guess that's what I get for not asking first. Man, it sucks, though. I was really looking forward to seeing him and catching up and everything."

I'd officially given up at this point. I was tempted to pull my kindle back out and start reading and hide away. Clearly, the universe wanted to dump dog poop on me and remind me of my curse. Not only had I slept with the one and only Slade a few days prior, but it seemed I'd kissed his brother a few days before that. And *now*, I was secretly dating my best gay friend behind everyone's back.

I'd seriously lost the plot. What was I even doing? I think I needed to have my head checked again. My life really was a sitcom!

The chuckle slipped out of me, drawing their attention. Once it was loose, I couldn't bring it back and more tumbled out. Bending over at the waist, I let myself laugh until I couldn't breathe, the high-pitched squeal leaving me as I tried to catch my breath. Everyone in the store looked at me now, but I didn't care, it had felt nice to laugh. Wiping my eyes, I calmed down and looked at the three people upfront, who were looking at me with varying degrees of concern.

"Sorry, it's just a little too much."

"You sure you're okay, sweetie? You're not trying to do too much after your injury, are you?"

"Yeah, Mom. I'm fine."

"Okay then. Now, give me some sugar, I need to head out and pick up Noah."

Walking over to her, I kissed her cheek and gave her a quick hug, her rose scent comforting. "I guess I'll see you tonight for dinner."

"Yep. I invited Thane and Simon as well. Hope that's okay with you," she winked. "Be good." She quickly made an exit before I could protest. Well, thank you very much, Mother! I couldn't believe she was matchmaking! Looking between the two men, they eyed one another.

"Um, so, yeah." It was all I could get out before the words just left me.

"Well, I'll let you get to your lunch with your *best friend*. I'll see you tonight."

I didn't miss how he emphasized best friend or how Simon's nostrils flared when Thane leaned down to kiss my cheek. I'd been too stunned to stop him at that point. Simon crossed his arms, an eyebrow raised as I watched Thane leave. Ignoring him, I walked around and grabbed my purse before hollering at Bubba.

"Taking lunch."

"Okay, sweetums, be good."

Laughing, I grabbed Simon's hand and pulled him out the door. I had a feeling lunch would be another difficult conversation I'd want to hide from.

"MOM, WHERE'S THE STRAINER?"

Robin James turned, an uncharacteristic furrow in her brow. "I'm sorry, what, dear?"

"The strainer?" I motioned to the pot I was currently holding up, waiting to dump. The movement caught her attention, and she jumped into action, grabbing it out of its new hiding spot. Sighing in relief, I dumped the pasta into it and tilted my head to avoid the steam. Once it was done, I put the empty pot down and tended to the noodles.

I'd come over early to help her with dinner, the anxiety coursing through my system all afternoon. Simon had been quiet at lunch, asking the bare minimum of questions and then barely giving me any affection when we parted. I felt like I'd already screwed up our relationship two days into it.

I was beginning to understand that I wasn't cursed. *I was the curse.*

"Okay, Mom. They're ready for you."

"Thanks, dear. Now, go and play with Noah. He's missed you. I'll holler if I need anything else, I promise."

"Yeah, okay."

Distractedly, I wiped my hands and headed out of the kitchen. I'd hoped being here would've settled my nerves, but my mom appeared as distracted as me. My phone beeped, and I anxiously withdrew it from my pocket. This dress was one of my favorites for that reason alone.

Except the text wasn't from Simon or even Slade, but Thane. I wasn't sure how I felt about seeing him tonight. Everything was jumbled in my head and heart, things having changed so much since the night we kissed.

Thane: I'm looking forward to tonight. It will be nice to meet your family.

Me: Yeah, I'm sure it will be awesomely awkward. You do realize my parents will be here? My dad and mother?

Thane: Yes, of course. Parents love me, you know. Just wait and see.

Me: It's that part that worries me the most. I'm sure mothers do love you. Mine already does. I mean, what's not to love? But we kind of just met… you know?

Thane: You're right. But also, I'm only in town

for today, and I really liked being with you the other night. I don't want to sound like the biggest dick but if your head wound was your way of blowing me off, then just let me know now. I just wanted to see if what we had translates outside a bar.

Me: …

His text confused me, and I didn't know what to say or how to respond to it. I hadn't lied and even told him I didn't remember until I saw him. Chewing my lip, I debated how to respond as I walked outside to where Noah was. When I didn't reply back immediately, he started to send me more, amping up my anxiety.

Thane: I mean, it's cool if it was. Just tell me, and I won't come to dinner. I'm not trying to be a stalker.

Thane: That's a joke, by the way.

Thane: Cherry, I'm not a stalker, I promise. Though I bet that's what stalkers say.

Thane: I can get you some character references if you need them. I was looking forward to meeting your family, but perhaps I jumped the gun and overestimated my charm. I'll leave you alone.

Me: Whoa, slow your roll. I was just thinking. Plus, I just got outside.

Me: Did I mention my dad is the police chief?

Thane: On second thought…

Thane: Kidding, I think that's awesome. I can't wait to wow them and Noah.
Thane: Honestly, I can't wait, Cherry.
Me: Awesome. I guess I'll see you later then.
Thane: Should I arrive naked, or is that later? That might be awkward at the dinner table, so definitely for later. Okay, good, got that cleared up. And my parole officer said I couldn't make friends.
Thane: Kidding.
Me: Why did I talk to you again? Your jokes are horrible.
Thane: I charmed you with my good looks first
Me: Oh yeah, you're right. You're just a pretty face. Now that I realize that, I'm good.
Thane: You're funny, Cherry, but I'm not letting you go that easily. I'll show you how irresistible I can be. I'll see you later. You already invited me, so no take backs, that would be rude not to keep it.
Me: Using my southern roots against me, I see. Talk to you later.

I pocketed my phone, an odd feeling in my chest. This would either be the best dinner or the worst.

NOAH and I were drawing outside with sidewalk chalk. We'd been working on a mural of the yellow brick road with Dorothy, Lion, Scarecrow, and Tin Man. He was working on the lion while I finished up the scarecrow. This was one of our favorite things to do together. We both enjoyed art and had started making chalk drawings when he was a baby. They've improved in their clarity over the years.

"You're doing it again," he muttered.

Sticking my tongue out, I ignored him and kept on humming. Noah hated when I sang songs. He gave me a complex on that end of things, but it was a habit I couldn't break. If I wasn't singing, I was humming, always a song in my head and heart.

Spread out on the driveway, a piece of chalk in my hand was how Thane found us twenty minutes later.

"Wow, is that The Wizard of Oz?"

"Mother of Pearl!" I screeched, clutching my chest. "Geez, you're quiet."

Noah laughed his little twelve-year-old head off at me, always finding it hilarious when I was surprised. I'd like to blame Thane, but it was just me.

Pulling my legs under me, I tried as ladylike as possible to keep my bum covered while doing so. It hadn't been a great idea to lay down in a dress, and I was kicking myself now over it. As I discreetly tucked my dress under, a hand appeared in front of me.

Like a knight in shining armor, Thane held out a hand to help me rise. His head was backed by the sun, and he looked like an angel with the gold light radiating around him. His smile twinkled like a toothpaste ad, and his blue eyes shimmered like the sea, and I wondered if he could be any more perfect.

Placing my hand in his, I gracefully stood before

wobbling a little when both my feet were under me. He reached out and steadied me, his hands grasping my hips, and I clutched his arms as I tried to steady myself.

"Who are you?"

Noah's voice cut through the air, and I found myself laughing, effectively breaking the spell I kept falling under in his presence. It was odd how disarming he was in person, when I spent little time thinking of him otherwise. Dropping his arms, I was surprised when I saw him grabbing my hand and linking our fingers. Looking down at them, I frowned. Was I okay with this?

"I, uh, this is my brother, Noah," I introduced when Thane didn't say anything to Noah's question.

"How do you know my sister, stranger?" Noah asked, tilting his head up, taking Thane in. He had an assessing glint in his eyes I'd never seen before, and I wanted to shout at him for being rude, but he wasn't wrong, and I found myself chuckling under my breath.

"Apologies, bud. I'm Thane." He smiled. "I met your sister the other night and saved her from sitting alone. Now, who drew this munchkin over here?"

His answer wasn't wrong, but something about it tugged at me. Noah surveyed him carefully before smiling and puffing up his chest in pride at his drawing. He'd spent almost a whole day working on his Lollipop Guild and it was really good.

"I did."

"Well, that's amazing!"

"Thanks," he blushed, and I knew Thane had endeared himself to my brother.

"I guess we should head in, little man, and see if Mom needs any help with finishing dinner."

Noah stood, brushing off his pants, and placed his chalk back in our container. Picking up mine as well, he gathered the items and carried them inside with us trailing him. When we started toward the sidewalk, Thane stopped and bent down to grab something. Quirking an eyebrow, I tried to look at what he was hiding.

"Did you bring something?

"I did, but you can't see it yet."

"Oh! Is it a gift?"

"You'll just have to wait. Now, come on. I'm famished!" He grinned wide, and I found myself feeling lightheaded again. Cheese on toast, this man was too charming. I'd need to be careful.

Mom was putting the last of the dishes on the table when we entered. Thane dropped my hand and pulled out the bouquet of flowers he'd hidden there. Smiling, I felt my heart take off at the gesture until conflicting feelings of guilt arose. I couldn't like another guy, especially Slade's brother, but more importantly, not now that I was with Simon. I needed to reign it in before I lost everything again. I didn't think I would survive it this time.

Mom looked up in surprise, and I couldn't help but like the guy. Anyone who could make my mom look that happy had to be a winner. Just not the one for me, I reminded myself.

"Mrs. James, thank you for allowing me to crash your dinner. I hope these are a presentable hostess gift."

"Oh, they are lovely. Thank you, and, please, it's Robin."

My mom took the flowers and walked back into the kitchen, giving me a look. It was then I realized how idiotic it was to keep me and Simon a secret. My family was going to be rooting for Thane now and not understand when I didn't reciprocate, especially if I kept giving off mixed signals like holding his hand. Distancing myself some, I watched as Thane turned back to me and smiled.

"That was really sweet. Thank you for making her smile."

"Well, I don't know if you know this, Cherry, but I kind of like you. And I did promise I was good with mothers."

"You're right. You did," I laughed, trying to avoid his mentioning of liking me.

"Well, thanks. My dad and Simon should be here soon as well."

"Ah, yes. The *best friend* and the police chief father."

"Who carries a gun at all times," came from behind him.

Thane froze, a flash of fear crossing his face for a millisecond before he wiped it clear. Ignoring the odd behavior, I ran over and hugged my dad.

"Hey, Dad," I breathed him in, his comforting smell of mint, a balm to my heart. My dad really was the best. "Be nice. Mom invited him to dinner, and he made her smile," I whispered in jest.

"Hmph," was the only response he gave, squeezing

me tight. He released me but held me at arm's length, taking me in.

"You doing okay, pumpkin?"

His childhood nickname for me always made my cheeks rosy. The past week had been stressful, and I knew he worried about me. Nodding, I smiled as I attempted to soothe his worries.

"Hey, sorry I'm late. I had to stop and get these."

Simon announced, walking into the room. I loved how, even after all this time, I still got lovesick butterflies fluttering to life in me. He approached me, but stopped midway with a pained look on his face, again confirming how stupid it was to keep a secret. Neither of us knew how to act now without feeling like we were being obvious, and in the meantime, stopping our natural affection toward one another. Deciding to save him, I walked and hugged him before taking the bag of gummy bears in his hand. Grinning wide at him, I popped a few in my mouth. These were so much better than flowers in my opinion.

I hugged him again in glee, but felt him hesitate this time and I started to pull back, worried I'd been out of line. Was our new relationship at stake? Could we not hug in front of others anymore? Thankfully, Simon pulled me tight to him a second later as I tried not to think about how our bodies were pressed together. I tried not to think about how good he smelled. I tried not to think about how safe I felt. I tried not to think of a lot of things, but I failed.

Because fudge, he smelt and felt good.

Now that I knew I had free reign to explore this

body and man, I no longer wanted to hold back. My hands had a mind of their own as they began to lower toward his ass, my cheek and nose rubbing against his shirt to get a good whiff. A throat cleared behind us, stopping me before the tiny moan slipped out.

I pulled back and found my dad, with his eyebrow raised, a tiny smirk on his face. "Dinner's ready."

Nodding, Simon and I followed behind him, and I imagined his face was as red as mine. When we got to the table, Thane, my dad, and Simon and I stood awkwardly as we all looked at one another. Thankfully, my mom entered with the last of the food, placing it on the table and saved me from having to make awkward conversation. Noah trailed behind carrying a bread basket, one already shoved in his mouth. When I looked at him, he shrugged and smiled wide with the bread peeking out.

"What? I'm hungry."

"Noah! Manners!" my mom admonished, reaching to take the basket. Noah ducked her arm though and pivoted around her to place them on the table, but not before stealing two more and backing away slowly with them.

The kid was too cute for his own good and instead of correcting him, we all found ourselves laughing as we began to take our seats. When I went to sit, Simon started to sit next to me and when he realized Thane had his hand on the same chair. He lifted an eyebrow, asking me what I wanted to do.

Fudgesickles, this was hard! Again, I realized how stupid it was to keep something like this a secret. They only hurt someone in the end. It was a lesson I'd learned many times. It was clear my mother thought she was helping by inviting Thane to dinner, but instead, she'd made it more difficult. If I made it through this without my head exploding, it would be a win.

While we stood there awkwardly attempting to figure out what to do, both their hands on the chair back, I noticed I still held the all red gummy bears.

"Oh, um, thanks, Si. You know the red gummies are my favorite."

"Peace offering for being a dickweasel at lunch. Can we talk afterward?"

I nodded, placing them on the counter before taking my seat. Simon gave in and walked around to the seat next to Noah, putting him across from me. I didn't know which I preferred. Him next to me where I couldn't touch him, but could feel him, or across from me where I stared into his gray eyes. They held a tremendous amount of emotion, but the one I didn't understand was the bit of pain I noticed.

Maybe he thought Thane was cute? Simon couldn't be jealous, could he? Thane was hands down the most attractive man I'd ever met, it made sense if Simon thought so too. I didn't know how Simon could ever feel insecure, the man was gorgeous, but I knew we all struggled with something.

Glancing around the table, I watched in fascination as my dad leveled Thane with a look. It was a sick hobby of mine to watch the guys I dated sweat under his interrogation stare. It had become a rite of passage over the years, only a few succeeding. Thoughts of the last person who'd passed had me sobering, and I focused back on my food.

Mom had gone all out making my favorites of mashed potatoes, corn casserole, BBQ pork chops, macaroni and cheese, and cinnamon apples. My stomach growled in anticipation, and I realized how hungry I was. I dug into the wonderful smelling meal, knowing the real show would start soon.

My dad liked to get his victims comfortable before springing his trap. I wanted to feel sorry for Thane for what was about to happen, but he'd been the one to insist on coming over and meeting the family after one kiss. I was kind of hoping it would poke holes in the whole perfect thing he had going on. It was hard not to like him, but the guilt was weighing heavy on me, and perhaps, if he wasn't as he seemed, it wouldn't feel like I was making the wrong choice. Not that Simon would ever be a bad choice in my mind, but the timing royally sucked to finally be faced with two great guys to date. It was the ironic twist of my curse striking me.

Simon smirked at me across from the table, knowing as well what was about to go down. I tried to ignore the hunger lingering there, making me want to skip the food and go straight for dessert. Preferably the one where he made me see stars… naked. I couldn't be thinking things like that at the dinner table, though, so I gave him a pointed look back, but all he did was smirk harder, knowing he was getting to me. I think he was also feeling some jealousy, and ready for Thane to be brought down a peg. Simon was well acquainted with Eddie James' interrogation techniques.

Just as I placed a bite of mashed potatoes in my mouth, my father launched his first sneak attack.

"So, Thane, is it? Outside of being Slade's brother, what is it that you do?" He'd inhaled his dinner, as always, and was now leaning back as he placed his napkin on his plate and waited.

Thane grinned, wiping his mouth before he answered, "I'm a veterinarian."

Internally, I laughed because I knew that would stump my father. "Oh, hmm," he sat up, resting his elbows on the table. "That sounds interesting. Competitive work?"

"No, not really."

"Hmm."

"So, you get to play with dogs and cats all day?" Noah asked, taking an interest.

"Sorta, sometimes, I have to figure out what's wrong with them too and make them feel better."

"That's so cool."

"And where do you live, Thane? Slade's never mentioned you before," my father tried again to gain the upper hand.

"Oh, well, that's a tough one to answer. Slade and I've not spoken in a few years. I'm trying to patch things up. I've been working out west and just moved here to improve our relationship. It's been a bonus meeting this cutie." He smiled at me. "Right now, I'm currently in Tennessee."

"What did y'all fight about?"

"Just a family disagreement. It's boring, actually."

Thane dropped his eyes, the first sign that he was hiding something, the pressure from him at my dad's questions getting to him. It bugged me, his response. Not that I wanted to dig into their history, but something about it felt wrong. My mother, feeling the tension, cut in my dad's game of twenty questions and ended it. After that, we finished dinner making polite conversation.

When dinner was finally over, I wasn't sad to be done. It had been exhausting hiding my feelings with Simon and trying to manage Thane's presence as well. Walking him out, Simon lingered back, giving me time to do whatever I needed. The unfortunate part was, I wasn't sure what. This situation was so strange.

"Thanks again for inviting me to dinner."

"Ah, but you kind of invited yourself, remember? Or through my mom at least."

"Minor details, Cherry."

I gave him a tight smile, my body tense at the nickname. He still made me lose myself when I stared into his crystal blue eyes, but the effect was lost when I wasn't. "Well, I guess I'll see you around the shop when you visit Slade?"

"Nah. I think I'll head back and try again another time. Don't mention it to him, though. We have things to work out, and hearing I was here mingling with his people might not go over too well. I'll tell him when we touch base."

"Uh, yeah, sure thing."

He went in for a kiss, and I turned, offering him my

cheek as I hugged him quickly. Stepping back, I did an awkward wave, leaving him with a farewell. "Be safe."

Thane looked at me oddly, hurt shone in his eyes, and I hated how it made me feel like a bad person. I had too many other things going on though, to worry about it right now. "Yeah, okay. I'll text you."

"Perfect. Sounds like a plan, Stan."

Cringing, I turned and made my way inside, wondering how I ended up in this predicament in the first place. Simon had been right. I never should've done online dating again.

My Starry Nox,

Can you believe it's been two years already since we first wrote? We're moving again, so I'll have to send your next letter from my new address. Every week, I look forward to your letters, they're the best thing in my life. You've definitely kept your end of the bargain, the promise you made to me.

For that, I thank you. So, I'm sending you a gift. Don't worry, it's not expensive or anything, just something I saw and thought of you. I do hope you enjoy it.

I'll keep this short since I need to finish packing, but I couldn't leave without getting this in the mail to let you know not to write back just yet. I don't want to miss a letter.

Your Blaze

MY DREAM HOUSE

NOX

Chapter Fourteen

LENNOX

I FOUND Simon in the backyard, swinging in the hammock, his head tilted back as he took in the sky. I approached with soft steps, enjoying the quiet as I watched him. This part of the backyard was thankfully out of sight from the back windows of the house, making me feel bold in my movements. How many times had I dreamed about making out with Simon in this very hammock? Too many to count.

The stars were out, and it made me yearn for the innocence of the girl who felt they were the cure-all. At one time, they'd been my connection to a boy, a shared pastime providing me comfort. Now, they were a reminder of how not everything that sparkled was gold. Sometimes, it was just the deceiving wrapper covering the poison in the middle.

I was almost to him, my hands out in front to pounce when his voice spoke into the night.

"Do you like *him*?"

Stopping, I dropped my head before continuing the rest of the way. Carefully, I positioned myself next to Si in the hammock, our fingers brushed, but nothing else. Exhaling, I turned my head to take in his side profile.

"Honestly? I don't know. I liked him when I met

him that first night. We had a lot in common, and he was easy to talk to. We shared a kiss at the end of it, but then I hit my head and forgot about the date until I ran into him again with the cat. That being said, I like how things are with us and that we're finally getting this chance. I wouldn't trade that for *anything*."

Simon turned, watching me, and I felt his body relax next to mine. His fingers wrapped around mine, joining our hands together, and I exhaled in relief.

"I like where things are too. I just didn't want you to miss out and then resent me."

"I could never resent you, Si. Don't you get it? You're the boy I've been in love with since I knew what boys were, probably even before. Lennox and Simon forever, remember? I might be attracted to Thane, but it holds nothing to the love and feelings I've carried for you for over ten years. I've only ever felt this way about one other person, and well, that was an epic fail if there ever was one."

His eyes held mine, something in them shifting at the mention of Blaze, but that was long ago history at this point and had no bearing on my future. He'd broken my heart, and it was now duct taped into pieces.

"You know what I realized?" I asked when he didn't say anything, the quiet of the night around us. He shook his head, lost in his thoughts. "Maybe I'm the reason for my curse. Well, that and you intimidating guys apparently, but… mostly me."

Simon chuckled, brushing a piece of hair back, leaving his palm on my cheek. I snuggled into it, liking the feeling of his hand on my face in this manner.

"You're not cursed, Lemon, not at all. Maybe your heart is a little battered, just waiting for the right one to seal it back together."

"And you think that's you?" I teased.

"I hope so."

His eyes did that thing where they dropped from my eyes to my lips, and I knew he was about to kiss me. The look before the kiss was my favorite, the moment where you knew your lips were about to collide, joining your hearts together. That split second where magic seemed to happen as everything hovered on that precipice.

Simon inched closer, his eyes fluttering shut as he did, and I sucked in a breath. We'd kissed the other night, but it had been one of pure passion. This one would be intentional, sealing us together as lovers. No matter what happened from here on out, if we made it or not, we would forever be part of one another's story.

I hoped it was forever.

Our lips met, and it felt like electricity crackled around us as we pressed them tighter. Simon's hand flexed in my hair, pulling me closer as the pressure built between us. Tilting my head, I opened my lips to allow him more access. Our tongues swirled, and with each flick, I felt our bodies roll closer to one another. The hammock swayed with us, and I realized how absolutely horrible of a place to get freaky this was.

When it swayed again, Simon pulled back, both of us laughing. "As many times as I'd fantasized about making out here, I never considered the actual physics of it. We're either going to get seasick, maim one another, or get twisted up in this thing and have to get my parents to cut us out. How about we either move locations, or I don't know, go back to our apartment where we don't have to worry about how loud we get?"

"That sounds like my kind of competition, the one where no one loses."

"Oh, there definitely aren't any losers when it comes to orgasms in my book."

"I think that's the dirtiest word I've ever heard you say, Lenn."

"Oh?" I blushed. The feel of his body pressed into me had my heart racing. I brushed my hand against his stubble, the movement bringing tingles to my palm. Simon closed his eyes, leaning into it. The moment felt so surreal in a way, my dream manifesting into reality. Rubbing my thumb against his cheek, he eventually opened his eyes.

"I don't think you know just how much I love you, Lenn."

"Oh, Si, I think I do. My heart beats in tandem with yours. I love you, Simon Fisher."

"I like hearing that and knowing it's more than just friends."

"Me too."

"I think we should head home now, or we might have to endure our second time together outdoors."

Popping up, I tugged his hand, dragging him with me. I had no intention of playing twister with the hammock, getting grass stains on my butt, or eaten alive by bugs. Nope, that was not going to happen. Simon laughed at my exuberance but went along with my pulling. Walking in the backdoor, I quickly detoured to the living room where my family were watching a movie.

"Welp, gotta head out. Thanks for dinner."

Hugging my parents and brother, I made a quick exit before they could say anything. Simon bid his own farewells and followed me out, a wicked smile on his face for only me to see, sending zingers through me. Once we were back outside, I turned to Simon, my keys already in my hand, ready to go.

"Race you back! But like, in a totally non-Fast-and-the-Furious way!"

I'd taken off as I shouted, unlocking my car as Simon strolled casually to his. His carefree attitude was frustrating, but I would make it home first at this rate. Jumping in, I started my car and took off, more comfortable with the gears now that I'd done it for a few days. I lost Simon a few streets over, and I felt smug at winning. Yet when I pulled into the complex, he was leaning against his car, a cocky look on his face.

Pulling in next to him, I couldn't even formulate the words as I stared. He laughed and took off toward our apartment. Shaking my head, I hurriedly got out of my car and locked it before I jogged and attempted to jump on Simon's back. I ended up only hanging from around his neck since I didn't get up high enough to wrap my legs around him. They made that look so much easier in the movies! Hanging like a backward monkey, I started to slide off, landing back on my feet. Si turned, amusement lit on his face.

"Lemon, were you trying to be my personal backpack or thwart me from entering the apartment first? The action was such a disaster. I can't really tell what your intention was."

Crossing my arms, I tilted my chin, my stubbornness coming out to play having missed my rounds with Tatzilla. I started walking, ignoring his question, swaying my hips as I went.

"Oh, is that how it's going to be, Lenn?"

Smiling, I kept walking, confident I had the upper hand. I made it almost to the door when arms wrapped around me, and squeals erupted out of me as Simon swung me up into his arms. Wrapping my arms around his neck, I grinned so wide, my cheeks hurt.

"Well, I declare, Mr. Fisher, are you trying to sweep me off my feet?"

Si cocked his head, a look of pure sex on his face as his eyes heated causing my breath to catch. "Oh, Lenn, I hope to sweep you, keep you, and heap you."

"Heap me?"

"Yeah, make you cum so hard, your legs leave you in a heap on the floor."

"Holy guacamole, that's hot!"

Simon chuckled, used to my nonsense prattles. He managed to unlock the door, kicking it open while still holding me. The moment the door closed and was locked, his mouth descended on me. Somehow, he managed to walk, because a few minutes later, my back hit a soft surface, and he followed me down.

"Oh yes, much better," I managed to get out as he attacked my neck. Everything became a flurry of hands and lips, his pelvis rocking into me. My legs wrapped around him, and I pulled him as close to me as possible, needing the friction and intimacy.

Simon pushed my dress up, finding his way under to pull my panties down, and I felt his nose run up the seam of my center.

"Oh yes, Si."

My hands weaved into his hair, urging him on. He began to lick me, and I threw my head back, the feeling so wonderful. When he started to rub my clit, I found myself close to the edge already, the pent-up sexual tension with Simon years in the making. When he pushed a finger in, I could feel him sliding it back and forth, coating himself. Looking down, I watched as he devoured me, and I couldn't hold it back anymore, the sight of him between my legs too much to take.

"Simon! Ahh!"

My body tensed, my legs trapping him between my thighs as I trembled. This time when I felt a wet sensation, I froze, unsure what was happening. Simon moaned, licking me up even more. When he was done, he looked up, his face covered in me. I stared, realizing I'd finally done it. I'd squirted on Simon's face!

"Um, sorry?"

Simon cocked his head, licking his lips as he did. "Why are you apologizing, Lemon?"

"Because..." I moved my hand around his face, unable to utter the words.

"I still don't understand."

"You really haven't been with any other girls, have you?"

"No, not after you and me, I mean, I kissed a few, but other than first base, it never went further. Why?"

"Well, first, how the hell did you know to do all that then?"

"Um, well, there's this thing called porn, Lemon," he purred, crawling toward me. "They even have bi-sexual ménage porn, and it was the best of both worlds. I watched it a lot, imagining you. I also researched it just in case, not wanting to fail, and now, I got to try what I've been studying for years."

He nuzzled my neck, kissing me before he pulled back, a look of doubt now on his face. "Why, was it bad?"

Shaking my head vehemently, I grabbed his face to make him look at me. "Not at all, Si! That was the best oral I've ever received, so much so you gave me the elusive girl unicorn of squirting. Like, that's never happened before! I'm embarrassed by how wet I got. I guess I worried you would think it was gross."

"Gross? Why would I think that? It's the greatest achievement in my mind. I made you cum that hard. My hands and mouth turned you on, babe. Nothing about that is embarrassing to me."

"Okay, good."

"Was it really the best?"

"Hands down." I nodded.

Simon smiled, and I realized how much he'd worried about not being good enough. Shoving him down flat on his back. I unzipped my dress on the side, pulling it off, and unsnapped my bra, tossing it aside. Simon was still in his clothes, so I pushed his shirt up and over his head. He'd lost focus, staring at my tits, his hand reaching out.

"Can I?"

Chuckling, I grabbed his hand and directed him to my boob. I watched in wonder as my best friend discovered boobs for the first time again. Flashes of us stumbling around in that tent years ago had me wanting to rediscover his body too. Back then, he'd been a skinny teen, but now, Simon was all man. As he rolled my nipple over his thumb, I focused on unzipping his pants and pushing them down.

His cock sprung free, almost hitting me in the face with how close I'd been. "Well, hello, big boy."

"Lenn, did you just talk to my penis?"

"Uh, yeah. It greeted me, and I felt it deserved a hello." Kissing the tip, I licked up the dot of pre-cum there.

"Fuck, Lenn."

Simon's hands fell from me, and I took the opportunity to lick down his length, rolling my tongue around him. I didn't know much about the mechanics of the male anatomy, but I swear his penis wasn't this big the first time. I was enjoying my time sucking him when Simon sat up, lifting me off him.

"I can't wait any longer, Lenn."

He slammed his mouth down on mine, and we tangled tongues, my body instinctively moving closer to him, straddling his waist. Wrapping my arms around his neck, I lowered myself down on him, his hands directing my hips as I went. Sinking down low, I groaned out as I impaled myself. We both sat for a second, staring at one another, taking in this moment.

This was us, Si and Lenn. We weren't kids anymore. From here on out, things would be different. We couldn't hide behind miscommunication or fear. Our hearts were bare, our feelings out in the open, and our bodies fused together.

Simon cupped my face, sincerity covering his, his soulful eyes capturing mine. "I love you, Lennox."

"I love you too, Simon."

In a synchronized move almost, our lips made the final connection, sparking our passion.

Simon grabbed my hips and started to lift me, and I assisted as I moved, my knees next to him. Throwing my head back, I braced my arms on the bed, offering more leverage. I watched as Simon fixated on my breasts, the movement jiggling them with each thrust our bodies moved, the pleasure overwhelming.

"God damn, Lenn. You're so fucking gorgeous. It's been torture these past few years trying to hide my feelings for you. Most mornings, I had to take care of myself before I stepped out my door. Other days, I'd manage to make it through breakfast only to stroke myself in the shower, your smell all around me. I can't smell your shampoo now without getting hard," he groaned.

His words were dirty and hot, and I found myself growing wetter with each thrust.

"Fuck, Lenn. I can't last much longer."

I moved back to him, my nipples rubbing against his chest, the rawness of them lighting with sensations with each pass. Whispering in his ear, "I heard you, but I never thought it was me you were thinking about. I used to touch myself at night, hoping you'd hear and come into my room to help."

"Oh fuck, Lenn, that's hot. I wish I had."

It was the last straw. Simon started to piston faster into me, his cock hitting me deep with each thrust, and I found myself clenching around him, my body exploding into a million nerve centers as I fell over the edge, cumming with him.

Simon fell back onto the bed, both of us panting as we laid in one another's arms. This was bliss and I didn't feel guilty about it this time.

Simon got up later, cleaning us both up and bringing me my phone to charge. I glanced at it, no messages from anyone. I quickly dismissed the disappointment I felt. I'd just had amazing sex with the love of my life. Why did I need to be greedy or be thinking of someone else? I didn't. It wasn't who I was.

A notification popped up, and I remembered I hadn't checked my blog in a few days. Logging in, I was floored for a moment when I saw I had over 100 messages from B.E.R. Scrolling through them, a pit formed in my stomach. Simon walked over, and I quickly shut it off, plugging it in on the nightstand. My hands shook, but I ignored them, not wanting to draw attention for fear he'd ask questions.

Laying back, I pulled the covers up, needing to feel safe. Simon climbed in, turning off the light, and pulled me close. I snuggled closer, happy just to be in his arms. He kissed my forehead, and I realized he had some soft music playing as he fell asleep. It was soothing, but I laid there, my mind whirling, sleep evading me. Sometime around 3 am, I finally fell asleep, exhaustion catching up to me. My prayer, a desperate plea on my lips.

Make it be gone. Make it not real. Make it be gone.

Nox books,

I didn't mean to be nasty, or sound judgmental. Maybe I need to give it another try. What book are you reading? Perhaps we can read it together?

What do you think makes people do those things?

What are you up to? Anything fun?

I'm so glad to have met you.

B.E.R.

Nox books,

Are you going to share it with me? I'm sorry if I offended you.

Looking forward to hearing from you.

B.E.R

Nox books,

Listen, you don't have to freeze me out. I know you feel the same way I do. You can quit playing games.

B.E.R

Nox books,

Well, if you want to be a whore, who am I to judge? I can fuck you just as good. Give me a call, baby, and we can have a good time.

B.E.R.

Nox books,

Seriously, I can't believe you're playing this hard to get. Come on, baby, give me a call. You know you want me. It's written all over your page.

B.E.R

Nox books,

You fucking slut! I can't believe you'd rather be with a gay guy than me! Don't you know he'll only hurt you and leave you? He wants what you don't have, baby. Come to me, and I'll show you how a real man is.

B.E.R

Nox books,

My patience is getting low, baby. Quit playing games and come to me. I'm waiting.

B.E.R

Nox books,

I like your new car, though you might want to watch for second gear. You're changing it too soon. Don't be a dumb bitch and ruin the transmission.

B.E.R

Nox books,

I've been nice, but I'm sick of seeing you flaunt your ass in front of me. You're begging for my dick, but you keep torturing me. If one more guy lays a hand on you, I'm coming for you all.

B.E.R

Nox books,

Last warning, baby. You're mine. Don't ever forget it. I thought I made that clear before? Perhaps you need a recap? Visit Duncan lately?

B.E.R

Blazey Blaze, my purple haze,

HOW IS YOUR NEW PLACE? DO YOU GET YOUR OWN ROOM? ARE YOU CLOSE TO THE OCEAN? I WANT TO SEE THE OCEAN. I THINK IT SOUNDS MAGICAL. ONE DAY, I'M GOING TO MAKE IT THERE AND PUT MY TOES IN THE SAND AND DANCE IN THE WAVES.

I DON'T EVEN KNOW HOW TO THANK YOU FOR THE NECKLACE. IT'S PERFECT. I LOVE IT. THE CRESCENT MOON NOW HANGS AROUND MY NECK, AND I FEEL LIKE A LITTLE PIECE OF YOU IS WITH ME. HOPEFULLY THAT DOESN'T SOUND TOO DORKY. SCHOOL STARTS BACK TOMORROW, AND I HATE THAT I STILL HAVE TWO YEARS. I KNOW I'M NOT SUPPOSED TO TELL MY AGE, SO JUST PRETEND YOU CAN'T DO MATH. I MEAN, IT'S NOT MY FAVORITE, SO THERE'S NO WAY I'D BE ABLE TO FIGURE IT OUT. NOPE.

I HEARD A NEW SONG TODAY AND I THOUGHT ABOUT SINGING IT AT THE TALENT SHOW. BUT THEN I TRIED TO PRACTICE IN FRONT OF MY BEST FRIEND, AND I COULDN'T MAKE IT PAST THE FIRST VERSE. I'M NEVER GOING TO BE ABLE TO IF I CAN'T EVEN SING IN FRONT OF HIM!

I'VE BEEN MAKING SOME PROGRESS ON MY SKETCHES THOUGH. I HOPE YOU ENJOY THIS ONE I DID OF THE NIGHT SKY. IT'S CALLED NOCTURNE BEGINNINGS. MY ART TEACHER TAUGHT ME ABOUT THAT WORD. IT MEANS A PICTURE OF A NIGHT SCENE, OR A SOFT ROMANTIC PIECE OF MUSIC OF NIGHT ON THE PIANO.

I found it fascinating. Now you'll know what my sky looks like. There's also a hammock where I often lay to look at the stars. That's me. But obviously, I'm the one laying down, so you can't see me. See? Still a mystery, even in my drawing.

You know what we haven't done in a while. Questions. So I'm going to restart.

1. What's your vehicle of choice? So, this might sound dumb, but I really want a Volkswagen Beetle. But not like the new ones, an old one and it needs to be yellow! I just think they're so cute. I know it won't talk to me or drive itself like Herbie, but I just think it would be fun, and totally be me.

2. Do you think it's better to tell someone something that might be hard to hear or keep it to yourself? I'm hoping you have an answer. I struggle with this every day.

3. If you were an animal, what would you be? I honestly want to say a dog, but I'd probably be more of the hairless mole rat, knowing my luck.

Hope your new view is good.
Shine bright Blaze,

Chapter Fifteen

LENNOX

NO AMOUNT of caffeine seemed to be helping this morning. My head pounded from the lack of sleep, dizziness sweeping over me. It was Friday, which meant it was busy and I alone had three piercings today. I really needed to keep my eyes open if I was going to make it through them, or I would become my dream version of myself with clients running out on me. Nothing like stabbing someone in the wrong spot to ruin your day, well, and theirs.

Of course, as luck would have it, it was also the day Slade decided to grace us with his return. He stormed into the shop like a thunder cloud, the darkness surrounding him like a visible cloak. The poor door closed quietly, too scared after being almost wrenched off its hinges to squeak in protest.

Everyone froze as we waited to see what he'd do, the prodigal bossnemy returning. Slade stomped past me, a glower covering his face, and headed straight to his office, ignoring everyone. The others had jumped out of his way, no one tempting his foul mood. Bubba arched an eyebrow at me once he was behind closed doors, but I didn't have it in me today to gossip, so I shrugged before turning back around.

The poor sleep, the anxiety over the messages I'd received, and now Slade's return had me wanting to run and hide. Perhaps a dark hole would suffice. Or a cabin in the woods. Oh, I know, one of those bunkers! I would definitely be able to hide from all my troubles there and hope they went away on their own. Sounded like a solid plan to me.

My phone vibrated on the counter, but I couldn't bring myself to look at it. Touching the darn thing instantly gave me hives, and I'd been avoiding it all morning. I couldn't read or even draw. I'd been staring at the door and answering the phone like a responsible employee all morning! It was kind of sickening. I needed to get past this before people started expecting it out of me on the regular. Carefully, I reached out for my phone to see who it was. It was a text message from Tatzilla.

bossnemy: My office. NOW.

Rolling my eyes, I had half a mind not to bother with it. If he couldn't say hello to me, what did I owe him? Nothing. He'd ghosted me, left me alone after a night together, and now demanded me to follow his instructions. Through text messages. Not even in person.

Nope. I was not having it today.

Slamming it down, I shoved it under some paper, going back to avoiding it. What had facing my problems ever gotten me anyway?

Outside of Simon, nothing! And *that* had just

happened two days ago. Clearly, it wasn't an accurate reflection of success. Twenty-five years of disasters were what I had to go on. One good thing did not void them.

So, no, thank you. I would not be facing my problems today. I'd go with hiding all the way. I much preferred to avoid broken hearts and trauma.

Twenty minutes later, my coffee was empty, and my eyes still wanted to close on their own. Pulling out a magazine from the other day, I casually flipped through it when a door slammed behind me, and Tatzilla marched up to me.

I could feel him breathing behind me, his eyes laser focused into the back of my neck, but I ignored him. Even when he moved into my periphery, I let him stew at the end of my counter, focusing on my magazine instead. If he wanted to talk to me, then he could treat me like a person.

"James!"

I jumped at his shout, my face flaming in embarrassment as everyone in the shop turned and looked as well. Turning my head, I narrowed my eyes at him, but I still said nothing. He was seething, and for a second, I feared what he might do. Covering the fear, I iced him out right back. I didn't say anything, giving him only my glare, waiting for him to tell me who'd peed in his Cheerios today.

"I've. Been. Texting. You."

Words have never been gritted out through teeth as painfully as now.

I kept my focus on him, reminding myself not to get trapped in his stormy eyes, the darkness swirling and calling to me. Raising one shoulder, I turned back to my magazine, nothing else to say to him. The more I thought about it, I was the one allowed to be angry, not him. He'd left *me* and then ignored me for days! I didn't owe him anything until he apologized.

My thoughts had distracted me from the Hulk-like man next to me as he wrestled with his rage. When his arms bracketed me from behind, I gasped, my air becoming lodged in my throat when he bent down to whisper in my ear. I had to focus on what he said, his breath heating my neck, pulling goosebumps to my skin. His woody leather scent invaded my nostrils, curling my toes as I succumbed to his sexual energy, his dominance rolling over me.

"*Peaches*, don't forget I know how to push all your buttons. I can make you scream, panting for me right here in front of everyone. Or you can move your sweet ass back to my office. I'm fine with either option. You have three seconds to decide."

"You wouldn't," I breathed, wanting to slap myself for sounding so breathless. What the h-e-double hockey sticks was I thinking? My mouth seriously needed to shut the fudge up, and my body needed to remember how much he hurt us. The part of my brain that apparently made logical decisions had decided to take a vacation.

"Want to really test that theory out, James? Three seconds. Starting now." His body left mine, his intoxicating essence leaving me, allowing me to think again. Sucking in clear air, my brain cleared from all the haze, realizing what was at stake. Fortunately, I only waited two seconds before I booked it to his office. I shut the door behind me right as he said three. Leaning against it, I folded my arms, not willing to give him any more leverage.

"I'm here. What do you want? I'm busy."

It was obviously a lie, and we both knew it, but I had to keep up some of the facade. Slade gritted his teeth, fighting with himself. "Sit down, James."

"I'll stand, thank you very much."

Crossing my legs, he took notice of my outfit, and I swear his head almost exploded. "What the fuck is that?" He gestured toward me, a look of utter disbelief on his face.

Looking down, I didn't understand what his problem was. "Um, jeans. You know the things you wear every day?" I cocked my head, not understanding his issue. They didn't have holes in them. They were just a typical pair of Levi's.

"But, but, but," he started, unable to find his words before he shook his head, a deep exhale leaving him. Planting his hands on his hips, he glared back at me. "What's wrong? For three years, I've painstakingly had to watch you prance around in skirts and dresses. Now, you're covering yourself up, so what happened? What's wrong?"

I was confused. Both by his words and tone. He sounded concerned, but also pissed off about the fact he cared. I hadn't realized what he was implying. Was I upset? Had I unintentionally dressed in jeans because of the stuff I'd shoved into the back of my mind? I didn't know, but I definitely didn't want to discuss it with Slade.

"It's not your concern. You made it perfectly clear what you think of me when you left me alone." I sucked in a breath, my words starting to tremble, a wobble in my voice. I held my breath, attempting to keep the waterworks at bay. I could not cry in front of him.

Slade watched me, his jaw clenching, as it looked like he weighed his words.

"It wasn't—"

I couldn't hear any more excuses or lies, so I cut him off. "It's fine. You told me, remember? Can I go now?"

His nostrils flared as his breathing increased, and I worried I'd finally pushed the bull too much. "Careful, Peach. I'm not feeling overly generous today. I'm likely to strike out and not care who I hit in the process."

"I don't know what that's supposed to mean, Evans. You threatened me to come back here. I'm here. So, what do you want, Slade?"

He slammed his hands on the desk, and I jumped. "I told you it would only be one time. Don't come crying to me now when you can't get enough of my dick, James."

Scoffing, I rolled my eyes, masking my hurt. "Get over yourself. You think you're the best I've ever had? Puh-lease. Now, tell me what was so *important* you had to call me back here. It's starting to look like you're the one who can't get enough."

"We both know that's a lie, James. But go ahead with whatever lies you need to tell yourself," he sneered, before blanking his face into a cold mask, devoid of emotion. "Make sure to follow up with the distributor today. We're getting low on ink, and we can't have you being incompetent and messing up all of the appointments for next week. That's all. You're dismissed."

The sneer at the end gutted me, his easy dismissal of our time and of my value at this job. Slade waved his hand, pushing me out of his office, and then returned to his computer. He sat there, ignoring my existence, and I realized I just couldn't take it anymore.

An alarming calmness came over me, and I dropped my arms before turning to open the door, knowing what I had to do. Pausing with my hand on the doorknob, I tossed my grenade over my shoulder before I exited.

"Sure thing, boss. And believe what you want, but you're wrong. I fucked Simon three ways to Sunday last night, so no, I'm not thinking about your cocktail wiener at all. While we're at it, this is my formal notice that I quit."

His face had grown slack at my words, and I calmly opened the door and left his office, shutting it quietly behind me. My breaths were quick as I stepped out, and I knew I had a limited time to either make it to the alley or bathroom. Considering the slamming and throwing of things in the office behind me, I chose the alleyway. I needed to get away from that angry hornet *now*.

Bubba saw me, the tears already started streaming down my face, and reached out to comfort me, but I shook my head, not willing to stop. "I can't," I whispered. "Just, don't tell him which way I went, please."

"Sure thing, sweetie."

His face changed, and the burly biker emerged, the bear officially pissed off on my behalf. I slipped out the back just as I heard Slade's office door open, slamming against the wall. He would seriously need to fix them all at this rate. I could hear him start another rampage as he shouted at everyone in his vicinity. When I could hear him and Bubba, I bolted, not wanting to be caught in the alley, my face full of tears and my bravado dissipated.

My luck appeared to be on my side for once, and I ran into Simon as he exited the salon.

"Hey, babe, funny meeting you here." Hearing his voice, I folded myself into his arms, when he realized something was wrong. "Lenn, what's wrong? Talk to me, pretty girl."

"Can you get me out of here? I can't be here right now."

"Yeah, of course. I have a free hour. I was coming to bug you, but this works better."

He pulled me around the front, and I jumped in his car, relief surging through me at being out of there. I didn't say anything as he drove, not caring where he went as long as it was far away from Emblazed Tats. When he pulled up to the Dairy Barn, I turned to him and a smile tugged at my lips, wanting to emerge at his thoughtfulness.

"I'll be right back. Grab a picnic table, okay?"

Nodding, I wiped my eyes and headed to the table in the shade. Simon returned a few minutes later, two shakes in hand. Having your best friend as your boyfriend had definite perks. He already knew all of your favorites and what made you happy when you were sad.

"Here we go." Simon sat next to me on the bench, and I leaned my shoulder against him as his arm wrapped around me. "So, who do I need to beat up?"

Laughing through my tears, I tried not to get snot on his nice shirt. Simon dressed well, and I didn't want to mess up his look when he returned to work. "Ugh, Slade returned."

Sitting up, I took the top off my shake and used the straw to play with the whipped cream, bringing it to my lips. I could feel Simon's gaze on me, but I took my time, debating how much I wanted to reveal. The rock I'd been hiding behind kept moving, and I would need to either brave it or find a bigger rock.

"He, uh, was really rude. Demanding me to come to his office, threatening me, and such. Then acted like I didn't know how to do my job, telling me to follow up with the distributor today, which if he'd been here, would've known I did on Wednesday! Ugh, he just irritates me so much. I couldn't take it anymore. He hurt my feelings and pissed me off so bad, so I quit."

"What? Wow, I wasn't expecting you to say that. I can't imagine him saying something that would upset you that much. What was it?"

I debated with myself, the truth right there on my tongue. "He asked why I was wearing jeans and then made some derogatory comment about his dick or something."

Simon looked down, realizing also that I was indeed in jeans. "Okay, he might have a point about the jeans.

That is strange. I think I've only seen you in jeans since the summer we were fourteen two times. I didn't even think you owned a pair. Are you feeling okay? Do you regret what happened last night?"

Rolling my eyes, I scooped out some strawberry milkshake and whip this time, shoving it in my mouth before answering. "Don't be ridiculous. Slade's just projecting whatever crawled up his butt. Last night was everything, don’t let him ruin it."

"I feel like I'm missing parts or something. What exactly did he say?"

He studied me quizzically, and I panicked. Kissing him, I took him by surprise as the cold of my milkshake had made my lips and tongue frozen. Simon pulled back after a few minutes, a goofy look on his face, and I distracted him from what he really asked.

"Who cares? It's Slade. He's hated me from day one without any reason. Each time I think he's a human being, he goes and does something doubly douchey. I'm tired of working at a place where I'm not appreciated or ever get to apprentice. Can you just take me home, and I'll work out getting my car later?"

"Yeah, okay. If that's what you want. I just think you should work it out with Slade. You love your job, and I don't think you hate him as much as you protest."

"Pfft. I so do!" I huffed like a child and realized how ridiculous I sounded.

"What was your one line in the ‘15-minute-Hamlet’ sophomore year? You know in the second part when it was two minutes?" He grinned mischievously, already knowing the answer since I'd made him practice it over a thousand times with me.

"The lady doth," I mumbled.

"Was that it? No, I think it was something else. A little louder, too, please. I can't hear you with all this noise around me."

I glared, his eyes lighting up in amusement. We were practically in the country, the one road to get here was quiet at this time. The crickets and cicadas were our only audience.

"Fine! 'The lady doth protest too much, methinks'. Happy?"

Simon roared in laughter, and I stood carrying my now empty milkshake to the trash. I took it back. Best friends made horrible boyfriends because they remembered *everything*.

Simon followed a few minutes later, a smile on his face, and I couldn't stay mad at him for long. When he dropped me off at the apartment, I had to borrow his key since I remembered leaving my belongings at the shop. Simon kissed me goodbye, but I didn't linger, wanting some time to myself before I had to face the big bad wolf again.

I crashed on my bed, taking a nap for a few hours. When I woke, I managed to shower and eat some crackers before I went back to sleep. I remember Simon checking in on me at one point, but I was a zombie to the world, the emotional turmoil having zonked me.

When I woke up the next day, I felt like a million bucks. I guess I really needed to sleep. All the events of the past week and my injury had caught up to me demanding it.

Dressing, I was surprised when Simon wasn't in his room. It was 7 am, so maybe he ran out to get some breakfast or had an early client. It was the perfect time to run by the tattoo shop, no one else would be in for hours, and I could clean out my area without having to face Slade again. I didn't even feel bad it wasn't a two-week notice.

Booting up my computer since my phone was still at the shop, I ordered a Lyft and avoided clicking on my blog. The red notification blinked 200 new messages, and I couldn't deal with it. Shutting it down, I jogged down the stairs to wait for the car.

The drive was quiet, my driver not in the mood for chit chat and it was something I appreciated about them. Five stars from me! When we pulled in front of the shop, I was startled when I saw Simon's car parked there. I guess he did have an early client.

Since I didn't have my phone, there was no way for me to check, so I decided to surprise him. Popping into the salon, there weren't many people in yet since it was early, more specifically, no Crystal. Peeking around the booths, I didn't find him as I waved to the other stylists I knew. Walking out the back, I started to feel a sense of deja vu as I made my way down to the tattoo shop.

Maybe Simon was there, but I didn't know why he would be when I wasn't since I didn't think he and Slade were friends. Though, now that I thought about it, Gladys had mentioned something that bothered me that day, but that I had forgotten in my excitement. It didn't make sense though.

Either way, if Simon was here or not, I needed to grab my stuff before I ran into Tatzilla. I wanted to be able to grab my phone and solve the mystery of Simon's whereabouts. The door was unlocked, surprising me since I hadn't opened for the day yet. Pulling it open, it was the sound of shouting that first caught my attention. The shop being lit up inside the second. Fiddlesticks!

Following the noise, I stopped in my tracks when I heard my name among the shouting. I was about to charge in there and give Slade a piece of my mind when I started to understand their conversation.

"What the fuck is wrong with you, Simon?"

"Me? Have you asked yourself that question lately? There's not a week that goes by where you don't say something rude to hurt her feelings!"

"You don't understand. It's the only way."

"I don't understand! I lied to her for nine years. I'm still lying to her, in fact. So, don't tell me what I don't understand."

"Yeah, well, that was your choice. She made her decision about me and then pretends each day to act like she doesn't know."

"You're wrong about her. Lennox would never do or say the things you told me. If you took your head out of your ass, you'd see that."

"I *know* what I *know*. Drop it. *Nothing* will change how I feel now."

"Yeah, keep telling yourself that, buddy. You're one

mean word away from either crushing her heart for good or professing your love to her, if you didn't already yesterday. What was that all about? I can't believe she quit! What exactly did you say to her?"

My head was spinning with everything they were saying. I didn't understand it. They acted so familiar with one another, and yet, Simon had never told me he knew Slade on this kind of level. And what was he talking about? Slade *liking* me? Even *loving* me? The pounding in my head began to increase with each comment that didn't make sense.

"I wouldn't worry about it. You got what you always wanted."

"Not *everything*." Simon's voice was quiet on that part, and I heard the sadness there.

"Yeah, well, last I checked, that was your choice too."

I heard someone move, and I took the chance to peek into the office. Simon had been standing in front of Slade's desk, and I watched as Tatzilla walked around, getting close to Simon, breathing him in.

"How's that one working out for you?" Slade rubbed his hand down Simon's back, and I kept waiting for him to say something, to brush him off, but he didn't. In fact, he melted into Slade's touch.

"Fucking excruciating." I heard the longing then, and it *hurt*.

"So, what are we doing? Why are we making ourselves miserable?"

"I don't know anymore. It all made sense a few years ago and seemed like the best option, but I don't know now."

"Do you ever think about it?"

"Us?"

"Yeah."

"All the time."

"I feel like everything I wanted is slipping away from me, the sacrifices I made meaningless. I don't want to lose you too, Simon." As Slade talked, he continued to explore Simon's body, his front pressed into his back now. It was *intimate,* and I was both hurt and turned on by their behavior.

"Maybe it's for the best," Si whispered, his breath catching as Slade rubbed his nose across his neck, eerily similar to what he did to me yesterday.

"How can you say that?"

It was clear there was a history here I didn't understand, sending pain rippling through me. The intense emotion triggered my memories, pulling them to the surface as everything began clicking and falling into place. In a rush, the memories hit me as the events of the fateful morning flooded me.

Spilling the milk, Simon leaving, Slade telling me I was nothing to him, getting coffee only to overhear Simon say he couldn't stand to be around me, crying and falling to the floor, Slade telling me I was weak. Then passing out and hitting my head.

The anger I hadn't felt that day raged through me as everything connected. They were both liars and had been playing this game behind my back for years. I was tired of being their toy to toss around. Simon might want me, but he clearly wanted Slade too. But like a train wreck, I couldn't take my gaze off them, and I kept watching them. With each gentle touch Slade placed over Simon's body, each sigh that fell from his lips, I felt a tear slip-free.

"We *can't*. I'm with Lennox."

"Won't you miss this, though?" Slade began to nibble on Simon's neck, and I stayed there taking it, feeling owed this torment. I should've told Simon about my night with Slade.

"Of course, but I'm not single anymore. I can't lie to her when I'm with her."

"Then one last time. You can give me that."

I watched as Simon caved, Slade pulling his mouth closer. Their kiss was aggressive and hot. I didn't want to like it, but I did. So, I stood there watching as my heart broke. When clothes started to be removed, I couldn't take it anymore. Shoving the door open, it slammed against the wall, ricocheting back toward me. I stopped it with my hand, the slap ringing out and sending sharp tingles through me. It gave me the dissociation I needed from the heartbreak to focus on. As I stood in the opening, my breath came quick as I watched them scramble back from the noise, looks of shock on their faces.

"Well, aren't you two precious? Looks like you've been keeping secrets from me. How about I make it really easy for you both? I'm done, and I'm moving out. There. Now, neither of you have to worry about me or try to figure out how to 'deal' with me. Stay the H-E-double hockey sticks away from me."

Turning, I ran to my desk and grabbed my purse out of the drawer. I had a few precious moments as they scrambled to put on clothes. I shoved my phone in my pocket and grabbed a few odds and ends laying around. I was already slipping out the door when I heard the first footsteps fall behind me. I jumped into my car and, miracles of all miracles, managed to take off without stalling before either of them had even exited the building. It could be due to the locks I clicked, or the bench I moved in front of the door in my mad scramble, but who was really to say. I watched in my rearview as they managed to get out, but they were dust in my rearview by then.

Fifteen minutes later, I pulled up to a red brick one-story house, confident they'd never look here. A few motorcycles sat out front, but besides them, you'd never expect a motorcycle gang member to live inside.

At least he said he was in a gang, but knowing Bubba, he just told me that to scare or impress me depending on the day. Knocking on the door, I wasn't shocked when it took him a while to answer it. It was early, and he was a notorious late sleeper. He was wearing clothes this time at least, so that was a bonus. I'd seen a little too much of his gingersnap when I'd shown up before, unannounced.

"Sugga? What are you doing here?"

He opened the screen door wider, and the tears I'd managed to hold back started to fall, and my lip trembled. For Pete's sake! I was sick of crying

"They've been lying to me and want to be with each other."

Or that was at least what I attempted to say. Instead, it came out more like a garbled mess of "EHhendnukdnfaeuahuha," through my tears. Bubba pulled me into his arms and shut the door. Once my tears dried, I texted my mom where I was, and then I shut off my phone, not wanting Simon to get desperate and try to use the 'find my friend' feature.

Bubba made me some breakfast and let me cry on his shoulder all day while we watched classic romance movies together. When he left to go to work, he promised not to tell them where I was, although I wouldn't put it past him to cave. So, I discreetly turned my phone back on and used the 'find my friend' function myself. Thankfully, Simon wasn't at home. I ignored where it showed him, not wanting to wallow in anymore grief today.

Quickly, I made my way to the apartment and picked up a few things, throwing them into a duffle bag. It was time I got out of dodge. Pulling out of the complex, the thought I tried to ignore surfaced. *Simon was at Slade's.*

My heart was crushed. My job and friendship were gone. There was only one place a brokenhearted soul like me belonged.

Nashville.

Ready or not, here I come.

I'm so ready to be done with school. I don't even know what I want to do with my life, just to be out there living it. Maybe I will travel, see the world? I don't care as long as it's away from here. My brother and I are officially not speaking. He'd been keeping something big from me. And let's just say, when I found out, I was furious. He violated the sanctity of brothers, and I don't know if I can trust him ever again.

Maybe it's that I've been sharing everything my whole life, and this one thing I didn't want to share. Perhaps that makes me a bad brother. But he's had everything come so easy to him, and I finally start to do well in one area, and he has to take it? Be glad your brother is younger, he can't hurt you like mine did.

If we were to meet in real life, what would we do? I often wonder about this. I'll see something cool and think, 'oh, I wish Nox could see this'. Or hear a funny joke, a song, or draw a new picture and I find myself wishing I could share it with you. Does that make me a creep?

I hung your picture up and now, I stare at it every night. I think of us sharing a night sky, and what that would be like. It's my favorite part of the day. I like that word too. Nocturne. It kind of reminds me of you, my Noxturne.

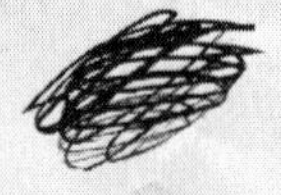

Maybe we can write things we'd do together, so it feels like we are. These could be in addition to our three questions or in place of one. I'll go first.

1. This week I wish I could show you this new store that opened. Arizona is weird, but this place is cool. It's a living art exhibit and anyone can go in and paint, draw, sculpt, spray paint, whatever they want on the walls. It's collaborative and each person adds on to the next person. I drew half a heart with wings and fire and stars, thinking about how you could draw the second half. They'd be different but connected. I like thinking that there would be a symbol joining us together even if we never meet.

2. If you had three wishes, what would your first one be? I'd wish for the impossible, for my mother to still be alive. It was hard enough her and Dad divorcing, it was even worse when she died 2 years later. I often wonder if I hadn't said anything about her cheating if she would've lived longer. I don't know what I'd do with the other two.

3. What's something you wish you knew how to do? So, I don't know how to ride a bike. I kind of wish I knew how.

On winged hearts, I'll meet you
under the stars, a song in my heart
only you can hear.

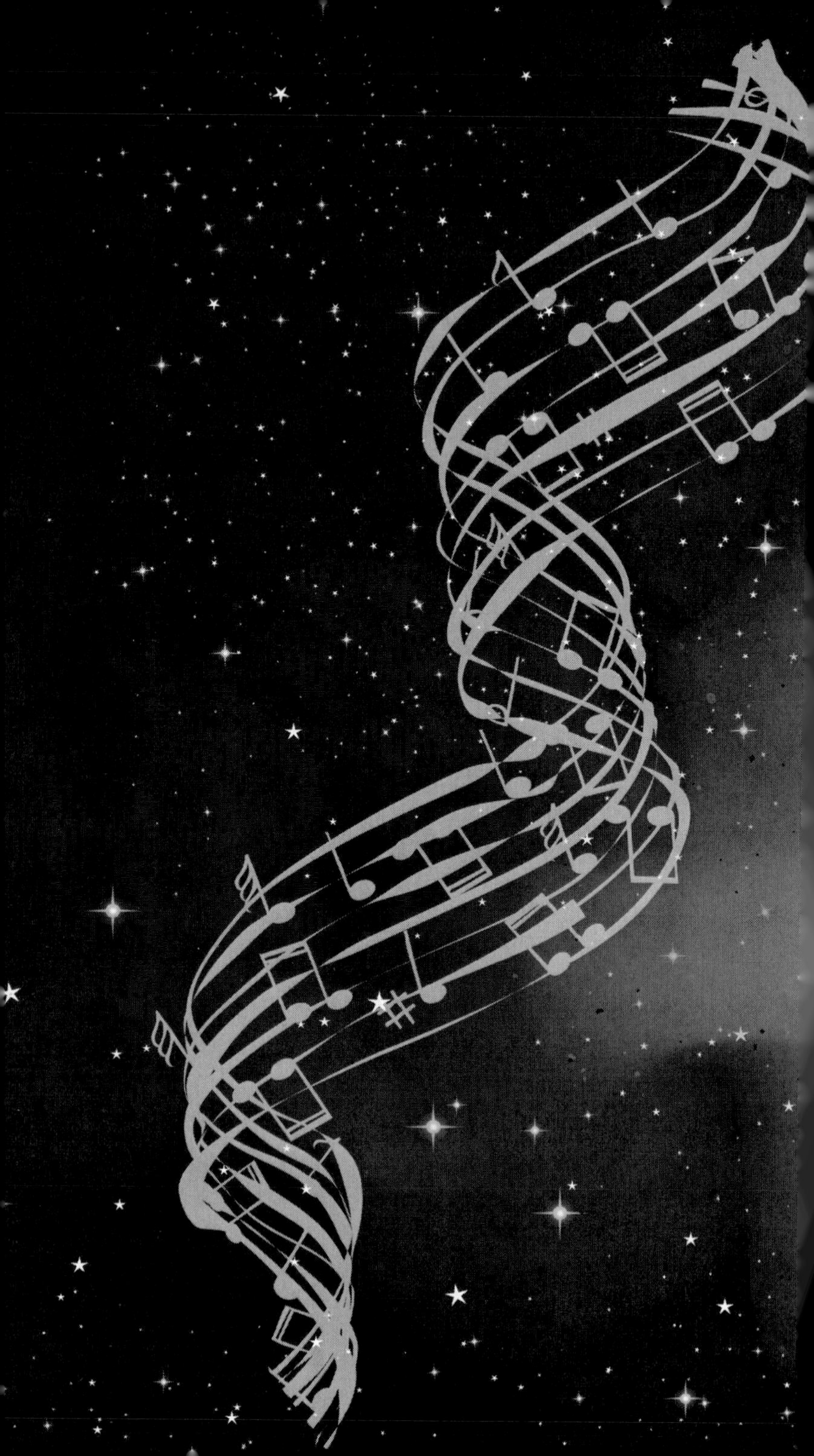

Chapter Sixteen

LENNOX

"LJ, your next appointment is here. I'll get them prepped."

"Thanks, Ethan."

I didn't turn my head but mumbled out my gratitude as I focused on the client in front of me. I was filling in the piece I'd been working on for a couple of weeks now, and today was the last part.

"You've gotten pretty busy. How long have you been at Equinox Ink now?"

"Oh, um, about two months, I think. It's all kind of blended together. I started in August, so whatever month it is now," I laughed dryly.

"Well, it's October, so yeah, two months," he chuckled. "You're good. I'm glad I found you when I did. I'm digging this full sleeve. I'm gonna have to get you to do my leg next. I'm still debating what I want."

"Yeah, no problem. Just let Ethan know and he can get you scheduled," I said distractedly, looking over the arm. "Well, I think that's it."

Turning off the gun, I looked back at the full image. It was one of the most intricate pieces I'd ever done and had taken me a couple of sessions to do. It was full of flowers, moons, and trees with a panther hidden in it. The colors popped, and the eyes glared back at me. I looked up, smiling at the man, pleased with myself.

"Thanks so much for trusting me with this beautiful piece."

"It's no problem, sugga. How about I take you out for dinner as a thank you?"

Shutting down my face, I adopted the expression I've worn since I got into Nashville. Fake kindness.

"Bless your heart," I gushed, "that's so kind of you to offer, but I'm afraid I'm a taken woman."

Smiling, I got up, stretching my legs and arms from the cramped position I'd been sitting in for the past hour. No one ever mentioned the weird, uncomfortable maneuvers you did while tattooing someone.

"I'll send Trudy over to double check my work and then Ethan will wrap it up for you. Thanks again, hun."

Quickly, I left the area, needing to get some air. What was it about guys, that the moment I wasn't interested in any sort of dating, they all started asking me out? I was beginning to think it was men who wanted to date the unattainable ones and not women. Popping into the break room, I grabbed a bottle out of the fridge, the cold water cooling my throat as it went down.

"You okay?"

Nodding, I kept drinking the water, not caring if any of it slipped out. The panic eased some as the water rushed down, and I pulled it back, wiping my mouth with the back of my hand.

"Yeah, I'm good," I answered, not turning to

acknowledge whoever was behind me. I headed back out to my next client, a smile plastered on my face.

Day in and day out, I did the same dance. Sassy, but polite with a smile on my face, and my accent exaggerated, I pushed through to the next day. I'd learned really quick I could get away with almost anything if I said it 'southern' enough. Most tourists wanted that true Nashville experience, after all.

After a few nights in a motel, my dad was able to find me a place after he'd called around and found out an old buddy of his had a place to rent over a tattoo shop. It was perfect timing as I'd been one night away from caving after itchy sheets, crappy water pressure, and cockroaches and heading back to Bowling Green with my tail tucked between my legs. Thankfully, it turned out to be the lucky break I needed and helped me prove to myself I could do this.

Once I was settled, I couldn't help but peek into the shop below, curious about the place. It wasn't as nice as Emblazed Tats, but it had some oddly strange similarities with the designs and layout. After a few days of poking about, Ethan started talking to me. He'd just taken over as manager for the store and once I'd shown him my designs, he agreed to give me an interview.

Within a few days, I had a willing subject to tattoo and an abbreviated apprenticeship under Trudy. Ethan and her agreed since I'd already worked in a shop for three years, I didn't need the normal apprenticeship of learning the ropes before I started, so they dumped me in headfirst. When walk-ins came in and they were willing to try a beginner for a lower cost, I got to practice. The shop had a good Instagram following, posting all their tats, and before long, I was designing and tattooing on a regular basis. I'd even started being requested by name. It felt nice to be validated in my efforts and that I was potentially good at something.

Overall, Nashville was good to me. Despite my heartbreak and missing my family, I was making it on my own for the first time in my life. No best friend, no parents, or an overbearing boss to tell me what to do. Each day, I made my own decisions, and I was doing something I'd wanted to do forever, no longer letting fear hold me back.

Granted it was lonely at times, but relationships hadn't ever done me any favors. I'd accepted I wasn't the type of girl to get a 'happily ever after', and as hard as it was to stop the wishful thinking and hoping, in the end, it was better this way. If I didn't wish for something, it couldn't be taken away from me.

Book boyfriends would have to suffice. I hadn't blogged since leaving, shutting down my site to avoid reading all the messages, but my kindle account got a hefty workout. And while I devoured my new favorite genre of reverse harem romances, I knew my life wasn't meant to be that way.

Checking my watch, I sighed, and greeted my next client as I headed into my cubby space. This was my life now. Tattoos and Books.

I tried to convince myself I was happy with it.

"GIVE a round of applause for our next singer, the one and only, LJ Star."

Smiling, I gripped the microphone, nerves constantly overtaking me every time I stepped onto the stage. I still got incredibly bad stage fright, but it was something I pushed myself to do, needing the outlet. I'd also found I craved the adrenaline of singing, so despite almost passing out from nerves each week, I showed up at this bar and sang. The band began playing behind me, and I found myself relaxing more and more as I sank into the music, the rhythm a balm to my heart.

The first note belted out of me, and I swayed to the music as it flowed through my body, sinking into the lyrics. The emotion was heavy in this one and I felt each and every word as I sang Lady Antebellum, "Need You Now."

Open mic night had become my safe haven to explore, even if it wasn't what I wanted to do with my life. I enjoyed it, and it filled the empty void my day to day had become. I never realized how much of my life had been wrapped around Simon until he was no longer in it.

He'd tried to call me, sent a bunch of messages, but they all went unanswered. I couldn't look at them, knowing I'd cave if I did. It was cowardly of me, but I also felt I deserved it in a way. Both as a punishment for not making the best choices in life, and as a chance to spread my wings on my own and see if I could fly without him there to catch me. Simon had become my safety net, and I often chose to hide instead of facing things, and while running was what led me here, I didn't regret it.

Music and singing were helping me find myself and had become the only moments I let myself feel. The song ended, and I stepped off the stage, the crowd cheering as I walked through them, offering me congrats. I found his smiling face at the back, the same one who'd been my comfort and biggest surprise in this city. His blue eyes sparkled, making me fall into their cool waters as they always did, and I found myself smiling in return.

Thane had wanted to pursue me and date when he found me one night alone at a bar. I'd committed one of my no-no's by drinking myself into a stupor alone, but was too heartbroken to care about safety. Thankfully, he'd been there to make sure I made it home safely. I ended up spilling the whole sordid affair with Simon and his brother, and he'd been kind and listened. After that he'd agreed to be friends for a time, and I was grateful. I didn't think I could've handled anything more.

But here lately, it seemed like he was running out of patience and wanted more. I was trying to rekindle the spark I had with him. He'd give me a look and I'd wonder if it could be more. Sadly, it didn't seem to be moving in that direction. The spark was dead, my hormones taking a backseat to my broken heart. I felt bad and I wanted to like him. Maybe it would be worth a try to get over them? It had been there before. It wouldn't just vanish, would it? The questions of uncertainty were what bothered me the most.

"Amazing as always, my southern princess."

Giving him a quick hug, I tucked my shorter hair behind my ear, smoothing it over my piercings, a nervous habit I'd developed. My hair was back to my natural color, and now chin length. It had been another attempt to find myself.

I'd changed my name, my hair, and my habits. Something had to stick eventually. I hoped it would keep me hidden longer and give me a chance to figure things out. I knew they'd come for me at some point, but my father and mother had sworn themselves to secrecy, promising not to tell Simon even under duress.

"Was that song about him, or should I say *them*?"

Shrugging my shoulders, I took the shot off the table, a new habit, my days of not drinking behind me. It had become so familiar now to toss the tequila back at the end of a song and the liquid slid down easily, maybe a little too easy, and I sank back into my chair to wait until my next song. A few of the usuals sang, and I zoned out, debating my next number. Thane left but returned a few minutes later and brought me honey tea for my throat, and I smiled in thanks. He'd gotten used to my zone moments where I shut out everything.

Blowing on it, I decided to be sociable tonight and not shut him out. "So, how was the clinic today? See any cute dogs for me yet?"

"No, not yet." He grinned. Thane was still the most attractive man I'd ever met, and while I would sometimes still get distracted by his beauty, I never felt like I wanted to jump his bones right then and there. But maybe, that was the point. Maybe all my dating relationships had been disasters because they were built on lust instead of love?

Even though I didn't want to admit that was wrong, I knew it was. I had loved Simon, and the one I didn't like to remember. Pushing aside my morbid memories, I focused back to the present.

"When are you going to let me come visit, anyway? I want to see the amazing Dr. Thane Evans in action!"

"Oh, you know how it is. It's hard to have people there that aren't certified. One day, when it's closed, I'll take you by. I promise."

Drinking my tea, I nodded, the same answer he'd given me before. "You coming over after? Or you need to get home?"

"Oh, I might be able to hang for a while."

"Cool. Your roommate still giving you trouble?"

"Yeah. I need to find a new place to live. I hate that you can't hang out there."

"It's fine. My place is closer to work anyway," I laughed. I didn't think it was weird I'd never been over to his place, but after two months, it was starting to feel that way, like maybe he had a secret family or something. It was probably just my overactive imagination, my broken heart seeing lies and deceit everywhere even when there wasn't.

"Give it up for Tom and his lovely rendition. Now, our next singer tonight at The Roof is a newbie. He's asked to remain nameless, so let's give him a warm welcome."

The lights stayed down as the music started, and

only a faint one lit the singer with a guitar on a stool. They were mostly in shadow, hiding their face from view. The piano started, the chords ringing out, and I recognized the song immediately. My interest perked up, and I leaned forward, wanting to be nearer the stage.

"You know them?" Thane asked, an edge to his voice.

"No, I don't think so, but the song…" I trailed off as the first note sung out, my voice stuck in my throat at the beauty of the sound. The words pierced the air, and I found myself barely sitting on my chair, the richness in their voice painful and deep as they sang Lewis Capaldi's, "Someone You Loved."

As they sang about heartbreak and love, I was mesmerized by their voice. Something familiar whispered in my mind, a tear rolling down my cheek as the song ended, and somehow, I knew it was Slade.

"It's your brother," I whispered. I turned to Thane, but he was no longer there. I looked at the door, and I barely saw his head pass through before he was out of sight. Picking up my phone, I called him as I headed to the back area, where I could hear better.

"Hello?"

"Hey, why did you leave?"

"I'm sorry, I thought you heard me. I got an emergency text. I've gotta go in. Dog in critical condition."

"Oh my God. I'm so sorry. Of course, be careful, and good luck saving the dog. Let me know how it goes and I'll talk to you tomorrow."

"Yeah, tomorrow."

"You sure you're okay? Are you upset about the dog? Or… your brother?"

"I gotta go. Bye, Cherry."

"Okay, yeah, bye."

The dial tone hit my ears before the last word left me. Wiping my eyes, I shook off the weird feeling the call had left me in and the emotional overhaul the song Slade had sung. As the heartbreak of the music faded, my anger returned. That wasn't fair. He couldn't come in here, to my open mic and sing a song thinking it would make everything okay. It didn't work that way.

Knowing what I had to do, I walked over to the emcee and gave him my number. I was up after Carrie, who was on now. I didn't see Slade behind the stage or in the crowd, but I knew he was there, and I bet Simon was with him. It was time they listened to *me*. All these years, and all the lies they'd fed me… Well, I had something to say about it.

"Alright folks, we get our last treat from crowd favorite, LJ Star, now. Let's remind her how much we like her singing for us."

Walking on stage, I smiled and waved, confidence filling me unlike ever before. I took hold of the microphone, ready to say my piece finally. Months I'd been wallowing, feeling gutted for the lies and secrets they held. They couldn't come here now and try to win me over with a sad song. That might've worked on 'before Lennox', but I wasn't that girl anymore.

"Good evening, folks. How are we doing tonight? Are y'all enjoying all the music? What about that new performer? Wasn't it just heartbreaking? Yeah, I thought so too. So, this one goes out to him and his friend."

Placing the microphone back into the stand, I glared daggers at the audience and belted out my anthem via The Chicks', "Not Ready To Make Nice."

The anger gave me a voice, and I felt vindicated in my performance. So many times I'd been told to 'sit down, be nice' or 'that's just how it is'. Well, I was tired of playing nice and accepting that my feelings weren't valid. When the song ended, there was an uproarious applause, and I almost did a mic drop, an emotional strength surging through me. I felt powerful as I walked off the stage, confidence rising up in me.

I wouldn't fold.

Nothing they could say would make me crumble.

He was waiting for me at the end of the hallway, and for a second, I faltered. It was unfair how good he looked. His hair shined under the lights, the silver a perfect shade. The only assurance I got that he might've missed me was his face looked like crap, his eyes full of grief.

"Lenn, can we, please, talk?"

"I think I said everything on that stage."

"No, Peach. I don't think you have."

His voice came from behind me, and I sucked in a breath. They had me cornered, not willing to let me escape this time. Folding my arms, I leaned back against the wall so he couldn't surprise me. Slade glanced at me, and, in a weird synchronization, they moved, facing off with me. Rolling my eyes, I decided to get this over with as quickly as possible.

"Fine. *Talk*."

"In order to do that, Lenn, we should head somewhere quiet."

Huffing, I stormed off, realizing I wouldn't get to sleep or get rid of them until this was over. Waving at the bartender as I passed, I slapped a tip down for my drink. "Bye, Bear. See you next week."

"Later, LJ. Be safe."

He eyed the two men behind me, his face asking if I was okay. I nodded, smiling as I kept walking. It was comforting to know I could make my own friends. I didn't talk as we walked out onto the strip, their footsteps heavy behind me. I could almost feel their eyes boring into my back and while I didn't necessarily want them staring at my butt, I knew the leather pants and jacket I wore accentuated all my curves, bringing a smile to my face.

My wardrobe, another big change. Since Slade had made a comment, I found myself not wanting to wear my normal dresses and instead, went down the hardcore, dark, bad mama jama route with dark jeans, leather, and old band t-shirts. In a way, I blended better with my peers, helping me fade into the background. It was easier in the background.

We made it to the shop, taking the back entrance and headed up the stairs. I didn't check once if they were following, that was their problem if they couldn't keep up. Once I was inside, I walked to the fridge and grabbed some water. I didn't offer them any, not feeling very hostessy at the moment and took up a spot on the couch, or well, the whole couch. Kicking my legs up, I made it impossible for them to join me, leaving their choice between a hardback chair or old recliner that smelled of refried beans.

Simon decided to sit in the chair, and Slade remained standing. It didn't surprise me, and I rolled my eyes as I twisted the cap off my water and took a long swig. When I was done, I set my eyes on them, ready for this to get over with. When they still didn't speak, I groaned, throwing my head back on the couch for good measure.

"For Pete's sake, we're here, so why don't y'all start talking already?"

Slade smirked, and I hated how it instantly made my panties wet. I didn't want to admit it, but from the moment I saw both of them, I'd been panting. At least I had confirmation that part of me wasn't broken. I just didn't see Thane that way anymore. It was a shame, but chemistry couldn't be faked. It would be so much easier if I could choose him over these two.

Slade grabbed another chair from around the table, spinning it as he sat in it backward, folding his arms on it.

"First, *Nox*, I think it's time you admit the truth."

I looked at him strangely, wondering why he called me that. How did he know that name? He stared, waiting for something, apparently wanting to make this the most difficult conversation in history.

"The truth about what? And why are you calling me Nox?"

"See, I told you, man. It wasn't her. It couldn't have

been," Simon piped up, turning to Slade with a pleading look, only confusing me more.

Slade gritted his teeth, ignoring him as he strained to keep himself in check before speaking again. I took another swallow of water which ended up being a mistake as he spoke his following words right as I did.

"So, you haven't known for the past three years that I'm *Blaze*?"

Spitting the water everywhere, I turned to him, my mouth hanging open, and shouted, *"What the fuck?"*

Blaze

I guess in a way I am lucky to not have that type of relationship with my brother. But I can't help but wonder if there's something you can do to fix things? Family is special and you shouldn't throw it away without trying. But I also don't know what occurred, so ignore it if it really is unforgivable. I just always have hope that people can be redeemed.

My best friend says it's a flaw I have. If I'm going to have one, I'll take believing in people over collecting toenails any day.

I think I feel that way because of my mom and the lies people say about her that aren't true. I think people see the version of others that is easiest for them. They don't have to question their beliefs if they can cast you as the villain. Small town gossip can be pretty grueling, and I've had my fair share of rumor mills. From someone who has made mistakes or been the victim of others, it's not always intentional or easy being on the other side.

I like this idea, our meetings in space! How cool would it be to have that as a tattoo? It would be like a friendship necklace, but forever. You have one heart and I have the other. I hope were friends forever. I think my life would be empty without you.

1. So, there's this place called the Dairy Barn and it's my favorite place to go. I'd take you there and blow your mind with the best milkshake ever! Trust me, it's amazing.

2. My wish is about my mom too. I'd wish for my mom to not struggle with her mental illness. The others, to be able to sing on stage, and to fall in love.

3. A skill I wish I knew… Well, I wish I knew how to skateboard, or play the guitar. Two things just for you!

4. What are your thoughts on piercings? I decided to pierce my upper ear the other day and it wasn't too bad. I now have three holes in my ear. So, fancy. I think I want to learn though. I think they're sexy on guys too.

5. Would you rather never find love, or lose love? This is hard… heartbreak isn't fun, but the reward is worth it, right? I hope I never give up on love.

I'll be waiting,

Chapter Seventeen

LENNOX

Three and half years ago

"I CAN'T BELIEVE we're finally going to meet Blaze after all these years," I beamed at Simon in the mirror as I perfected my cat-eye. He was lounging on my bed in his usual pose, reading a comic.

"Mmm-hmm."

"What? You aren't curious?"

"Maybe?" he shrugged, still not meeting my eyes. Turning in my chair, I leaned against the back, taking him in.

"What's up? You're all, I dunno know. *Shifty*."

"Shifty?"

"Yeah, shifty. You've barely said two words since you've been here. Do you not want to go?"

He sighed, sitting his comic down and turning, his legs now on the floor. Bracing his elbows on his knees, he looked at me. "It's not that, Lenn. It's just… I don't know. Something feels off. Why now? What's the cause?"

I shrugged, not wanting to admit the reason for the sudden meeting, my last letter to him a swan song. When he'd replied back instantly, asking to meet, hope filled me at the chance. But I couldn't admit that to Simon.

"He said he's in town. What does it matter?"

I tried to hide the stars in my eyes, mostly because I didn't want them to be noticeable, but also, I wasn't supposed to have stars in my eyes. I shouldn't be hoping this was the moment I'd dreamed about finally happening with my pen pal, not now anyway. Fortunately, I'd gotten good at concealing my feelings. Between Blaze and Simon, I was a closet full of repressed emotions.

I knew feeling this way would only get me in trouble, and that I shouldn't. I did have a boyfriend, after all. A perfectly good one too, a great one in fact. Almost as if he knew my mind had started wandering, Duncan walked into my bedroom, reminding me of his presence.

"Hey, LJ."

I sighed, hearts leaving me as I took him in. He was tall, dark, and handsome, the whole freaking package. He was the epitome of everything you'd want in a boyfriend. Duncan was attentive, sweet, and thought I hung the moon. I'd met him through my dad, surprisingly, and we'd been dating for almost a year. He was a few years older than me and a rookie cop.

I didn't know what our future held, but I could see babies and white picket fences with Duncan. I just needed to get rid of this crush I'd held for my pen pal for the past eight years. It was the one thing I believed holding me back from saying yes to Duncan. I'd already accepted Simon wouldn't happen. He was gay, and there was nothing I could do about it.

"Hey, Duncan," I cooed, the loved-up sound leaving me. Immediately, I felt guilty for the lingering feelings I had for Blaze. Duncan bent over and kissed me on the cheek before turning to Simon.

"Hey, bro. What's up?"

They did the classic bro handshake, and Duncan sat down next to Simon on the bed. They'd been friends before Duncan and I started dating, having met through some nerd convention they were both into. I was just glad their relationship hadn't changed when we'd started dating. Simon had even given me his seal of approval. Duncan and I's relationship was the type of dating experience I'd always wanted, and after the disastrous love life I've had up until now, I felt I was owed.

"So, y'all excited about meeting your friend? What's his name again?"

"It's Blaze. Or well, that's what we've known him as. It could be something completely different."

"Well, I think it's cool you're getting to do this. It's a long time to have a friendship."

"Yeah, it is. I'm excited too. What about you, Si?"

"Oh, yeah. Me too," he answered distractedly. He was on his phone, and when he felt my stare, he looked up, guilt there. "Uh, I need to take care of something. I'll meet you back in an hour to leave, okay?"

"Yeah, sure," I frowned. "See you in an hour."

Simon left, and I watched him walk out the door, concern warring with my excitement. Duncan's words broke my stare off with his retreating figure, and I turned back to him.

"Everything okay?"

"Yeah, I hope so."

I twisted back around and finished getting ready while Duncan regaled me with one of his funnier moments this week as a cop. He was always telling me stories, which made me feel like I was part of it.

"Wow, LJ, you look hot. You sure I don't have anything to worry about?"

I walked over, wrapping my arms around his neck, my hands trailing up it. At this level, we were almost eye to eye. He smiled, and placed his hand on my hips, but dropped them down to my thighs, traveling up the back of my legs.

"You have nothing to worry about, babe. You know I like to dress up, so this isn't something new. Besides," I whispered, "you're the one I'm coming home to later. It's okay still if I stay over, right?"

"Mmhm," he mumbled, nuzzling into my neck. I wanted to give in to him, but I knew Si would be back soon, and I didn't want to redo my makeup. Pulling away, I kissed him briefly and left him with a wink as I walked off. I watched as he adjusted himself with a cocky smile on his face.

"I can't wait until *later*. I love you, LJ. You're my shining star."

"Love you too, Dunc."

I blew him another kiss, and he caught it, making me giggle. I was still waiting for the other shoe to drop or for his warts to appear, but the more time I spent with him, I just kept finding out how perfect he was. He followed me out, and I waved when he headed to his car, and I got into Simon's, who had just pulled up at the curb. Centering myself, I looked at my best friend, remembering his earlier weird behavior. He seemed back to normal now. I smiled when he glanced over, ready to meet Blaze.

"Duncan good?"

"Yeah. He's the best."

"I can't believe how cool he's being about everything."

"What's there not to be cool about?"

"Come on, Lenn. Even I could tell you had a crush on Blaze."

"Well, yeah. *Crush*. I'm curious to see if that translates in person, but it doesn't mean I'm just going to throw everything away. I think a small part of me has been holding back from Duncan because of this unknown, so now I get to answer it. It'll be what I need to settle down, start a family and all that, next year after I graduate college."

"If you say so."

"I do say so."

"Well, okay. Let's hit the road. You have the place we're meeting him at?"

"Yeah." I glanced down at my phone, a new message coming through. "Oh wait, looks like they were full, so we're to meet them at the Tavern instead."

Writing back, I smiled and tucked my phone away. Time to meet the last whisper on my heart, and open myself up to the future before me.

Based on the ring I found last week in Duncan's drawer, it was just around the corner.

THE WATER GLASS had officially soaked the napkin it sat on, the condensation long gone. It was an hour past when he said he'd be here. Simon had dropped me off, wanting to let me have time first, but as I sat alone at the table, the pitying looks from the waitstaff, I regretted his thoughtfulness. At least if he'd been here too, I wouldn't look like the stood-up loser I currently was. I picked up my phone again, sending one last message, the others mocking me at their unread status in the chat app.

ME: Hey, I'm here. I'll grab a table.
ME: Everything okay? I'm the one in the star dress, your necklace around my neck.
ME: I'm starting to get worried. Are you lost? The one on Broadway was the right one, correct?
ME: Did something happen? Blaze? I'm worried.
ME: It's been an hour. I'm guessing you're not coming.
ME: It's really shitty of you to stand me up like this. You could've just told me you didn't want to meet. It was your idea, after all.
ME: I don't think I can talk to you anymore. I want friends who will respect me and honor their words. I thought I knew you. Goodbye, Blaze

Motioning to the waiter, I grabbed my check and paid the bill. I'd ordered an appetizer at least, so I wasn't starving. A text came through right as I stood up to go. With my heart in my throat, I opened it.

> **Blaze**: Wow, I can't believe you showed! Guess I lost that bet. Did you really think I cared? Honey, I've been catfishing you for years. I don't care about you. Simon was in on it too. Just ask him. He's never stopped writing to me. It wasn't even me the whole time. I let my friends write to you too, and we laughed at your letters. I used to read them every morning over the intercom about the poor little country girl with the crazy mother who fell in love with her gay best friend and the imaginary boy across the world. You're pathetic, and I'm tired of pretending. Smile, you're on camera.

Tears streamed down my face, and I looked up but didn't see anyone. He was probably lying, hoping I'd make a scene or something. Wiping my cheeks, I held my head high like my momma taught me, and I walked out of there. At least it had done the one thing I'd wanted—removed all doubt, leaving me open to Duncan.

Simon entered the restaurant as I was exiting, and the pain I felt in my heart splintered. When he saw my face, he rushed to me, reaching for my arms, but I stepped back, not wanting him to touch me.

"Lenn, what is it? Tell me, what's wrong."

"Is it true?"

"Is *what* true, Lenn?"

"You've been writing to Blaze this whole time behind my back?"

His face dropped, the guilt evident, and I watched him swallow hard before nodding. "Yes, but I can explain."

"No need, Blaze did it for you. I'll find my own way home."

Running out into the crowd, I lost myself amongst the throngs of people, blending in as I weaved, my short stature aiding me in my escape. When I found a Honkey Tonk bar with music playing, I ducked in, I found a quiet hallway and hoped I'd lost Simon. Pulling out my phone, I leaned against the wall and called the one man I could count on.

"Hello?"

"Dad?"

"Pumpkin, is that you? What's wrong?"

I slunk down and cried as I tried to explain everything to my dad through my tears. After a few minutes, he managed to cut me off.

"Okay, Lennox, listen to me. I'm going to grab Duncan and send him to get you, okay?"

"But he has to work. It's fine. I'll just grab a car or something."

"I don't want you riding with a stranger for that long, especially if you're upset. Just grab a drink wherever you are, and I'll send him to you as quickly as possible. It might be a few hours, but he'll come."

"Okay, thanks, Dad. You're the best."

"No problem, pumpkin. Be safe. I love you."

"Love you too."

Walking to the bar, I grabbed a stool and ordered a drink. It was time to get wasted. Nothing like a broken heart to make you want to drink.

SEVERAL DRINKS LATER, things were feeling better, and all my tears had dried. I'd even gotten on stage and sung a karaoke song with a new friend I'd made. Who needed long-distance friends anyways? Because, apparently, I was a freaking riot, making friends all over the place. I even bumped into an angry bad boy earlier, and he'd smiled at me, saving me from falling on my face. I was winning at life.

My new friend I'd been dancing with pulled me closer, whispering in my ear. His hot breath fanned over my skin, and I didn't like it. I tried to push back, but his arms were locked. Letting go, I leaned in to hear him over the music, hoping he'd let go once he got out what he wanted to say.

"You're so pretty. Want to come back to my place?"

"No, that would be bad. I have a boyfriend. I've already told you that, Chad," I slurred.

"Oh, come on. I know girls like you just say that. You don't really have one."

"But I do. I swear."

"Nuh-uh. Come on, I'll show you a good time."

"Nope, can't do it."

"Don't be a bitch. Besides, you're all over me. I

could do whatever I wanted, and no one would believe you otherwise."

Fear curled up my throat, peeking through the alcohol haze I'd been in. I'd thought it'd been fun, flirting a little, just having a good time. Apparently, I'd been sending signals I didn't want to send, and now, I was stuck with *this* guy.

Just when I worried about what to do, the bad boy from earlier appeared, my tattooed angel saving me again.

"I think you should leave her alone."

His menacing stare was enough to make the douche back up, scurrying off the floor and the relief I felt was palpable.

"Looks like you saved me again." I grinned, the alcohol sloshing around in my body. A vague recollection of the Tattoo Angel giving me a drink, followed by one from Simon when he found me, and I threw them back one by one. I'd had so many by that point, it was hard to keep count. When Simon tried to talk to me, I ran off again, not ready to face anything else tonight.

Everything after that began to bleed together, the haze of the night a blur, and I began blinking in and out of consciousness, only aware in pockets of moments. The next time I came to, I was in the hallway, braced against the wall, a guy I didn't recognize leaning over me, his hand around my throat. Though it was hard to tell who he was, his face swirling in front of me as he became two.

"No, leave me alone. I need to go back out there. I have a friend coming. My boyfriend, too."

"Now, honey. You can drop the act. I know there isn't a boyfriend."

Panic crawled up my throat. This was bad. I was alone. I'd run away from Simon, and Duncan hadn't appeared yet. I didn't know what time it was, but it felt longer than it should've been for him to arrive.

I tried to push the guy off me, but my arms went weak, my legs heavy, and I found myself falling back against the wall, unable to move as he loomed over me.

"Now, be a good girl, and just take it, why don't you?"

"No," I slurred again, trying to stop him, but my body wouldn't move.

"I think the girl told you no. I'd back away if I were you."

"Fucking slut, fine. She's not that hot anyway. Too fat for my taste, they're just usually the easiest to bag."

"You're disgusting. I'd leave before I use your skull to paint the hallway, buddy."

The guy scoffed, dropping me, and I fell to the floor, my head hitting the wall as I went down. Blinking, the man in front of me came into focus, his blue eyes feeling safe and familiar, a warm feeling spreading through me.

"Hey, gorgeous. Are you okay?"

"I dunno. He wasn't very nice. I can't feel my legs."

"Okay, just wait here, and I'll grab some water, okay."

Nodding, I hit my head against the wall again. "Ow."

He chuckled as he got up. "Be careful, gorgeous. Don't hurt yourself."

"Do I know you?" slipped from my tongue before everything spun around me, the music too loud and the lights too bright. When a shadow appeared over me, I felt relief as the lights dimmed. When a hand smacked my cheek to rouse me, I blinked open my eyes, expecting to find the kind stranger. Instead, it was my tattooed angel, come to save me again. Looking at him full-on, my breath caught, his dark eyes intense.

"Tattoo Man. Ow, that hurt. You're not so nice right now, but you're really hot. Are you here to save me again?"

My eyes started to close again, whatever I'd drunk affected me fully now, and the world kept going black. I felt a slap again, and my eyes popped open. He'd bent down, eye to eye now as he stared intently at me, an emotion I didn't understand on his face, too drunk to try.

"Starry Nox?"

I raised an eyebrow, or attempted to, at his question, the movement unnatural as my faculties had left me. I went to ask a question, but instead, when I opened my mouth, vomit spewed all over me. I watched in horror as his face turned up, disgust written there. He let me go just as the stranger came out, giving him a strange look.

I fell to the ground as they talked, words exchanged over my head I couldn't make out, and I barely remembered muttering, "jerk," before passing out.

When I woke up next, it was to the sounds of sirens wailing, a clicking sound in the background, and screams. Someone was jolting me, trying to get my attention, and I realized I was hanging upside down.

Blinking, I came to find myself hanging from my seat belt, Duncan under me, begging me to wake up. I reached up a hand to cup his cheek, and I saw the relief in his eyes at my gesture. The movement hurt though, liquid running down my face, altering my ability to see him fully. I blinked, attempting to clear my view as he cut something away, and then my body free fell into his arms. Cradling me, he pulled me out of what I now realized was wreckage. The world spun, the colors not making sense, and a constant ringing sound in my ears, as I tried to come round to stay present.

More wetness dripped down my face, obscuring my eyes completely, and my arms and legs hurt. It was challenging to breathe as well. The air became clearer as Duncan moved me, though the jostling hurt with each step. When he cleared the car, I didn't remember being in, he kissed me, not caring about the blood. Tears streamed down his face as he spoke to me, but I couldn't make out his words as he handed me off to the paramedic.

I reached my hand out, wanting to bring him with me, needing him by my side. I watched his lips move again, but I still couldn't make out any sound, the ringing overwhelming me, a rushing of blood to my head. Everything happened so quickly after that.

Duncan never took his eyes off me, speaking to me even though I didn't know what he said. He walked backward, blowing me a kiss, not paying attention to where he was when a car jumped the barricade. I tried to scream, to shout, but nothing was moving or working, no sound leaving my mouth, just silence.

I watched in horror as he blew me one last kiss, not realizing the danger ahead. He turned to do whatever he'd been going to do when the car struck him, his body flying up in the air before landing in an odd position on the road. It all played out in slow motion, and I was powerless to stop it.

Hands shoved me down before something was injected into me, my eyes closing as my tears slipped free, and a prayer that it had all been a horrible dream.

WAKING THE FOLLOWING MORNING, I knew my wish hadn't come true. This nightmare was all too real, the pain in my body proving it. My mother's sniffles were the first sound I heard, the beeping of the monitor the next. I tried to lift my arm, but the cast on it stopped me, noticing the one on my leg next. When I opened my eyes, I found my mother and Simon close to my bed, holding my hands. I didn't care anymore about the stupid fight I had with him, the reason not seeming as important anymore. I wanted comfort from my best friend, to believe what I'd witness wasn't real.

When they both took me into their arms, we cried together, and I knew I couldn't deny it any longer.

Duncan was gone.

When Dr. Barnes came by later to tell me about my injuries and the care I'd need, he'd crushed my heart a little more when he told me they'd found traces of GHB in my system and would need to do a rape kit to make sure I hadn't been assaulted as well. He told me to expect some memory loss, that my recollection of the events would be fuzzy due to the level of alcohol and drugs in my system.

He was right on one part. I could barely remember anything after calling my dad, the drinks, and things I'd done in that time span, a black hole. The one thing I wished would fade away, was the vivid memory of Duncan blowing me a kiss before…

Shutting my eyes closed, I decided to push this all away too, to go back to a time when none of this pain existed. If I pretended it didn't hurt, then I could go on living.

Who needed love when your heart was already battered and beaten? Not me. I'd stay home, work a job, and be there for my family. Every time I tried to be happy and in love, disaster struck. It would be better to pretend this never happened instead of focusing on the hurt and grief. I wouldn't survive it. Losing Blaze was hard enough, losing Duncan was too much. I wasn't strong enough to face them both.

Resolute in my decision. I put on a smile and focused on getting out of here, hiding my grief away until it disappeared.

Six months later, I found myself walking into a tattoo shop for an interview. It was my latest attempt to find something I'd enjoy. Sticking out my hand, I greeted the owner before delivering the pitch I practiced over and over with Simon.

"Hey, I'm Lennox, and you should definitely hire me."

"And why should I do that? I doubt you've got the skills to work here."

"Well, that's where you're wrong. I'm quite good at stabbing things, and everyone needs a little Lennox in their life."

"I don't know about that, but I'm willing to see if you can convince me with your pitch."

Sitting down, I began my spiel and all the valuable assets I could offer. He regarded me as I spoke, grilling me with questions, but I answered them all, determined to get this job, even if he was a bit of a Tatzilla. This would be my new beginning.

Blaze

It's been eight years and I find myself wondering what it all means. You're my best friend in so many ways. And yet, I've never seen your face, or heard your voice. Are we setting ourselves up for a lifetime of unhappiness?

Maybe we've grown out of pen pals. Maybe I'm just sad because I had another amazing date and yet, I can't find it in me to be happy. Why is that? Am I sabotaging?

I know he wants to move forward with our relationship. I found a ring last weekend. I'm still in school though. Only 22. But most girls are getting married here at that age. Maybe it's not so crazy?

In some ways, I feel so mature and old, living a life of deep moments and experiences. In other ways, I still feel so naive and young. I think I need to take some time to figure it out without you as my crutch.

Because you are Blaze. You're the piece of me I'll never have whole.

A smudged line on my heart that will never heal.

I don't want to do this. But I think I must.

I have to let you go, Blaze. It's time.

Goodbye Nox

Starry Nox,

LET'S MEET. I'LL BE IN NASHVILLE. WE CAN SETTLE THIS ONCE AND FOR ALL. I CAN'T LET YOU GO. NOT YET. YOU'RE MY BEST FRIEND TOO, AND THAT MEANS SOMETHING TO ME.

Your Blaze

Chapter Eighteen

THANE

I WATCHED from the shadows as Slade and Simon swooped in, stealing away my southern princess. For two whole months, I'd had her all to myself, and it'd been the best period of my life. From the moment I met her, I knew she was the one for me.

It took some time, but I'd eventually been able to track her down after that first day. I'd saved her brother, our souls bonding in that moment, forever connecting us to one another. It was pure luck I'd even been in the parking lot to begin with. My father had stopped off in the town, and I'd gone wandering as I do.

The mall was only a few minutes' walk from our hotel, so I'd made my way there, hoping to find something to pass the time. If anything, I could blow some quarters in the arcade, or maybe I'd be lucky enough to score. Women or drugs would be welcomed.

When I'd come upon her, I didn't think, jumping into action. It was a rush I'd never felt before. Locking eyes with the girl, I felt something in my chest stir, and I latched onto it, afraid of letting go of the first thing that had made me feel human since my mother died. I liked how it made me feel to be needed like that.

Dad was lost in his grief, and my brother was a troublemaker, one arrest away from spending the rest of his teenage years in juvie. The demands I felt placed on me overwhelmed me, but I found relief and hope when I looked into her eyes. For the first time in weeks, I could breathe.

When the sirens started, I panicked, not wanting my father to catch me out, so I left, not thinking about getting her number.

It had been a big enough story, though, that I was able to figure out who she was in that small town. *Lennox James.*

My crush began, diving into her history and learning everything I could about her, and soon an obsession was born. She was perfect, and I wanted her. I hated that her peers turned on her after the event, but it made my job easier as well. I tried to weed out everyone until I was the last one standing. Then she'd have no choice but to choose me.

Each year, I found myself able to learn more info about her. We traveled enough through her town that I was able to stop and watch her a couple of times a year. Sometimes, I'd brave it, and I would approach her, but she never seemed to recognize me, brushing me off like some tourist.

Spying was easier that way, and I gathered intel like a fiend. I learned about her failed relationship with Simon, and it helped me cross one name off my list. I'd still need to divide them, but it was easier if there wasn't a love connection. When she talked about Blaze, I knew I'd found my actual competition.

It took me a while to realize he wasn't a peer at

school, and I wanted to laugh when I discovered he was a pen pal. How much competition could he be? They didn't even know one another and had never met. But as the years passed and their connection grew, I knew there would come a time where she would wonder, and I needed to be prepared.

It was easy enough once they switched to email, and I cloned her phone one time when I was following her. Once I had access to all of her accounts, I didn't need to worry. Hours and hours went into reading their messages and learning everything I needed to about them. It was sickening how this Blaze lusted after my girl. He didn't deserve her, and I would make sure he knew it.

The first time I hacked into her account, I tested it out and found I could mimic emails. So, I sent strange ones, and then replied back about being hacked or leaving my phone somewhere. I set up a baseline, your basic standard procedure so it wouldn't seem odd later down the line. Then I waited.

Every day, like a ritual, I would read their messages and observe. Oh, how I learned so much through their love letters. Even if they denied it, I could clearly feel their bond. At first, I was envious, but then I used it to become the perfect version of the three men I found my Lennox falling for, even if she wasn't aware of it.

Because there were three, well, there once had been four, and I thought another had taken himself out of the game, but it looked like Simon had been a sleeper.

Their whispered deceit was riddled with lies, their scribbled confessions mine to tangle.

For years, I waited until the right moment and planned. I would periodically get on and insert myself in their chain of letters, mimicking one another's speech patterns until I could flawlessly do both. I put myself in their lives, making friends with my competition, and giving me all the insider information I needed. I had full access to their lives now, and I could shift the playing field in whatever direction I wanted.

I tried different approaches, hoping to have my southern princess fall in love with me organically. We met once at a bar and it had been great, until it wasn't. I tried by engaging with her through her blog, but she'd already been poisoned by them at that point, spouting that ludicrous belief she could love more than one person. Each time things went haywire, my anger would rise and I'd lash out. There had been a few times I'd even gotten a little desperate, and overplayed my hand, having to re-strategize each time once my anger cooled.

Fortunately, the other two numbnuts had dug their own grave, leading her right into my arms. I couldn't have planned that one better myself. I really owed them for it, setting it up perfectly. All the lies and betrayal I'd planted over the years, finally coming to fruition.

But now, they were back and wrecking the careful work I'd laid the past two months to make her mine. I could feel her caving, giving into the bond we shared, and knew it was only a matter of time now. If she fell back into their grasp though, then I'd have to get rid of them too.

I'd already gotten rid of one lover and moved the pieces into motion for the other three.

It was my time now. I wouldn't let them steal my Cherry.

Because Lennox was mine, and I had no intention of sharing.

Flipping on the computer, I logged into the camera feed I'd set up in her apartment. The computers around me hummed, the familiar sound a comforting background noise. I put on my headphones, turning up the volume to hear what they were saying, what lies I'd need to defuse once they left.

She hadn't immediately caved to them, and my heart skipped a beat, excitement building at winning her over.

I could make her love me. I could kidnap her and lock her up until she realized I was the one for her. I'd almost succeeded once at it. But call me old fashion, I wanted her to choose me. It felt sweeter to win that way.

I was so close; I could taste it.

To be continued in Smudged Lines

Letter from the Author

Thank you for reading Lennox's story. I hope you enjoyed it. This story was built from my reader group and the polls they answered. From naming the characters, to where it was located, the details were forged there and then they became alive in my mind.

If you enjoyed this story, you might want to also check out my other books while you wait for part 2. I have a completed winter sports contemporary RH, a standalone fairy tale retelling, and a dark contemporary mafia romance.

Thank you Emma for reading and cheering these characters on. Your surprise on everything spurred me to keep thinking creatively. And yeah, I did create a true psycho character for once. You're welcome!

To Kayla, Becki, and Tori, thank you for reading through it and loving Lennox's sass, Slade's angsty ass, Simon's sweet nature, and well, Thane's crazy.

To Brenda, Sandy, and Amanda, thank you for

helping make sure the storyline was consistent, and making it more southern.

To all my readers, new and old, thanks for picking up another book of mine! I keep writing and you guys keep devouring. I appreciate you all so much.

Kris Butler writes under a pen name to have some separation from her everyday life. Never expecting to write a book, she was surprised when an author friend encouraged her to give it a try and how much she enjoyed it. Having an extensive background in mental health, Kris hopes to normalize mental health issues and the importance of talking about them with her characters and books. Kris is a southern girl at heart but lives with her husband and adorable furbaby somewhere in the Midwest. Kris is an avid fan of Reverse Harem and hopes to add a quirky and new perspective to the emerging genre. If you enjoyed her book, please consider leaving a review. You can contact her the following ways and follow Kris's journey as a new author on social media.

Also by Kris Butler

Tattooed Hearts Duet

Riddled Deceit

Smudged Lines

Dark Confessions

Dangerous Truths

Dangerous Lies 11/13/21

Dangerous Vows *Feb 2022

Book 4 *May 2023

The Council Series (completed series)

Damaged Dreams

Shattered Secrets

Fractured Futures

Bosh Bells & Epic Fails- as part of the Christmas Wishes : A Christmas Anthology

12/10/21 *Preorder for 0.99 cents*

The Order (Council Spinoff)

Stiletto Sins *Summer 2022*

Sinners Fairytales Series (Shared world/standalone)

Pride

Made in United States
North Haven, CT
09 June 2023